BAD BLOOD WILL OUT

An Ashmole Foxe Georgian Mystery

WILLIAM SAVAGE

Ridge and Bourne

BAD BLOOD WILL OUT

by William Savage

For my many helpers, especially Jenn and Janet

T he man looked up at the sky, noting the heavy clouds moving in from the west. There was going to be a storm. The air was humid, pressing down on him, sliding around and clinging, so his skin and his clothes felt damp. There was something rancid about it; a metallic taste in the mouth. However much he breathed in, it never felt enough. He could have sworn the air was being stripped of its life-giving properties, leaving him struggling and winded. It was getting dark early too. What had begun as a pleasant enough evening — a good evening to go to the playhouse — would most likely end in thunder and torrential rain.

Was that thunder now? The man strained his ears, but he couldn't be sure. Whatever it was, it was a long way off. Maybe there would be time for him to finish work for the evening and get home before the storm broke. The play must be nearly over by this time. Then people would stream out of the theatre, see how dark it was, and start looking for him and his friends to light them home. The streets of Norwich were bad enough in daylight: filthy, uneven, slippery with mud and worse. Few people maintained a light outside their houses at night as the by-laws demanded, so you would be lucky to get home without a fall along the way. That is, if your pocket wasn't picked and you weren't robbed.

The threatening storm promised a good night for business if you were a link-man like him. People wanted light to help them along their way, which is exactly what his flaming torch offered them. Sometimes the dozen or so link-men waiting outside the old White Swan Playhouse would be lucky to get two or three customers between them. Not tonight. Tonight, everyone would be engaged at once. The younger, more energetic ones might be able to return two or three times for more custom, if their initial journeys were short enough. Not him though. He was old and tired, not feeling too well either. One customer and then home, he told himself.

The link-man looked at the sky again, trying to guess how quickly the storm was approaching. The air was still at ground level; just one or two occasional gusts and small ones at that. Up high, where the clouds were, it might be far windier. He narrowed his eyes, trying to see between the buildings. So far as he could judge, the looming mass of darkness to the west was considerably closer than when he had looked at it last. He glanced down at his lantern, checking the candle inside was alight. He needed to be quick off the mark when the show ended. If he wasn't outside the main entrance, with his torch lit ready, others would get the customers and he'd be left standing. Even on a busy night, that wasn't what any link-man wanted. If a customer reckoned you hadn't got someone else eager to hire you, they'd start haggling over the price. Mean bastards! They'd spend a shilling, or even two, for a place on one of the benches inside the theatre, then try to cheat you out of a few pennies afterwards.

He was getting too old for this game. His back was giving him hell tonight. Normally it was his knees which plagued him, making him walk oddly and threatening to give way as he stumbled over the ruts and pot-holes in the streets. It was all the standing about that did it. Time was he could trot along beside a chaise or a cart, earning good money for helping prevent the horses getting into trouble and lighting the way when the rich folk descended from their carriages to go inside. Not anymore. These days he often struggled to keep up with many of his customers. Then his tips went down and some threatened to pay less than they had agreed, saying he hadn't done his job properly.

What time was it? The church clock had chimed the hour not long ago, so he'd probably got forty-five minutes. More than enough time to rest his backside on one of the mounting blocks at the front and come back later to have his torch lit by the time people were ready for him. Yes, if he tucked his lantern down here, close to the pile of everyone's torches, he could forestall the younger ones and save a minute or so more. Seeing him without a candle, they'd dismiss him as competition for the early customers. Then if he slipped away before them, they'd take no notice and he could be back to get ready and light up before they realised what he was doing.

The man bent over, wincing at the pain in his back, and set his lantern down carefully, selecting a spot where its light was shielded by a pile of rubbish. No one would notice it there. After that, he limped away around the corner towards the front of the playhouse building.

Ten minutes later, a gust of wind from the fast-approaching storm blew the lantern over, its door opened and the lighted candle inside toppled over into a small puddle of oil and tar which had dripped down from the unlit torches. In moments, a thin, blue flame rose, fanned by one or two more gusts, and set fire to the pile of rubbish. Soon after, the whole pile of torches was alight, sending a plume of thick, greasy smoke up the side of the building and sending a good deal of it inside through an open window. Before anyone noticed, the wall of the playhouse against which the torches had been stacked also began to smoulder, as did the thatch on the eaves above. As the storm bore down on the city, the White Swan Playhouse was already well alight.

❦ 2 ❦

TWENTY YEARS LATER

'Damn and blast the man!' Ashmole Foxe barked. 'Trust Cousin Henry to come up with an idea like this! It's quite spoiled my breakfast.'

He leant over and looked for the bell he usually kept handy for calling a servant. Not there. He must have left it in his library last night.

'Molly! Molly!' he yelled. 'Come here, girl! What are you doing when I want you?'

Molly could have told him she was busy cleaning the grate in the parlour, but she had more sense than that. She simply stood and waited for him to decide what she had to do.

'Fetch Mrs Dobbin here,' Foxe said. 'Quickly, now. Tell her I need her at once.'

It was many years since Mr Ashmole Foxe had received any communication from his cousin, the Rev. Henry Foxe D.D., Rector of Ashington Magna in Kent. Now, as he re-read the letter which had arrived from him that morning, he could not help wishing the gap in contact had continued for longer still.

When Mrs Dobbins, his housekeeper came in response to his message, he flung the letter down in front of her.

'There!' he said. 'Isn't that a piece of the most damnable effrontery? No polite request to find out if it's convenient. No suggestion I might have something more important to do with my time. Cousin Henry has decided, so I must jump to carry out his will, whether it suits me or not. What do you think of that, eh?'

Since Foxe had failed to tell her what it was his cousin wanted from him, Mrs Dobbins was hardly in a position to comment. Being a sensible woman, and well used to her master's occasional rants, she merely enquired who Cousin Henry might be, since she had never heard his name mentioned before.

'Henry is the son of my father's only brother,' Foxe told her. 'A clergyman of a most disagreeable kind who lives in Kent, sharing his home, now his wife has died, with my only other cousin, his sister, Harriet. There you have the sum total of the living members of my family. No, I mislead you. There is another person, one I have little knowledge of. Listen and I will read out what Henry says.'

'My Dear Cousin Ashmole,

'It has become clear to me that when a young man is possessed of a modicum of intelligence, robust health, a good education, and sufficient money to meet his daily needs, but has no employment adequate to his abilities and means, he is bound to become a nuisance to his family.

'Such is the case of my son, Nicholas. It does not seem to have occurred to him to consider whether his present mode of life might prove a hindrance to the happiness of those about him. He flits from occupation to occupation, never settling on anything and pursuing it long enough to derive a benefit. His latest thought is to become some kind of man of business. That is, at least, better than the last, which was to enter the navy — a mode of life for which he is possibly the most ill-equipped personage you could imagine.

'I am sure you will understand that, as a member of the clergy, my own grasp of buying and selling is of a most tenuous nature . . .'

'Get to the point, Cousin,' Foxe snapped. 'You never could use a plain expression when a deluge of complex, rambling words would serve instead. It must be all those years of boring your parishioners to death with your sermons.'

Mrs Dobbins gave a delicate cough. Fortunately, it was enough to urge her master onwards without more comment of that type.

'. . . of a most tenuous nature, as befits one whose mind must be set on heavenly, rather than worldly matters. I am therefore unable either to advise my son or command his respect for my opinions. He dismisses all I say with the convenient excuse that I have neither knowledge nor experience in the field.

'It has occurred to me that you, Cousin, might well be a suitable person either to set him on the right path or dissuade him from a venture that could well prove disastrous. As I recall, your own business is tolerably successful . . .'

'Humbug!' Foxe muttered. 'He knows I am a good deal better placed in society than he is, for all his pretence of being accepted into the circle of the local squire and his cronies.'

The truth was Foxe's bookshop was doing better than ever before under the guidance of Mrs Crombie; so much so he now hesitated to enter it too often, lest his interference should upset things. His other business, the buying and selling of rare books, also produced a steady income; while the most it demanded was for him to wait for some improvident gentleman to be in such need of funds that he was eager to sell the best volumes in his family library. Foxe also owned several properties throughout the city, all managed for him by his attorney with little but occasional supervision. He was also a sleeping partner in the successful shipping and wherry business run by his closest friend, Captain Brock.

Mrs Dobbins waited as patiently as she could to find out what all this was leading up to. It was all very well her master criticising this cousin for being too free with his words. Mr Foxe could have spared her this lengthy reading if he'd told her at the start what it was all about.

'. . . so he may — I do not say he will — be disposed to take some notice of what you can tell him about life as a merchant. I have therefore despatched him to Norwich, trusting in your family affection to take him in for a while and allow him to experience something of the life you lead. He will be arriving, I imagine, not long after this letter.

'I remain, Cousin Ashmole, your most devoted and affectionate kinsman,

'The Reverend Henry Foxe D.D.

'Rector of Upper Massington, Kent.'

'Damn the man!' Foxe said again. 'He may be pompous, thoughtless and self-centred, but he isn't lacking in cunning. He's left me no choice but to take his son in. It is either that or turn him away to wander the streets and get into who knows what trouble. By sending letter and son almost together, he's denied me any chance of refusal.'

'I'll have a room prepared for the young man right away, sir,' Mrs Dobbins said. Why all the fuss, for heaven's sake. They had plenty of space for visitors. Most of the time, Mr Foxe lived alone in his great house. There were sometimes young women, but generally only for the night. His 'pets' the servants called them. There hadn't even been so many of those recently either. 'He can sleep in the rear bedroom above yours, I think. All it needs is for me to air the bed. Will the young man need anything else, do you think?'

'My reverend Cousin Henry, Mrs Dobbins, lacks the innocence of the dove but assuredly has the cunning of the serpent. Witness his letter telling me of young Nicholas's imminent visit coming only this morning, when his son must already be well upon his way.'

'Not an act you would expect of a clergyman, Mr Foxe—'

'Yet precisely what I would expect of Cousin Henry. He is my senior by many years, Mrs Dobbins, and well matured in guile. When she was alive, his wife — a woman of saintly patience and something of a favourite of mine — managed to exert some control over his baser tendencies. She, however, went to what I imagine must be a particularly well-deserved rest some twelve months ago, leaving her husband unrestrained. Well, we must make the best of things. I just hope Nicholas, whom I have never met, is not made in the image of his father. Henry's letter gives me hope in the matter, for he appears to have little tolerance or affection for his son.'

'That's a terrible thing to say, Mr Foxe.'

'A truthful one though. It seems Nicholas has no idea what to do with his life save, I imagine, to avoid becoming like his father. If his latest notion is to enter the world of business, I am not sure whether Cousin Henry wants me to aid him in this endeavour or put him off—'

At that moment, Charlie Dillon, Foxe's apprentice, knocked at the door seeking Mrs Dobbins.

'Sorry to interrupt you, master, but there's a cart outside with a clothes-press on it. The carter is asking where he is to put it. He's blocking a good part of the road and there's already a long line of other carts unable to get past. Some of their drivers have started to turn nasty. If we don't get him on his way quickly, there'll probably be a fist-fight.'

Mrs Dobbins jumped up at once. 'You recall you agreed to let me get you a new press for your clothes, Mr Foxe, after Alfred noticed your present one was showing signs of the woodworm. Those little devils can spread faster than a false rumour. If we don't get the old press taken out and burned, we'll have wormholes in every piece of wood in the house. I'd better go and sort this out at once, begging your pardon.'

By rights, Charlie should have gone as well. Instead he lingered.

'Well, lad?' Foxe said. 'What d'you want? Spit it out.'

'I need to go and talk to the Cunning Woman,' Charlie said. 'Missus Tabby has sent me a message. She's a good friend to the street children as you know, master. A good many of them would be in their graves if she didn't tend to their ills. Never asks for payment either — not that most of them have any money if she did. Some people say she has the Second Sight as well. I don't know about that, but she's a wonder with herbs and charms.'

'Don't ramble,' Foxe snapped. 'You say she sent you a message. What did it say?'

'One of the children brought it, master. She says I'm to go to her as soon as I can. She . . . um . . . wasn't quite clear . . . I mean, she didn't say precisely . . .'

'Charlie,' Foxe said, fixing the poor boy with a most intimidating stare. 'I'm going to lose my temper in a moment if you go on like this. Why are you asking me anyway? I've told you before to go to Mrs Crombie if you need permission to be absent for an hour or so.'

'It's . . . well . . . Missus Tabby says it's about you, master. Something about you needing her advice bad, the message was. I didn't think you knew her — her being kind of not someone quite respectable, like.'

Foxe rubbed his hand across his chin and wondered how much to tell the boy. 'I've known Mistress Tabitha Studwell since before you were born, my lad. There was a time . . . well, forget about that. I wonder why she didn't ask me to visit her?'

'The message said you would be too busy, master, seeing you'd be dealing with the mayor's urgent request most of the day, then with your visitor tomorrow.'

'Damnation take the woman! How did she know about my visitor? Come to think of it, what urgent request from the mayor? I've had no such communication, for heaven's sake.'

That was when Molly the housemaid came in. 'Alderman Halloran's man is here, sir,' she said. 'The alderman wants you to go to see him right away. There's a matter he needs to discuss with you most urgently. It's on behalf of the mayor, he says.'

'I didn't hear you knock, Molly,' her master said.

'Oh, but I did, master. You must 'ave been talking.'

Foxe could have sworn Molly spent time practising that look of total innocence in front of a mirror. 'Very well,' he said. 'I'll believe you — this time. Just remember it for the future. Go and tell Alfred to have my coat and outdoor clothes ready and get me a chair to take me to Colegate. Now, Charlie. I'm sure you know where Mistress Tabby lives. Go and talk to her and find out what this is all about. Tell Mrs Crombie I said you could. Be careful how you do it too. She has every right to be cross with you for coming to me first. Off with you both. I'll go to see the alderman.' He shook his head. 'What I don't see is how Tabby could have known any of this.'

'It's the Second Sight,' Charlie told him. 'I told you what people say about her.'

'Nonsense, boy! There's no such thing. Probably servants — or apprentices — with too much time on their hands gossiping about their betters. Tabby has many talents — or had — but foretelling the future isn't one of them. If she could do so . . . never mind. That's another story, and not one for your ears either. Now get on your way and stop bothering me with nonsensical talk of Tabby having magical powers.'

3

Charlie Dillon ran as fast as he could through the streets and alleys beside the Market Place, heading for the river Wensum, which divides the great city of Norwich into two unequal parts, the northern third always referred to by natives as 'Across the Water'. This area had not been settled until two hundred years before, when persecution by the French king in the Low Countries sent the Protestant Huguenots fleeing for their lives. Many came to England, encouraged by Queen Elizabeth, bringing a good many of the skills of cloth working and dying on which the prosperity of the city of Norwich now stood.

The closer Charlie got to the river, the worse the roads and the traffic of carts, horses, and people became. The ground beneath his feet was fouled with a mass of mud, the droppings from the horses, and the refuse thrown out from the houses on either side. The way was so narrow and the press of traffic so great, he was forced up against the walls of the buildings, first by a huge wagon weighed down with wine casks, and then by a post-chaise driven with utter recklessness through the press of people.

As he turned from Wymer Street down to the Coslany Bridge, Charlie found the way blocked by a mass of angry people, some shouting and waving their fists, others trying to push their way through by sheer force. The bridge was blocked by a brewer's dray drawn up in the middle of the roadway. The post-chaise, which had so recently splashed Charlie with mud and forced him to jump for his life, had come up to the brewer's dray as it was crossing the bridge. Enraged by the slowness of the heavy vehicle before him, the young blade in charge of the post-chaise first yelled abuse at the driver of the dray, then tried to urge him on by cracking his whip over the fellow's head. Whether by accident or design, the tip of the whipcord caught the drayman's ear and drew blood.

Now it was the turn of the driver of the dray to let out a bellow of anger. Stopping his vehicle in the middle of the bridge, he took up a great cudgel from the seat beside him, climbed down into the road and made his way back to the post-chaise, where he began to belabour the driver about the back and head until the young man, fearing for his life, took to his heels. There was now a general argument amongst the crowd as to how best to clear the chaise out of the way. Some were for unharnessing the horse and turning it loose, then tipping the carriage into the river. A few wanted to take it and the horse to the nearest inn yard and leave it for the young man's return. The driver of the dray yelled he didn't care what was done with it, since he was on the right side of the blockage and needed to be on his way. That caused those on the other side to start abusing him, so he took up his cudgel again and swore to smash the head of the first man who tried to stop him getting on with the job he was paid to do. Fist-fights now broke out, stones were thrown, and two market women, trying to cross the bridge in the opposite direction, set about the driver of the dray with kicks and blows. The road looked as if it would remain blocked for several hours to come.

Despite his curiosity to see the outcome, Charlie pressed on, weaving and threading his way through the crowd. He managed to cross the Coslany Bridge by jumping on the dray and climbing over the front to drop onto the road beyond. Then, nimbly avoiding the fight now underway between the driver and the market women, he turned and darted down a narrow pathway between the houses which over-looked the islands dividing the river upstream of the bridge.

Many of the houses in this part of the city remained as they had been built hundreds of years before: large constructions of solid oak timbers, infilled with wattle and daub, a few now wearing a thin skin of brick designed to make them appear more like the grand merchant houses close by on Colegate. A narrow pathway ran between two such houses and Charlie made his way along it to where someone had built a far more modest dwelling, a thatched cottage, timber beamed, surrounded by its own garden. This was where Mistress Tabby lived. The house, though old, was more than large enough for her needs, and the garden proved ideal to grow the many herbs she used in making up her potions. What did not grow there, she found on the banks of the river itself, so she rarely needed to travel further into the countryside to collect her supplies.

Charlie didn't bother to go up to the house and knock on the door. Though the day was overcast, with more than a hint of rain in the air, he knew he'd be bound to find Mistress Tabby working in her garden. There she was, just as he expected, wearing an old woollen cloak to keep out the cold and kneeling on the pathway to pick out the weeds from amongst her precious plants.

Charlie knew better than to interrupt her work more than was necessary, so he squatted down beside her to find out why she'd asked him to come.

'Come inside, Charlie Dillon,' the Cunning Woman said, standing up to stretch her back. 'It's too long since I've set eyes on you. The others told me you'd fallen on your feet and Mr Foxe, the bookseller, had taken you in. Now you're his apprentice, are you? It suits you, I can see. You were such a scrawny, wretched little creature. Now you're almost as sleek as my cat, Sammy. Right. Sit down and listen to me carefully. I've heard quite a lot about your master recently. More than enough to tell me he's heading down the wrong path. If he doesn't listen, he's going to cause himself — and others — a great deal of disappointment and frustration.'

Much of what she said after that made little enough sense at the time. Fortunately, Charlie had an excellent memory, so he was able to relate it all, almost word for word, when he returned to his master's house.

She began by telling him his master must understand Providence had designed us to suit purposes beyond our understanding. It was not up to us to decide to frustrate what had been laid down. We are as we are. Our job in this world is to make the best of it. It was high time Mr Foxe gave up moping and settled down to be and do what he was best at. It was also total nonsense to be sulking as he was, just because a few people had laughed at him.

'Listen closely now,' she told Charlie. 'This is vital, so don't get it muddled up. You're to tell your master he's going to encounter two problems and he has to solve them both. No excuses. This is the best opportunity he's likely to get to set himself back on the right path for the future. Tell him to remember everything I taught him and start applying it again. Those cats aren't coming back. There were good reasons why he acted the way he did and nothing has changed. You can't catch your quarry if it can see you coming and knows what you're up to. Now, have you got it all?'

'Yes, Missus Tabby. I've got it. But what if he asks me what it is you think he's best at? What do I say then?'

'You tell him from me he already knows what his job is. He just has to do it, using his natural talents, the skills I taught him and the experience he's gained since. Forget everything else and—'

She broke off and her body stiffened. Charlie could see her eyes were fixed on some point far in the distance, as if she were now somewhere else, no longer talking to him, no longer concerned with him, no longer conscious of his presence.

'Death,' she said, in a low voice. 'Murder. It's started . . . reaching out from the past, full of hatred . . . black, bitter hatred . . . so much lust for revenge, so much pain, so much innocence destroyed, so much greed . . . it cannot be borne. . . too much hurt . . . too much anger . . . Oh Lord, so much killing! Tell Ashmole . . . tell . . .'

She gave a small sigh and fainted.

❧ 4 ❧

'Sit down, Foxe. I've asked for coffee.' Alderman Halloran looked tired and harassed. He must have been with the mayor, Foxe thought. Why does our civic leader panic so easily? Every time there's a problem to be handled — and that's often enough in a turbulent city like Norwich — the man is overcome with anxiety.

They were sitting, as usual, in the alderman's fine library, the walls lined everywhere with bookshelves of oak, save where long mirrors were set to reflect the light from the three tall windows back into the room. It was a place which invited calmness and quiet, which might be why the alderman usually chose it for talks with Foxe.

'You asked me to come quickly, Alderman,' Foxe began.

'Let's drop this Alderman business, shall we, Foxe? Lot of stuff and nonsense really. Just call me Halloran and I'll stick with Foxe? Much simpler.'

The mayor must really have been a nuisance this morning, Foxe reflected. The alderman was proud of his status and usually a stickler for protocol as well.

'This is the nub of the matter.' The alderman couldn't seem to sit still himself, preferring to get up and start a perambulation of the room. 'Ah, here's the coffee. Just put it down there, will you, Betty. We'll serve ourselves.'

He seemed glad of the interruption almost, taking his time to pour out the coffee and add sugar in copious amounts.

'You were going to explain the problem you've called me here to talk about, Ald— Halloran,' Foxe said. If he didn't urge the fellow on he'd be there half the morning at this rate.

'Yes . . . well. You know Edward Mordifort, of course.'

'Not personally, but certainly by reputation. He's a brewer, isn't he? Quite a prosperous one too.'

'Brewer, maltster, grain merchant and heaven knows what else. One of the richest men in Norwich, by all accounts. He's been murdered.'

'When? How?'

'He'd arranged a private ball, rout, whatever you call them, at the Assembly House last night. Select guest list, invitation only, you understand. The man is — was, I should say — eaten up with ambition to be made an alderman. He's been on the Common Council for years; never got any further. Anyway, he's been currying favour with those he thinks might be willing to support him when the next place for an alderman comes up. This . . . let's call it a ball . . . was for his cronies and supporters. Throwing his money about, you see. Making himself out to be a rising power in the city. There had been dancing in the first part of the evening, then at about eleven o'clock, the dancing stopped for a supper banquet to be served. Everyone rushed towards the room where the food was laid out, causing a crush in the doorway. As they did, someone — it turned out to be Mordifort — cried out and seemed to faint. It took a few moments to clear a space and then the fellow was seen to be lying on the floor, on his back with his left arm twisted underneath him. Staring eyes, grimace on his face, you know the kind of thing. Obvious he was dead.'

'Didn't anyone try to revive him?'

'Dr Proudfoot and Dr Hamilton were among the guests. Both physicians. They bustled up, took one look and agreed it was too late for anything like that. Man was stone dead. Proudfoot said it was obviously an apoplexy. Hamilton claimed the corpse bore all the signs of seizure.'

'Which was it?'

'Neither, of course. One of the other guests pointed out he could see blood starting to form a pool underneath Mordifort's body. They turned him over and found a knife sticking in the left side of his back. It must have gone straight into his heart and finished him off instantly.'

'What kind of knife?'

'A sort of dagger, so the mayor was told. One with a small handle and a long, thin blade.'

'Easy to carry and conceal.'

'I agree, especially since the affair involved everyone wearing those masks and long cloaks — dominoes, they call them, don't they?'

'Hmm.' Foxe took a few moments to think. 'I doubt this was a spur-of-the-moment killing. You don't usually carry a weapon of that kind to a masked ball — at least, not unless you're either mortally afraid of someone or out to commit murder. I suppose the mayor wants me to look into it?'

'Man's in a complete panic this morning. Mordifort was important, you see. Lots of influence amongst the right kind of people. Friend of the Townshends and the Walpoles. Doesn't do to be seen to waste time when someone like that is murdered in our city; especially when he's killed in what's almost a public place. Will you do it, Foxe? If you say no I swear the next corpse we'll have on our hands will be the mayor. I wonder what they'd put on his gravestone? "Died from panic" perhaps; or "died of overwhelming anxiety".'

'You can tell the mayor I'm quite willing to take it on, Halloran, so he can stop worrying on that score. Now, what can you tell me about Mr Edward Mordifort?'

Aside from the previous information about his widespread business interests and considerable wealth, the alderman's knowledge didn't amount to much. It was obvious the two men had avoided one another for some reason. Foxe suspected Mordifort had been too eager to promote himself, too pushy. Halloran, who was one of the old school when it came to polite behaviour, would have hated that. It was also likely Mordifort was a Whig to Halloran's Tory. About the only useful information Foxe could extract was that Mordifort was known as a tough, aggressive businessman with few scruples; the kind who believes the ends justify the means — especially if the ends involve extra profit.

'Did he have a family?' Foxe asked.

'A son and a daughter, as I recall. Mordifort claimed his son — Peter, I believe he is called — was a worthless nonentity, who spent his time writing foolish books about antiquities instead of learning how to make more money. I don't know much about the daughter, except that she married against her father's wishes. I do know he never saw eye-to-eye with his son-in-law.'

'Why? Do you know?'

'Too like himself, if you ask me. Another ambitious thruster, desperate for money and influence, only not as successful. If I recall correctly, he's a ship's chandler. Something like that. Alfred Henson's the name.'

'You don't know anything more about his wife?'

'My wife might. I'll ring for the maid and send her to see if my wife can come and tell us what she knows. I think she's about the house somewhere. I know she and the two girls were planning to go to your shop again today. Back to your circulating library, I imagine. They read more books in a week than most people get through in six months!'

Mrs Halloran was indeed in the house and was quite willing to tell Foxe what she knew of Dorothy Henson, née Mordifort.

'A tall, angular, sharp-featured and sharp-tongued young woman,' she said. 'My husband says her husband is ambitious. If you ask me, she's the one pushing him on all the time. When she was young, she was always restless; never satisfied with what she had and trying to get something better or more expensive. She dressed in far too rich a style for her position too. I wonder her father was willing to spend so much on her, for her wardrobe must have cost many hundreds of pounds and she was always having new clothes made. The trouble was, they were wasted on her. Whatever she wore, it always looked too big. I remember once she came to a ball in an evening dress with a neckline which would have revealed far too much — only she had nothing there to show off. She must have known all the other women of her age were laughing at her, but she still strutted about trying to flirt with the best-looking young men.'

'Your husband said she married against her father's wishes,' Foxe said. 'Can you tell me anything more about that occasion?'

'Her father wanted her to marry into the nobility — mostly to further his own interests, of course. She was to wait until he selected the right person and then do as she was told.'

'Her mother agreed to this?'

'She died quite a few years ago. I think Dorothy would have been no more than nine or ten at the time.'

'But when it came to it, Mordifort's daughter wouldn't do as her father told her?'

'She wouldn't wait. As soon as she saw several other young women in her circle were drawing all the attention by announcing their engagement or getting married, she wasn't going to be left out. She might also have picked up on the talk which was going around.'

'What were people saying?'

'That her father had been forced to double her dowry and offer a cash payment of a thousand pounds to anyone from amongst the eldest sons of the nobility who would be willing to take her on. I doubt if it was true, of course. More likely to be a piece of malicious gossip spread about because nobody liked her much. You see the problem about waiting until her father found someone for her, don't you? All the time she was without anyone known to have asked for her hand, the rumours were going to strengthen that no one would have her.'

'But Mr Henson was willing,' Foxe said.

'Mr Henson was up to his ears in debt at the time. His father had recently died, leaving him the ship's chandlery business. Unfortunately, young Henson has no head for business. What he does have is a taste for recognition, even if it means buying it by throwing what little money he has around. Dorothy stalked him like a cat with a mouse, somehow got herself pregnant — she said it was by him, but who knows? — and presented her father with an ultimatum. Let her marry the man of her choice or have a bastard grandchild. He gave in, as she knew he would, and she married Henson. The child was still-born, and she never conceived again, so that put paid to any dynastic hopes.

However, her dowry settled Henson's debts and she revived the business by the simple process of controlling the purse-strings and telling her husband exactly what to do, down to the smallest detail. That's how their marriage works. She doesn't care if he has mistresses — so long as they don't cost too much — as long as he continues to obey her instructions. However, the word is she's started to lose her grip on the fellow and he's found ways to lay his hands on some of the money too. His latest mistress is not the kind of woman to accept second-best in what he gives her.'

When Foxe left the Hallorans' house, he had a good deal to occupy his mind. He'd forgotten to mention he was soon to have an unwanted visitor, so Halloran would assume he could devote all his time to investigating this murder. No matter, really. If Nicholas truly wanted to understand the business of being a bookseller, he'd be better off talking to Mrs Crombie anyway. Of course, it would have been better if he hadn't been involved in an investigation during Nicholas's visit — heaven knows what his puritanical father would make of him being in a household where violent crime was discussed — but that couldn't be helped. If Nicholas or his father didn't like the situation, it was of no matter to him. He hadn't asked the young man to come, had he?

5

Early in the afternoon, Charlie returned home, but found Foxe absent. His message for his master from the Cunning Woman would have to wait. Since, like most boys of his age, Charlie was always hungry — especially so that day, having had no chance to scrounge anything from the kitchen at midday — he went through to the servants' quarters to wait. There, having persuaded Mrs Whitbread, the cook, to take pity on him to the extent of a mug of small beer and a huge portion of bread and cheese, he took his prize through to the servants' hall to eat it in peace. Instead, he found several of the other members of Foxe's household, together with Mrs Crombie.

Though Mrs Crombie was the junior partner to the master of the house in running his bookstore, she'd always taken great care to make herself agreeable to the servants. She never acted in a superior way or put on airs and graces. They had therefore become used to her coming into the house and now accepted her as part of the household, though she didn't live under the same roof. She had her own house, where she lived with Jane Thaxter, the dumb woman she'd taken into her home after one of Mr Foxe's earlier investigations, but she often joined the servants around the middle of the day for a drink and some of Mrs Whitbread's excellent cooking.

Charlie took a seat and, in between mouthfuls, began regaling the others with a description of his trip 'across the water'. Now he paused, with the natural instincts of a storyteller, at the point where Mistress Tabby had talked of death and slumped to the floor. His audience, of course, were now agog to hear the rest of his tale; even Alfred, the manservant, who had been leaning back in his chair, looking out of the window, while trying to maintain an attitude which suggested scepticism and dislike of dealings with anyone who strayed outside the realms of religious orthodoxy.

'What happened after then?' Mrs Crombie asked Charlie.

'I ran to get Bart, of course,' Charlie said, his mouth full of bread.

'Bart?'

'He's a kind of adopted son, who looks after Missus Tabby. People say she found him as a half-starved toddler, many years ago, clinging to the body of his dead mother at the side of the road. Nowadays he's enormous and strong as an ox, though he's a little weak in the head and doesn't talk too much. Missus Tabby made sure his mother had a decent burial, took the baby in and nursed him back to health. He's been totally devoted to her ever since. I tell you, it would be more than anyone's life is worth to try harming Missus Tabby when Bart is nearby - which he nearly always is. They say he punched a man who was trying to force his attentions on her so hard his jaw was broken. Another time he picked up a notorious robber and threw him up into a tree, where he hung for almost half an hour until his friends could get him down. Anyway, Bart came at once, picked Missus Tabby up as if she was a baby and laid her on her bed. I'm glad to say she began to wake up about then.'

'Why's that?'

'The way he looked at me. I was sure he thought I'd done something to her. My knees were knocking, I can tell you. Fortunately, Missus Tabby was able to assure him it was none of my doing.'

'This Bart fellow sounds like a menace to me,' Alfred growled. 'The master oughtn't to have let the lad go to see this so-called Cunning Woman. He might have been hurt.'

'Don't be such a misery, Alfred,' Mrs Dobbins said. 'Bart was only protecting his mistress. Anyhow, nobody came to any harm and

Charlie brought back some important news. There's going to be a death and the master will be involved in finding the killer. You know dealing with one of his mysteries puts him in a good mood. He's been getting crabby of late. Probably bored.'

'That's only if you believe in this witch-woman,' Alfred retorted. 'Prophecies and second sight! A load of rubbish I call it!'

Charlie turned on Alfred in a fury. 'Stop calling her a witch!' he yelled, 'or I'll . . .'

'Enough!' Mrs Crombie said. 'You mustn't be so disrespectful to Mr Horsfall, Charlie. He's a senior member of this household and you're only an apprentice. You must remember that.'

Alfred Horsfall looked smug until Mrs Crombie rounded on him too. 'As for you, Alfred, you should be ashamed of yourself. The master would never call a woman like this Mistress Tabby a witch, I'm sure of it; and what's good enough for him is more than good enough for you. If you can't find anything more helpful to say, I suggest you get back to your work. The rest of us are trying to help Mr Foxe, if we can. I'm quite sure we can manage to do so without you.'

For a moment, it looked as if Alfred would let his temper get the better of him and say something he would regret. But he must have remembered the high regard in which his master held Mrs Crombie, his own status as a servant, however senior, and the likely response of Mr Foxe to any complaint from her. It was also clear from their faces all the others were ranged against him. Alfred might be a bit of a misery and a traditionalist to his core, but he wasn't a fool. He had to work with these people. Best to keep his mouth shut.

Mrs Crombie turned away from the deflated manservant and went back to Charlie's story. 'Tell us about the message you brought back,' she said.

'There will be two problems — that's what she called them — for the master to solve. He must solve them both to put him back on the right track for his future.'

'Good,' Mrs Crombie said. 'Now, Molly has some news as well, haven't you?'

'The alderman sent for the master in a great hurry this morning.

The servant he sent told me he'd heard someone important had been murdered last night—'

She was interrupted by the sound of furious banging on the front door, as if somebody was trying to break it down. Alfred rose to his feet to go and investigate. After a few moments, they could all hear someone loudly demanding to see Mr Foxe and Alfred protesting his master was not presently at home. A few moments later, the manservant returned, quite obviously much annoyed by the visitor's refusal to accept what he had told him.

'It's Mr Postgate from the White Swan Playhouse,' Alfred said. 'I told him several times the master isn't in and I don't know when he will return, but he won't go. He says he must speak with the master and he'll stay in the hallway until he does. He keeps shouting there's been a dead body found in his theatre, and he needs the master to find out how it got there.'

'Death,' Mrs Crombie said. 'That's what the Cunning Woman foretold, wasn't it? Two deaths, in fact. Now here they are.'

'Two problems,' Charlie cried. 'Exactly as Missus Tabby foretold. He has to solve both, she said. No excuses.'

'The master doesn't like that there Postgate fellow,' Alfred said. 'Never has. Thinks he's a rogue and a bully who's not fit to be in charge of a theatre. Worse still, the master heard the man regularly expects the favours of every young woman who works in his theatre. If she won't yield to his demands, he throws her out. He's also been known to kick and cuff the street children — except those girls who'll let him do what he wants without payment.'

'It's true enough about him abusing the street children,' Charlie added. 'They've learned to keep as far away from the man as they can. Even the girls who'll generally go with anyone for money won't go near him. They say he's nasty and cruel and wants them to do disgusting things.'

'The master hates cruelty towards any creature,' Alfred continued. 'Bullying and abusing children makes him wild with anger.'

'You know the master went to the playhouse one time and told Postgate he'd take a whip to him if he heard of him abusing anyone else,' Mrs Whitbread said. 'If you ask me, Postgate can stand in the hall until he takes root and I'm sure the master still won't see him — unless it's to carry out his threat with the whip.'

'I'm amazed Mr Postgate has the cheek to come at all.' Mrs Dobbins was keen to add her two pennyworths, her face now flushed with anger. 'You stay here, Alfred. I'm not going to allow some foul lecher to stay in this house a moment longer. I'll go and tell him to leave — and make sure I've got a sharp knife in one hand. If he tries anything with me, I'll mark his face, sure enough.'

'Calm down everyone,' Mrs Crombie said. 'Please go back, Alfred, and tell him I'll be through in a moment. If he agrees to act in a civil manner, I'll let him tell me his story and I'll pass it on to Mr Foxe. That will be the best way. Charlie's right. Mistress Tabby mentioned two mysteries, not just one. This must be the second. There are killers to be caught and we all know he's the best person to do it. Just make sure you stay in the hallway with me, Alfred. I doubt this Mr Postgate will behave towards me in an improper way, but it's best to be sure. His type are nearly always bullies, preying on those they think cannot fight back. I'd tell you to throw him into the street, if it wasn't for the fact some poor person has died.'

'Two mysteries at once!' Mrs Dobbins said. 'Do you think the master can cope with that? He's never done so before, so far as I know.'

'The master can do anything! Just you see.' Molly hadn't spoken until now.

'We all know you're sweet on him,' Alfred said to her. 'Mrs Dobbins is right. Two problems at once sounds like a tall order.'

'I am not sweet on the master, Mr Horsfall, and well you know it. Not like Flo here and Charlie. She's always making sheep's eyes at him.'

'I am not—'

'No, she ain't—'

There might well have been a furious argument at this point had not Mrs Crombie reasserted her authority.

'Quiet, all of you! First of all, we need Mr Foxe to agree to get involved. Let me go to hear what this Postgate has to say for himself.'

MR POSTGATE, FACED WITH A LADY, BEHAVED TOWARDS MRS Crombie in a manner so oily and fawning any sensible person must have felt sick. He was a fat, pasty-faced creature, his dirty wig and worn clothes too young for him, his coat straining across a belly which indicated where his heart — if he had one — truly lay.

Summoning up all her reserves of resolve, she asked Mr Postgate to tell her what he had come to talk to Mr Foxe about, explaining yet again Mr Foxe was presently away from the house. Postgate smirked and nodded and began to tell his tale in such a wheedling voice she longed to smack him across the face and tell him to be a man. Then, when he had not passed the halfway point, he seemed to gain assurance from her willingness to listen and began, once again, to ask to see Mr Foxe in person. Mrs Crombie lost all remnants of her patience.

'I have told you several times, Mr Postgate,' she said, her voice sounding as if it came directly from the snowy wastes of the land of the Greenlanders, 'Mr Foxe is out and therefore unable to receive visitors. The choice before you is simple. You can explain your problem to me or you can leave now. I have already promised I will pass on what you tell me as soon as Mr Foxe returns. When that will be, I cannot say.'

'But my need is urgent, madam. You must understand me on that point.'

'I understand one of the actors appearing in your playhouse has been found dead and his death appears suspicious. You have also told me the local magistrate has been informed, as has the coroner. If matters proceed as they usually do, I assume an inquest will be held either tomorrow or the day after. Now, Mr Postgate, where is the urgency? The poor man is dead and will not come to life again.'

'Oh, I wish I could speak with Mr Foxe! He would understand it at once.'

'Let me hear no more of that tune, sir, I beg you. It will not serve any purpose, save to hasten your departure, willing or not.'

The flamboyance of the theatre seemed to have passed Postgate by completely, to be replaced by a kind of cringing urge to avoid the kicking he so richly deserved. An actress having a tantrum he could have dealt with easily. To be confronted by a respectable, intelligent, and confident lady who dealt in facts, not emotions, reduced him to a jelly.

'Come, come, sir. Surely it is not so difficult? You tell me your problem is urgent and your livelihood depends on a solution. All you need to do is explain why.'

'Because it's in the theatre!' Mr Postgate wailed. 'Because we are dealing with actors. Because some fool began to talk about a ghost.'

Mrs Crombie was startled. He'd not mentioned the ghost before. 'Whose ghost is this?' she asked him.

Finally, in fits and starts, constantly interrupted with deep sighs and more protestations of imminent ruin, the full story was told.

Some twenty years before, part of the playhouse had been destroyed by a terrible fire. It had broken out more than halfway through the evening's programme, fortunately in the backstage area, so the audience were able to escape the flames. Some of them even stayed to help fight the fire. Backstage, things were much worse. Some of the cast had been on stage, others in their dressing rooms; the stagehands had been busy moving scenery or carrying props; and everyone's attention had been on the stage, ready to move into action as the final part of the programme — a farce called 'The Innocent Country Maid' — headed towards the final scene. In the ensuing chaos, as some tried to fight the fire and others tried to escape with their lives, two people died, overcome by the smoke: one of the leading actresses, a beautiful woman barely twenty-five years old, and her baby son, lying in his cot beside her.

It was after the fire the stories of a playhouse ghost began, Mr Postage explained. They said it was the spirit of the dead woman, searching for her lost child. Over time, fewer people claimed to have seen the ghost, so the story started to fade from people's minds, including those who worked in the playhouse itself.

'Now the story has been recalled?' Mrs Crombie said.

'Indeed, it has madam. Please understand. Actors are terribly superstitious. People are saying Mr Chambers, the actor who has died, was killed by the ghost. Those who have seen his body — and I'm glad to say I have not — report his face seemed frozen in an expression of terrible fear. Apart from that, he has not a mark upon him. This too is being taken as the sign of a death caused by super-natural means.'

'But why should this ghost, assuming it exists, kill Mr Chambers?'

'In revenge. You see, Mr Chambers was part of the company on that fateful night. He has always suffered badly from stage-fright. According to those who had seen him, he had been drinking heavily in an effort to calm his nerves. Many blamed him for starting the fire, saying he was stumbling around in his dressing room, upset a bottle of brandy and knocked over a candleholder which set the brandy alight. From there, the flames spread to the curtains, the make-up, some of the costumes, and finally the fabric of the building.'

'So, he was blamed for the death of the actress and of her child? That is how the story goes?'

'It did not until now. Indeed, he had every reason to mourn those deaths. It was well known at the time he and the actress, Miss Margaret Lindsay, had been . . . um, shall we say intimate friends? . . . for some time before the accident occurred. He also claimed the son she bore was his.'

'You say he claimed it? Was there some doubt?'

'Plenty. For a start, several other men would have had an equal claim to have sired the child. All had been enjoying Miss Lindsay's favours. She was, I regret to say, somewhat free with her person, espe-cially if the man concerned came from a wealthy family. At first, Miss Lindsay declined to say who the father was, if indeed she knew. Then, soon after she arrived in Norwich, a young gentleman, a Mr Daniel Lambetts, appeared on the scene, having followed Miss Lindsay from London. This Mr Lambetts was heir-presumptive to a baronet, a rich landowner in Hertfordshire. The young fellow was also said to be deeply in love with Miss Lindsay, to the extent of hoping she would marry him. Whether he really did intend matrimony, I do not know. He must certainly have known her for a little time, for she began to claim he was the father of her child.'

'In fact, nobody knew who the father was.'

'That is correct. However, Mr Chambers persisted in his claim of paternity. You see, Miss Lindsay was the star, while Mr Chambers did not seem likely to rise above playing supporting roles. The cynics said he hoped to be able to benefit from a continued association with Miss Lindsay. Miss Lindsay, however, rejected his claim and was supported in this by a Mr Edwards, another actor, who stated Mr Chambers had always been rebuffed by Miss Lindsay. Whatever the truth of the matter, these two actors conceived a deep hatred for one another; so deep they could no longer perform in the same theatre or be members of the same company.'

'And it is Mr Chambers' body that has been found?' Mrs Crombie said.

'It is. But there is worse to come. The company in which Mr Chambers is now a member was due to put on a final performance tonight. Then they were to be replaced by another company, of which Mr Edwards is a member. The second company arrived a day early. Yesterday, last night if you will, was the first time, since the fire I told you of, that the two actors have been in the same theatre at the same time — and Mr Edwards was seen entering the playhouse at the start of last night's performance.'

❧ 6 ❧

Neither Charlie's explanation of the message from the Cunning Woman nor Mrs Crombie's attempt to interest Foxe in Postgate's story went well. Charlie's description of what transpired at Mistress Tabby's house was met with polite thanks for bringing the message and nothing more. Mrs Crombie fared worse. Her hopes of Mr Foxe agreeing to investigate both deaths at the same time were quickly dashed.

Foxe had returned from speaking with the alderman with his mind full of questions and possibilities concerning the murder of Mr Mordifort. There was no way he wanted to start thinking about a second mysterious death if he might avoid it. Mordifort was an important man in Norwich. If Foxe stepped aside to investigate the death of an actor — and not a good one either — he would face a great deal of criticism from influential people and embarrass Alderman Halloran and the mayor. When he heard the request for him to get involved came from the hated Postgate, his mind was made up at once. He had an important commission from the mayor, which must take precedence over everything else. Postgate could go to the devil.

So, Foxe listened to her politely, while his expression throughout her narrative was one of resigned patience, bordering on martyrdom.

She had concluded by asking him if she could tell Mr Postgate to come around and explain what he wanted in his own words. Foxe's response was instant. He wanted nothing to do with Mr Postgate or the strange death in his theatre.

'The man Postgate is a septic boil on the backside of this city,' Foxe said, 'and I regret the dead body in the playhouse is not his own. Help him? I'd rather see him rot in hell. I am sorry about Chambers. He was a promising actor once, before he started to lose his looks and turned to the grog. Now he'd been reduced to getting what parts he could amongst the small companies. No more leading roles. He was lucky to get to play Falstaff. When he did, unkind people said it was because he was tailor-made for any role which portrayed an ageing, drunken old man running to fat.'

'Had you heard about the fire?'

'I would have been only a boy at the time of the fire that ball of horse dung, Postgate, told you about. I suppose I must have heard something about it — my father printed one of the local newspapers of the time — but it can't have registered in my mind. As for the preposterous tale of a ghost taking revenge, I must have been to the White Swan Playhouse many times over the last few years, but I've never heard anything about such a ghost. I'm not going to help Postgate and there's an end of it. I'm sorry, Mrs Crombie. It was extremely kind of you to allow the wretch to tell you his story. You mustn't think I don't value what you've done and my decision is no reflection on you. Even if I was entirely at leisure — which is far from the case — the answer would be the same. If the coroner and the magistrate have been informed, they will deal with it.'

It was clear Mr Foxe was not to be moved, so Mrs Crombie nodded to show she understood and took her leave. The others would be as disappointed, as she was, that Mr Foxe would not take on an investigation into the actor's death. She knew Mr Foxe loved the theatre and everything it involved. She felt sure he would never have turned away, never have refused to try to resolve the unexplained death, if only it had not been the hated Mr Postgate who had made the request.

Very well. Mistress Tabby had said Mr Foxe must deal with both problems and it was vital to his future well-being that he did so. Just as she was correct about the two deaths, she seemed to have anticipated some difficulty in bringing this about, else why would she have said there must be no excuses? At present, it would be hopeless to try to change Mr Foxe's mind, so they would have to find another way. What if they started to investigate themselves, without mentioning it to Mr Foxe? They knew the kind of steps he usually took at the start of an investigation. If they went over the same ground, they could at least get things underway. Later, if they thought of some way to persuade him to take on the investigation himself, they could tell him what they had discovered so he'd have a head start.

Mrs Crombie decided she would put this idea to the others when they gathered in the servants' hall as usual next day. If everyone took a share in the work, they could fit it in easily with their other jobs. Mr Foxe wasn't a terribly exacting master and keeping the house clean and tidy didn't demand a great deal of effort when there was only one person living there, aside from themselves. She could help as well, if she left Cousin Eleanor in charge of the bookshop on occasion.

Now it was high time she set Mr Foxe's mysteries aside and returned to the business of selling books. The carrier was due tomorrow with the new books she had ordered from London for the shop and the circulating library. He should also have collected fresh supplies of the most popular medicines from the makers, most of whom seemed to reside in the capital. If he didn't, she would have some exceedingly unhappy customers.

Back in the shop, she couldn't help noting with pride the many changes she had made. The great, semi-circular counter was still there, as were the bookshelves reaching up to the ceiling; those all dated from the time of Mr Foxe's father, when the business had been as much a printing and publishing house as a bookseller. He had also put in the fine bow windows looking out onto the street, where she was able to display the prints and caricatures which sold so well. Her contribution had been to add such touches of comfort as made customers wish to linger, chat amongst themselves, and convince one another that if each bought a copy of the latest, most fashionable novel and shared them out, they could look forward to several weeks of entertainment for a modest outlay. As she had told Mr Foxe many times, nothing increased their sales more than people's desire to gossip. That was why she had put some chairs and sofas in suitable places, so the more elderly customers could take their ease, while the younger ones perused the shelves, or sought out fresh supplies of paper, ink, and pens for sketching or writing letters.

The patented medicines sold well too. Mr Foxe had been quite dubious about introducing them, perhaps fearing complaints from the city's many medical practitioners, perhaps estimating only artisans and the poorer shopkeepers would be drawn to them. He was wrong, of course. It was one thing to pay the high fees of a physician, or buy expensive preparations from an apothecary, if someone was truly sick; quite another to lay out so much money for day-to-day remedies for headaches, colds or upsets of the stomach. Poorer people came to buy the medicines for themselves, wealthier ones sent in their servants, but they all bought nonetheless. The newspapers were full of advertisements for patent medicines of all kinds, for there was no shortage of sickness in the city, real or imaginary.

She beckoned to Cousin Eleanor and asked her to begin the process of packing up for the day, then went upstairs to ask Miss Gravener in the circulating library to do the same. That done, she went into the workroom behind the shop to see her hair was tidy, put her hat and outdoor clothes ready, and told Charlie to start clearing up whatever he had been doing. She and Jane had promised themselves a fine dinner of mutton pie that evening, followed by second helpings of the rhubarb tart they had started yesterday. Jane would be sure to have it all ready at the usual time, so it wouldn't do to be late. Dear Jane! When she'd offered to take the girl in, it had been a simple act of charity. Now she counted it as one of the best things she had ever done in her life so far. She couldn't imagine living without Jane. To say she loved her was to understate her feelings. Best of all, she knew them to be reciprocated in full. So long as they had one another, neither needed anyone else.

WHEN THE HOUSEHOLD WAS GATHERED AGAIN NEXT DAY AND THEIR

midday meal had been quickly consumed, Mrs Crombie explained her idea. At first, there was considerable scepticism from those who had not been involved before in collecting information for Mr Foxe. Alfred protested he knew nothing about investigating crime and was most unwilling to become involved in any way with such 'ungodly activities'. Both Mrs Dobbins and Mrs Whitbread, the cook, echoed his uncertainty about being able to help. Besides, they told Mrs Crombie, their duties kept them in the house for most of the time. Molly and Florence were obviously worried about offering to take part without the express approval of the housekeeper and cook. In the end, only Charlie expressed enthusiasm for the scheme.

'Very well,' Mrs Crombie said at last. 'I quite understand some of you doubt whether you have the time or the opportunity to help in the ways I have suggested. It is not something we have done before, save when Mr Foxe has asked one or two of us to undertake specific tasks for him. I definitely do not want anyone to take part who is not willing and eager to do so. Charlie and I have helped Mr Foxe on many occasions with his investigations, so I am going to suggest he and I go forward with my plan. The rest of you will go on with your normal duties. However, I will ask you to keep your eyes and ears open, in case you should learn of anything which might prove helpful. Remember, we are not trying to supplant Mr Foxe in any way, nor compete with him. The sole purpose of our quiet collection of facts is to be able to hand it all over to him when he decides to take up the case himself — as I am sure he will, given time. He is too inquisitive to stand aside and leave any mystery unsolved, especially one connected to the theatre.'

When the two of them were safely back within the confines of the bookshop, Mrs Crombie told Charlie to accompany her into the workroom, saying loudly that it was high time she tested him on his progress with reading and writing.

'I don't want anyone else in the shop to know what we are doing,' she told Charlie, once they were seated together. 'There are too many opportunities for them to gossip with the customers. I am quite able to get them to share any useful information they may pick up.'

Charlie grinned. When Mr Foxe was involved in a mystery, the apprentice had a good many opportunities to be away from the shop himself. It wasn't that he disliked the work; he enjoyed dealing with the customers, when he could, and he knew he was becoming almost proficient at repairing damaged books from the circulating library. He just didn't like being indoors so much of the time; probably a legacy of his time living on the streets.

'Just you and me,' he said happily.

'You, me, and your friends on the streets,' Mrs Crombie said. 'Don't forget them. I'm sure we'll need their eyes and ears before long. Here's my plan. I'll see what I can discover from the gossip amongst our customers. You put the word out we need to know as much as we can about the details of this death at the theatre. At this stage, any information will be useful. Later, as we are able to sort out what may be important from all the rest, we can ask specific questions. Do you have any other suggestions?'

'No, Missus Crombie. That seems right to me. I'll slip out right now and see who I can find to pass the message on to the others.'

'Oh, no,' Mrs Crombie said, dashing his hopes of an hour or so on the loose around the Great Market. 'First I want to see what you have written and hear you read to me. That's what we came in here to do, isn't it?'

'But Missus Crombie—'

'Half an hour won't make any difference in getting your "troops" mobilised for action. You thought I didn't mean it, when I said I was going to test your progress, didn't you? You were wrong. Let me see. Yes, I just happen to have a suitable book in my pocket. Turn to the first page and begin reading aloud. After we've dealt with reading, you can show me the practice you have done in writing, and I'll give you one or two sentences to write down while I watch you. Come on now. Stop pouting. The quicker we start, the sooner you'll be finished.'

7

Foxe had woken after a night spent tossing and turning, part of his mind planning how he might best approach investigating the murder of Mr Mordifort, the other part returning again and again — and quite against his will — to the dead body in the old theatre. If only it hadn't been that wretched man, Postgate, trying to get him involved. Of course, he shouldn't be considering undertaking anything else until the matter of the Assembly House murder had been cleared up. It was for that reason he had sent Mrs Crombie away when she tried to interest him in the matter, and why he had refused to let her tell Postgate to come and explain more fully. People like Postgate were always looking for a convenient back upon which to place an unwanted burden. It would not be his.

Yet for all his brave words, he kept coming back to the playhouse and its dead body. He would tell himself to forget it, to think of something else, to remember the magistrate and coroner were already involved and it was none of his business. Five minutes later, he was turning the few facts Mrs Crombie had given him over in his mind, looking for connections and hints of areas for investigation. The trouble was he could never feel at ease with an event he could neither explain nor understand. If only he could somehow numb his sense of curiosity; his feeling the incompleteness of unanswered questions and unexplained events was an offence to his most deeply held values, an inner itch he must either scratch or suffer to drive him slowly insane, until he could put Postgate and his playhouse out of his mind for good.

As Alfred helped him shave and dress in a clean day-gown, Foxe reached another decision. Young Nicholas would probably arrive that day, expecting to find a competent, experienced merchant with all aspects of his business at his finger-tips. The truth was Foxe had scarcely set foot inside his bookshop these days and had only the most general idea of how Mrs Crombie was managing it. He told himself this was because he trusted her and didn't want to interfere, but that wasn't true. The main cause of his disinterest was boredom. He'd never found the details of running a shop of great interest, which was why the place had languished, neglected, until Mrs Crombie came to give it a new lease of life. However, it would never do to let Nicholas see what a careless fellow his father's cousin had become. If he was anything like Cousin Henry, he would be censorious by nature; ever ready to discover the faults in others and delighted to catalogue and reveal them to the world.

Foxe therefore decided he must ask Mrs Crombie to give him a detailed report on all aspects of the bookstore and circulating library. If she was put out by this, he would explain their visitor would expect him, as the main partner, to be able to discourse correctly on the nature and progress of the business. So far as Foxe knew, the lad intended to undertake a business career and had been sent to understand all which doing so might involve. Trying to catch up on months of business results and activities should also be enough to put the White Swan and its body out of his mind. Once he'd finished with Mrs Crombie's report, he would set himself to write to the other members of Mr Mordifort's family — his son and heir, the daughter and her husband — explaining what the mayor had asked of him and requesting a little of their time to ask some questions about the dead man.

The first part of his plan of action completed, the second would be to talk with whoever carried out the post-mortem examination of the body. There might be something useful to be gleaned there. He'd told

Alfred to find out when and where the inquest would be held. It would most likely be this afternoon. If so, he would have to miss it and catch up later. It would be much too impolite to be absent from home deliberately when a visitor was expected.

Poor Mrs Crombie was taken aback by Foxe's sudden interest in the minutiae of the bookshop and its takings and the success of the circulating library. Even when he explained the reason, she remained resentful because he had not warned her in advance of what he wanted to discuss. As a result, she had been thrown into providing him with specific information without being adequately prepared.

For more than thirty minutes, she struggled on as best she could, wracking her mind for details of the relative profitability of the book sales compared with the patent medicines and the supplies of writing and sketching materials. She thought she had managed remarkably well and expected some compliment from Mr Foxe to that effect. Instead, she noticed his questions growing less pointed and his responses vaguer and more general. It was as if something, somewhere, kept dragging at his mind, drawing him away from what she was saying, clouding his attention with some other matter of equal or greater importance.

Her own mind had begun to wander too, assisted in its lapses of attention by Foxe's growing indifference to what she was telling him. It was while she was attempting to concentrate on explaining the usefulness of personal recommendation in securing a growing number of regular clients for the circulating library, that another idea about the death at the White Swan sprang into focus.

For some time now, Mrs Halloran, Alderman Halloran's wife, and their two nieces, had been frequent visitors to the bookshop, especially to the circulating library. All were prodigious readers. They bought some books, but the cost of new volumes was too great to allow them to meet all their needs in that way. The circulating library was the ideal way for them to replace their reading matter on a regular basis. Because of the regularity of these visits, she and Mrs Halloran were now on easy terms with one another, and she had been invited to their grand house on Colegate to take tea with Mrs Halloran and her nieces on two occasions.

A fresh consignment of books for the library was due to arrive that day or the next. It would be but a small kindness on her part to send Charlie to the alderman's house with a message for his wife to say if she and her nieces came right away, they would have the best choice from the new volumes. That would bring them running!

She could then have a quiet word with Mrs Halloran and see what she might discover. Alderman Halloran was a close confidante of the mayor and would be bound to know a good deal about any recent killing, leaving aside the usual crop of murders amongst the poor, of course. They were always killing one another in quarrels over their women, the few pence in their pockets, competition for work or theft, and, most often of all, as a result of drunken brawling. The constables usually laid hands on the killer within hours and the only involvement of the magistrates was to see him or her properly tried and sentenced to death or transportation.

Mrs Crombie was so delighted with this plan she quite lost the thread of what she was saying and stopped in some confusion. Fortunately for her, Foxe must also have been far away, so they both sat in silence for a few moments, each trying to recall what they had supposedly been discussing.

It was into this silence that the sound of knocking at the front door came. Mr Nicholas Foxe had arrived.

※

IT'S OFTEN SAID THAT THE FIRST IMPRESSIONS OF A PERSON CARRY most weight in forming someone's view of another's character and worth. If the saying is true, Foxe's first impression of his cousin's son, Nicholas, was a long way from what he had expected. He had imagined he'd be confronted either by a puritanical religious fanatic, or by someone feeble, scholarly and bookish, pale from long periods spent indoors, his back and shoulders bowed bending over his books. In short, a younger version of his cousin Henry, who was both of those. Cousin Henry's domineering nature and self-centred outlook were hidden behind an appearance which suggested a minister of the more retiring sort.

What Foxe saw before him now was a tall, well-built young man of athletic appearance; the kind of fellow you might see riding to hounds or impressing the ladies at a country ball with the grace and vigour of his dancing — to say nothing of his strong thighs and well-turned calves. It's true his dress was rustic and conservative — that could be easily remedied — but Foxe couldn't help taking an immediate liking to the fellow.

For his part, Nicholas behaved with proper deference to his host, enquiring after his health and apologising for the unexpectedness of his arrival.

'Are you sure this will be a convenient time for my visit, sir?' Nicholas asked. 'If it is not, I will, of course, return home at once and await a better occasion on which to make your acquaintance and learn what I may about your business.'

Foxe reassured the young man this was as convenient a time as any and bade him a hearty welcome. That done, he turned to practicalities. 'I suggest you go into the dining room,' he said, 'where one of the servants will bring you something to eat. I'm sure you must be tired and hungry after your long journey from London. Afterwards, I will ask my housekeeper, Mrs Dobbins, to show you to the room prepared for you, where you may set out your things as you wish and perhaps take a little rest. If you would like some fresh air, you are quite free to walk in the garden, for it is a fine day and a warm one too. Now, if you will excuse me, I am much preoccupied with certain matters laid upon me by the mayor of this city.'

It was a lame excuse, but Nicholas's early arrival would leave him free to attend the inquest on Mr Mordifort after all. Foxe always liked to be present at these occasions if he could, since you never knew what might arise during the questioning of any witnesses, especially the medical examiner. Foxe knew the medical evidence was not always given in full at an inquest, since the purpose of the hearing was only to determine the cause of death, not suggest who might be to blame — unless it was obvious from the evidence, of course.

This inquest, however, turned out to contain little more than the minimum of formalities required by law. Mordifort's son gave evidence of the identity of the body and a Mr Hamilton, who had been present at the Assembly House that evening and close to the point where the killing occurred, deposed that he had heard Mr Mordifort cry out and fall to the floor. It was then the turn of Mr Dangerfield, the surgeon who had carried out an examination of the corpse.

He stated the deceased had died as a result of a single wound inflicted with a sharp-pointed, thin-bladed knife. The knife was shown to the jury and Dangerfield continued with his evidence.

'The blow was struck from behind to the left side of the deceased's back,' he told the coroner. 'The knife was then left in the wound. I found it had penetrated the right side of the heart, causing immediate death.'

'The knife was driven into the left side of the man's back,' the coroner said, 'yet you found it had penetrated the right side of the heart. Can you please explain how this might have come about, for I confess to feeling somewhat confused by the evidence on this point?'

'The blow must have been struck from the left and slightly below the point where the blade entered the body,' Dangerfield said. 'The blade then passed between two ribs moving in an upwards direction from left to right. Like this. Imagine I am behind and to the left side of the deceased.' He picked up the knife and made a thrust upwards, the blade moving to his right as he did so.

The coroner still looked puzzled. 'For a blow to have been struck in such a way, Mr Dangerfield, would the murderer not have had to be standing well to the left of his victim, as well as behind?'

'He would, in my opinion.'

'Yet evidence has been given there was a crush of people trying to pass through the doorway at the place where the deceased was attacked. I find it hard to understand how the murderer could have found sufficient space to strike a blow as you have demonstrated.'

'He could have bent his arm, sir, and held it closer to his body, like this.'

'Indeed so, Mr Dangerfield. But to strike a firm blow from such a position — firm enough to penetrate the deceased's clothing and pass through the flesh and muscles of his back into his heart — would surely demand unusual strength if the arm was bent up in the manner you described. Do you not agree?'

'I do,' Dangerfield agreed. 'Either way seems awkward. To stand to the left allows the blow to be made with ample force but must surely have made discovery certain, given the number of people present. To stand to the right, or directly behind, would create such a lessening of strength behind the blow as to make penetration to the heart, through the muscles of the back, quite uncertain.'

'I see. If the murderer had been close behind his victim, he could have hidden what he was doing by placing his own body in the way. However, your evidence goes against this, since he would have been forced to bend his arm across the front of his body and strike from that position. To stand to the right would make the posture still worse. To strike with sufficient force to penetrate to the heart, he must have been to the left of the place where the wound was inflicted. If so, his hand would have been in view of anyone who happened to be looking that way. Do I understand you correctly?'

'You do. Perhaps he was simply lucky or calculated no one would be looking in that direction at that time. I cannot offer any other explanation. The track of the knife blade is certain, since it was still in the body when I first began my examination. To be sure of its path towards the heart, before I removed the knife to allow me to unclothe the deceased, I inserted a thin strip of wood into the body alongside the blade of the knife. I am therefore convinced what I am telling you is correct.'

'Thank you, Mr Dangerfield,' the coroner said. 'You showed admirable sense in what you did. Let me express the court's gratitude for your care and attention to your task. You may step down.'

The coroner did not refer to this puzzle again, probably judging it to be irrelevant to the question facing the jury. Instead, he told them there could be no doubt Mr Mordifort was murdered and the only other matter they had to deal with was whether there was sufficient evidence to suggest who was responsible. Since no evidence had been given on this point at all, there was, in his view, only one possible verdict. The jury, declining to retire, murmured between themselves, with much nodding of heads, and the foreman then stood to deliver their verdict; Mr Edward Mordifort, merchant, had been murdered by a person or persons unknown.

Foxe pondered this anomaly in the medical evidence all the way home, but failed to find a satisfactory answer. The coroner hadn't mentioned many of the ladies present would have been wearing dresses with wide skirts, which might have obscured any view downwards to some degree; nor that one or two people could still have been wearing the cloaks which were common at masked balls. Wearing a mask must also restrict a person's vision to a significant extent. It would have required only a second or so to put the knife into the right position and push it home, so the killer was not taking too much of a risk in a crowd of people with their minds on the forthcoming banquet. It was certainly a puzzling finding, but there was no reason to suppose it to be of major importance.

Once he was back in his house, Mr Foxe went at once to his library, where he took up paper, pen, and ink and wrote identical letters to all three members of Mordifort's family. In each, he expressed suitable condolences for their loss and explained, briefly, the mayor had asked him to conduct certain enquiries into the circumstances of Mr Mordifort's death, with a view to bringing a successful prosecution against his murderer. He ended by asking for a few minutes of each person's time to ask certain questions pertinent to this undertaking.

That done, he called Alfred and told him to see the three letters were delivered as quickly as possible.

❧ 8 ❧

Foxe and his young second cousin, Nicholas, did not meet again that day until they sat together to take dinner in Foxe's fine dining room, the candlelight glinting off the silverware, the crystal glasses, and the mirrors set into the wall between the windows. Foxe had instructed Nicholas's place should be set at his right hand, for, had he been seated at the opposite end of the table, conversation would have been difficult without shouting, given the table's length. Even so, it was a silent meal for much of the time. Foxe's mind was still working on all he knew about Mordifort's death and Nicholas did not yet know how he might best conduct a conversation with a wealthy and clearly important man like Mr Foxe. It was not, therefore, until they were finished with their food, had emptied their wineglasses, and seen all cleared away by Molly and Florence, that there was an opportunity to speak at any length.

Foxe now took up the cut-glass decanter Alfred had set at his elbow and prepared to pour some brandy into their two glasses. 'Would you like some brandy, Nicholas?' he said. 'It is quite a fine vintage.'

'My father says strong drink is the work of the devil, sir,' Nicholas replied. 'He will not have it in the house. I have never tasted brandy.'

The wistfulness in the lad's voice as he said this awoke a small devil

in Foxe's mind. How typical of his Cousin Henry to ban spirits in his
household. Many Anglican clergyman were well noted for their
connoisseurship of intoxicating liquor in all its forms and only a pig-
headed puritan like Cousin Henry would take the opposite view. Foxe
had no time for puritans and killjoys of any sect. Indeed, he had
precious little time for any of the cant associated with religion. There
and then, he decided it was high time young Nicholas should be introduced to the good things of this world.

'Well, you may try it now,' he said. 'Your father is not here and I
will not tell him, if you do not. It will do you no harm at all. Indeed, it
is a pleasant conclusion to a meal at any time and a good thing on a
cold night. Only when alcohol is taken in excess is it harmful, be it in
the form of spirits or any other.'

Nicholas hesitated a moment, then took the glass Foxe offered.
Having sniffed at its contents, he was unwise enough to take a good
mouthful and gulp it down. As a result, he experienced a long spell of
convulsive coughing and spluttering. After he had recovered his breath
and wiped the tears from his eyes, Foxe counselled him to drink the
brandy in smaller amounts in future, though he smiled as he said it. In
a strange way, the episode proved fortuitous. Both found the previous
sense of formality and restraint between them had been lessened.

'Tell me, Nicholas,' Foxe began. 'What do you have in mind for
your future? Business is a wide field. To be successful in it, you need
access to capital. Yet I do not recall Cousin Henry has any great wealth
at his disposal.'

'Indeed not, sir,' Nicholas said, shaking his head sadly. 'My father
lives primarily on the income from his tithes. So far as I know, he has
no resources available to him otherwise. Indeed, I would not have
been able to attend the University had it not been for the kindness of
our local squire. It was he who paid for my time at Oxford, urged on,
no doubt, by my father. It has always been my father's dearest wish I
should follow him into the church. I believe he and the squire were in
agreement that I would take holy orders and become my father's
curate, then succeed him as Rector when he should decide to retire.'

'And you do not wish to do this?'

'I do not. To be honest with you, sir, I think I would rather starve.'

'Given such a definitive statement, I think we must rule out the church as a way of you earning your living. What of the other professions?'

'For my father, all would be second best or worse. However, for me to enter one of the other professions — medicine, say, or the law — would at least be acceptable. Unfortunately, I have discovered no taste for either. I am far too squeamish to get involved in the cutting up of cadavers and the other gory elements of the physician's work. The law I think too boring to contemplate.'

'Having ruled both of those out, you have therefore reached what feels like an impasse. Have you any idea at all what you would like to do?'

'I confess I have none.'

Foxe paused. There was something nagging at the back of his mind. If Nicholas had expressed no interest himself in a future in business, and Cousin Henry had no capital available to launch his son on such a course, why the sudden desire to send him to Norwich, supposedly to learn more about the world of business? There was something untoward here. He had always known Cousin Henry to be a devious man. Just how devious, he was about to find out.

'Well, I will be happy for you to stay here for a little while, Nicholas,' Foxe said at last. 'You may learn whatever you wish about the bookselling business. If it appeals to you, we will see what can be done about setting you upon your correct path in life. Tomorrow morning, I will introduce you to Mrs Crombie, who is both my partner in the business and the widow of a respected bookseller in this city. She is best placed to explain to you in detail all that takes place, both in the bookshop itself and in the circulating library which she has established. My own involvement in it is quite limited. I do take an interest in the buying and selling of rare books, but that's something in which it would take you many years to become established. Not only must you acquire a considerable knowledge of such volumes, you must also gain a reputation amongst book collectors — especially those who are most discerning and demanding— since only they are willing to pay enough for their purchases to afford the seller any significant profit. What is more, they do not wander into bookshops merely in the hope of finding something to add to their collection. They know who is likely to have the right books for sale, just as I know which people in this area are most likely to have suitable books they wish to dispose of. You would need to become well-established as a bookseller of the conventional kind, before you could consider adding the sale of rare and collectable volumes to your portfolio.'

Nicholas looked decidedly downcast. 'I understand,' he said. 'Nevertheless, you have my most sincere thanks for your helpfulness in this matter. I am sorry to put you to such trouble — and your partner Mrs Crombie too. To be blunt, I have no notion whether bookselling would appeal to me. It is true I love books, but to love reading books is, I imagine, rather different from the business of selling them.'

'Yes, you could say as much.' Foxe hesitated, unsure whether to push further at this time to discover the real reason why his cousin Henry was so keen for Nicholas to come to Norwich. In the end, he decided to risk all and plunge in.

'I think,' he said, 'Cousin Henry had another reason for sending you to Norwich. Perhaps I am being too suspicious — and I must hasten to say you are welcome here, whatever the reason for your visit — but there is a question in my mind which will not give me peace until I know the answer. Others will tell you I have a most decided curiosity. It has also been said it leads me into trouble — I cannot deny it — but it has also taken me into many of the most interesting and exciting experiences in my life to date. So, Nicholas, let me ask you this. Why did Cousin Henry send you here? I cannot believe the reason I have been given is all there is to know about the matter.'

'If my father wished to deceive you, I can see he has failed entirely. I don't say whatever reason he has given you is false. I would never accuse my father of telling an outright lie. What I suspect is he has not told you the whole truth. My father has decided to re-marry. It must have been quite a sudden decision, though that is only based on my limited understanding. He may indeed have had it in mind for some time. His chosen bride is a woman, conservative and religious in her habits, who lives in a village not far away; a lady whose years are far less in number than my father's. By my reckoning, she cannot be much more than ten years older than I am.'

Foxe was amazed. Cousin Henry must be well into his fifties. The young man sitting next to him looked to be in his early twenties. What could persuade a woman of thirty or so to marry a man so much her senior? Not a rich man either.

'This is indeed surprising news,' he said. 'Can you tell me any more about this lady?'

Nicholas hedged. 'I think my father has little taste for living alone.'

'But he does not live alone. Your Aunt Harriet lives in his household.'

'I do not think such a consideration counts for much with him. I love my Aunt Harriet dearly. She is a kind and gentle lady, who has always tried to supply me with the affection and understanding of a mother. That is why my father's treatment of her sometimes causes me pain. It is not that he is actively unkind, you will understand. It is just that he does not seem to notice her much of the time, though without her the household would grind to a halt.'

'A sad state of affairs indeed. However, you have not answered my question about the lady your father intends to marry.'

'I am not sure what I can tell you, for I have only laid eyes upon her two or three times.'

Foxe waited and Nicholas gave in.

'As I said, she is about thirty-two or three. She is . . .' He paused, searching for the right words. '. . . I would say she is a lady who is, unfortunately, rather plain. She also has a retiring disposition. I feel quite reluctant to add any more, sir, for I feel I may be doing her a great disservice in describing her in this way. However, from what I have grasped via the village gossip, many are saying they never expected her to find a husband at all.'

'Does she have a dowry?'

'That I cannot tell you. She may have, for her father is a gentleman with a substantial mansion and surrounding estate. He has several other daughters, all of whom are married, and, I believe, two or three sons. It is my understanding he acquired his wealth through business overseas — in the sugar plantations of Jamaica, I believe — then handed over his business to his sons to run and bought himself an estate where he could live out his later years. The only other thing I know about him is he too is an extremely religious man. I believe he devotes a good deal of his time to obscure theological studies, though he is not ordained and holds no position in the church. He is, however, so my father assures me, a great favourite with the bishop and is known to exercise influence in the matter of senior appointments within the diocese.'

All was now clear to Foxe. For a start, his cousin wanted Nicholas out of the way before he got married. It would be too dangerous to have a handsome young fellow in the household, especially when he himself was so much older and far from being a fine physical specimen. He must also have his sights set on ecclesiastical preferment, which he hoped his new father-in-law would be able to arrange for him. Provided the bride's father's wealth was not already exhausted by his other children, it was also likely a reasonable dowry would be forthcoming — if only to ensure this final unmarried daughter found a suitable husband. There was likely to be little affection in this marriage. It was a marriage of convenience for both, though Cousin Henry's convenience had obviously taken precedence.

It was time, Foxe considered, to turn to another topic. 'There is something I need to explain to you, Nicholas, since it will affect the amount of time we can spend together over the next few days or weeks. From time to time, I have assisted the mayor in the investigation of certain crimes of importance to the well-being of this city. Generally speaking, it is left to the injured party to bring a prosecution in a case of theft, and for family members to do the same if the crime is murder. However, there are sometimes situations in which the mayor believes those who direct the fortunes of this city have an equal interest in seeing justice done. Do you follow me?'

'I think so, sir, though I have no great understanding of how the law courts function in our land.'

'That is of little account. What I wish to explain is this. An important merchant and member of the Common Council was murdered three nights ago. You could say to kill such a man is an affront to the city, as well as to his family and the rule of law. The mayor has therefore asked for my help in tracking down the assassin and collecting the evidence needed to sustain a successful prosecution. This afternoon, while you were resting, I attended the inquest. I hope tomorrow, or the day after, to be able to question the man's children about him. To the best of my present knowledge, all were present when he was struck down.'

'I did not realise this was something you became involved in,' Nicholas said. 'Does my father know?'

'Probably not,' Foxe said. 'Unless you want to be summoned home instantly, you would be well advised to see it stays that way. There is no reason you should become involved in any way —'

'But—'

'— so he has no reason to fear your morals might be contaminated by contact with any potential criminals. I merely tell you so you do not wonder if I am suddenly absent. Since Mrs Crombie will be looking after you when you are in the bookshop, I will be able to leave you in safe hands, if the need arises.'

'If it is not an impertinence, sir, may I ask that you tell me what you can of your investigation from time to time? I should be most interested. Most crimes, I believe, are committed amongst the poor, usually by what my father refers to as the criminal classes. To hear of a crime which has taken place amongst persons of quality is an opportunity I should not want to miss.' He paused. 'I will be sure not to mention it in my letters home.'

Though their acquaintance was so brief, Foxe had already decided to like young Nicholas. He agreed to keep him informed, telling himself privately he could easily omit any details likely to shock.

Later, as he lay in his bed that night, Foxe found yet more problems had taken up residence in his mind, each determined to keep him awake as long as it could. One arose out of his conversation during the evening with Nicholas and concerned his cousin Harriet, whose life after her brother's marriage looked to be headed towards still greater neglect and servitude then she was suffering at present. On the face of it, there was no way Foxe could interfere. He might be fond of Harriet and concerned for her welfare, but Cousin Henry would not take kindly to any complaints from Foxe about his treatment of his sister. Indeed, interference might make things worse, given Henry's general pig-headedness and belief in his own correctness about everything.

Harriet's state was not so unusual. It was an unfortunate fact many unmarried women found themselves in similar situations once both parents had died. Few of them possessed their own resources. Their failure to marry — often caused as much by one or more parent using them as housekeeper, then nurse, as from their own choice or lack of attraction — left them dependent on one or more brothers for a place to live and the means to sustain themselves. Since brothers usually had families of their own, making provision for a spinster sister was often seen as more of an imposition than a duty undertaken willingly through affection. Foxe felt sure Cousin Harriet was in exactly such a situation, now about to be made worse by the arrival of a young wife, who would take over the responsibility for the household which had been Harriet's until this point. Still, try as he might, Foxe could see no way of interfering in this situation, so he set it aside as something to be dealt with at a later date.

His other concern, of course, was this murder the mayor wanted him to solve. He had done all he could for the present about this. Until he was able to speak to the members of Mordifort's family, there was no way to proceed further. The medical examiner's evidence at the inquest was puzzling, but offered no separate way forward. The murderer had chosen an excellent time and place to commit his crime, for if no one came forward to say he or she had seen some part of the murder taking place, the number of people present must itself defeat further investigation. According to the alderman, Mordifort was the kind of man to amass many enemies, either through his business deal-ings or his open ambition for high office in the city. There would be many who would not be sad to hear of his death; though whether any of those would go so far as to stab him in the back was doubtful. Besides, the masked ball at the Assembly House was a select gathering for his friends and political allies only. Was it really an occasion on which you might expect to find one of the man's enemies present with murder on his mind?

That left the death at the White Swan Playhouse. Despite his refusal to get involved, Foxe found he could still not put the matter entirely from his mind. It was the sheer mystery of the thing which bothered him. Had it been a straightforward killing, say a person attacked in the street by a cutthroat, or a quarrel between two actors resulting in a sudden blow, he could have forgotten about it more easily. To find an actor dead, apparently with no outward sign of what killed him, demanded an explanation. Foxe didn't believe in ghosts, so he dismissed such explanations out of hand. It might, of course, have been a natural death; a sudden paroxysm, a seizure or perhaps an apoplexy. The inquest might make that clear, provided the medical examiner could find sufficient evidence, only he could not attend without being seen by Postgate; nor, he told himself for what must be the hundredth time, should he be giving time to an investigation he was determined not to undertake. He had enough to keep him occupied in dealing with Mr Mordifort's death. Something might turn up to throw light on what had happened at the theatre. If not, the answer to what — or who — had killed the actor, Mr Lemuel Chambers, would probably never be known. He had no way of seeking the information needed to satisfy his curiosity without letting the hated Postgate know he was carrying out an investigation, despite his denials. Damn! Damnation and hell take the man!

It was with a sense of helpless bitterness and frustration that Foxe finally succumbed to sleep.

❧ 9 ❧

After breakfast the next day, Foxe decided to take Nicholas with him to his favourite coffeehouse. He hoped he would have responses to his letters to members of the Mordifort family during the day, but he could not count on it. They must be grieving and shocked, and might well decide they could not contemplate talking about the event until after the funeral.

They left Foxe's house and walked through the surrounding maze of narrow streets lined with old buildings made of timber, their fronts jutting out into the space above the roadway and their sides leaning on one another like drunkards reeling homewards, until they came to the edge of the great marketplace. The market that morning was not especially busy, but Nicholas was still impressed.

'I don't think I shall ever get used to the size of this market,' he said to Foxe. 'I've never seen anything like it before. There are so many people and so much noise; and the smells . . .'

'The smell can be somewhat overwhelming, I agree,' Foxe said. 'We are not far from the fish market here. You should try coming on a hot summer's day. It almost stops your breath. The meat market is down there, next to the Shambles.' He waved a hand towards the far, left-hand part of the market place. 'You can imagine how that area smells too, to say nothing of the rats, cats, crows, ravens, and kites which flock there to feed on the offal. To be honest, this market is not especially busy today. At this time of the morning, most of the inhabitants of this city must be at their work, spinning or weaving the fine cloth for which Norwich is famous. The people you see before you offer a poor estimate of how populous this city is.'

Nicholas shook his head in wonder. 'I've never been anywhere as large as this before, same for my brief stop to change coaches in London on my way here. The biggest city I have been in is Canterbury. The cathedral there is splendid, but the rest of the place is small compared with this. I must confess I have never seen a city which has so many churches either. The inhabitants must be unusually pious.'

Foxe could not help himself laughing at this remark. He hoped Nicholas would not be offended, though he was reaching the view that little or nothing of Cousin Henry's excessive religiosity had rubbed off on his son.

'It's true there are a great many churches in Norwich, Nicholas,' he said, 'but I suspect it has more to do with our forbears' superstition and love of display than their piety. Look, before us stands St Peter Mancroft, one of the finest of them all, while the church of St Stephen is not far beyond. No, I do not think Norwich can claim to be a particularly pious city, unless you count the large number of dissenters who live amongst us. You will find buildings used by almost every kind of sect, cult, and religious leaning within our streets somewhere.'

'My father has a loathing for dissidents of any kind, sir, so I have no experience of them or their beliefs. He would have all kept in obedience to the established church or face the consequences. It's true we have small congregations of dissenters in the villages round about us, but they make little impact.'

'Here the newly-built chapels of the dissenters rival the churches in grandeur. Remind me to show you the Octagon Chapel, built to serve a large congregation of independents and led by some of the most learned men in the land. Come, we will go this way, so you may see two other fine buildings constructed by the same architect as that one — a local man too.'

They made their way beside the church of St Peter Mancroft and away from the Great Market until they reached the Assembly House and the Grand Concert Hall hard by it.

'There, Nicholas. Before you stand two of the finest buildings which have been constructed in Norwich in the last twenty years or so. Are they not beautiful?'

Nicholas declared himself duly impressed.

'Sadly, the murder I told you of took place in the Assembly House before you. A foul deed in a beautiful setting. Now let us hasten to the coffeehouse. It is not far away now.' They turned to their left and started walking parallel to St Peter's Church. 'This open area we are passing is the Chapel Field, a good place to stroll on a pleasant evening, and down there lies the Hay Market—'

Mr Foxe broke off his speech at that point and lunged forward to grab the arm of a dirty little boy, who was, as it seemed, merely passing by on his way somewhere else.

'Not so fast, Tommy,' Foxe said in a stern tone. 'This gentleman is a friend of mine. Give him back his purse.'

Nicholas clapped his hand to his side. Sure enough, his purse was gone! The boy, held securely by one arm, pulled Nicholas's purse from his breeches and handed it over without argument.

'I'm sorry, Mr Foxe, truly I am,' the boy said. 'I didn't know as how he was with you. Otherwise I wouldn't 'ave done it, 'onest I wouldn't. You do believe me, don't you?'

'This time I do,' Foxe said. 'Yet you know me well enough to understand what would have happened had you run off with the purse, as you were about to do.'

'You won't tell on me to Charlie, will you, Mr Foxe? If he 'ears I've stole summat from a friend of yours, I'll be in right trouble. I didn't mean to do it, Mr Foxe. I thought 'e were just some stranger.'

'Fair enough, I suppose. He is a stranger here. Still, he shouldn't have that kind of trick played on him on his first day of exploring our city. Now, here are two shillings. I'm relying on you to share it out fairly and make sure all your friends have a good meal today. It's a few days since I've been out walking, so I suspect many of them have been going hungry. Now, off with you!'

Throughout this exchange, Nicholas stood silent and amazed. He could not understand how his purse had been taken without him feeling anything. Nor could he grasp how Mr Foxe came to know this scruffy boy's name, or why he should have given him money, when he was plainly a thief. Should he not have handed him over to the constable at once? As it turned out, a still greater shock was to come, for they had scarcely walked a dozen yards further when Mr Foxe turned aside to speak to a girl, whose profession could easily be deduced from her scanty clothing and the brazen approach she was making to every man who came near her. Indeed, Nicholas could not but feel ashamed he had noticed her at all, let alone that he had allowed his eyes to dwell several moments too long on those firm, rounded breasts which were almost fully exposed by the neckline of her dress. She was a pretty girl, no doubt, but he should have been more resolute in turning his eyes away.

'Good day to you, Mary,' Mr Foxe said to the girl. 'Are you feeling better? The last I heard of you, you were poorly.'

'The same to you, Mr Foxe,' she replied in the strong accent of the county. 'I'm me old self again, right enough. And who's this fine young gentleman by your side? If he's a friend of yours, you know I'd offer 'im a special rate.' She sidled nearer to Nicholas, well aware of the effect her charms were having on him. Indeed, she managed to lean forward a little to afford him a better view. 'Wouldn't you like to 'ave these bubbies in your hands, sir? Many a man has paid me a full sixpence to let him fondle 'em, but you could do it for nothing, seein' as you're a friend of Mr Foxe 'ere. Give me . . . oh, ninepence, say, and you can run your hands anywhere you like — an' I'll take your yard in me 'and an' give you the kind of pleasure I reckon you've never 'ad afore. There's a good spot down the alleyway there, sir, where none will see or interrupt us.'

Nicholas's face was, by now, so hot and red it was a wonder his shirt collar hadn't started to scorch, while the sweat was pouring from his brow as if he'd been running hard. Foxe decided he'd had sufficient fun at the lad's expense and stepped in to save him from anything worse happening.

'Mary, my dear,' Foxe said in the gentlest way imaginable, 'leave the poor fellow alone. You can see how embarrassed he is. He isn't used to such treatment. Indeed, I'm quite sure this is the first time he's know-ingly come this close to a whore, let alone one as pretty and shameless as you are. Put your titties away now, there's a good girl. They're magnificent, as you well know, but quite overwhelming to a well brought up lad, who's been living in a rectory. Now, how are the others in your group? Jane and Maude and . . . Kitty, isn't it? . . . and Betty, Ruthie and all the others?'

Mary turned away from Nicholas at once. 'We lost Betty, Mr Foxe. It was cold an' the wasting lung disease took her, not three weeks past. The rest is as well as you can expect, though Ruthie got a bad dose of the clap and Maude found her belly swellin' and 'ad to visit Mother Hendry for the cure. That always tears a girl up, that do.'

'I'm sorry to hear about poor Betty,' Foxe said. 'She deserved a better life than she had. Now, here's four shillings for you, Mary. Make sure you and the other girls have a good meal today. Use anything left over for medicine or anything else you need. Keep your eyes open to catch me if you see me going past.'

As the girl turned away, Nicholas could restrain himself no longer. 'That girl. . .' he blurted out. 'She . . . she's a . . .'

'The word you want is whore. Yes, Mary is a whore — a good one too, as I understand it — but she's still one of the street children, as is Tommy who stole your purse. They all live where they can, for they have no homes to go to. Most of the girls either beg or sell themselves to get money to eat. The boys tend to steal. I do what I can to help them. None of them want to live like this. They have no choice. And don't be misled by the maturity of certain parts of Mary's body. I reckon she can't be any older than fourteen, if she's that.'

'But, sir! To speak in the street with such people; thieves and . . . whores. Surely it is demeaning to a gentleman?'

'They are still children,' Foxe said gently. 'They sleep in doorways or in the churchyards, at constant risk from ruffians, disease, and cold. It's a hard life, as you can guess. They're here because they've experi-enced much worse from their families, their masters — if they were apprentices or servants — and the poor houses and orphanages to which many of them were sent. No one cares about them, for few can see past the dirt, the crime, and the misery to the child beneath. If I recall my New Testament correctly, the people of his time berated Christ for associating with publicans and sinners. Were he here today, I do not imagine he would turn away from a child such as Mary, whore or not.

'I don't know if you've met Florence, my kitchen maid. I found her on the streets, too. She didn't sell herself though — or says she didn't. Her nickname then was "Quick-Fingers" Flo from her dexterity in picking pockets. One day I caught her picking mine, felt sorry for her and found her a place in my household, if she agreed she would not steal again. She has kept her promise and become a most useful servant. Charlie Dillon, my apprentice, was also once one of the street children. Indeed, though he lives now in the old stables at the bottom of my garden, he still has a good deal to do with them. They see him as a kind of leader, though many are older than he is. I get him to let me know if there are any in particular need. If so, I send them what money I can through him. On days like today, as I am walking in this area, I keep my eyes open and check up on those I can. Since I have been kept at home for some days of late with a cold, they will have missed the small amounts of money I can give to them. That's why you saw me give Tommy and Mercy so much to make up for the days I missed. Usually I avoid large amounts; the temptation to use it to buy drink or waste it in other ways is too great. Still, Mercy has a good head on her shoulders and can probably be relied upon to do as I asked. Tommy I am less sure about, but I had no choice.'

'You make me feel ashamed, sir,' Nicholas said. 'I have heard of charity many times — my father is fond of preaching about it - but I have to say I have never seen it in action as I have now. Many talk about helping the poor, but only at a distance. None would dream of speaking to those children in the way you have. You may be sure I will remember this, sir, and act upon it when I can.'

By this time, the two had come to the door of the coffeehouse. Foxe led the way inside, walking quickly to his favourite table, nodding and murmuring greetings to various people as he passed them. The owner immediately left his place behind the counter and hurried up to greet this most favoured customer, clearly relieved his absence had been temporary only and he had not transferred his custom elsewhere.

Their coffee came in an instant and Foxe and Nicholas sat down, expecting to enjoy it in peace.

It was not to be. A gloomy-looking man of medium height came over a moment later and sat himself down without a word on the empty chair on the other side of Mr Foxe from where Nicholas was sitting. 'Foxe,' the man said. 'Here you are. I haven't seen you for some days. Where have you been?'

Foxe clearly knew this man, for he ignored his question and the impoliteness of his manner, turning instead to Nicholas. 'Let me introduce our unexpected — and uninvited — guest to you. This is Mr Sebastian Hirons, the editor of the "Norfolk Intelligencer", which I'm sure he will tell you is the most important and best-managed of the several newspapers produced in this city. Hirons, this is Mr Nicholas Foxe, the son of my cousin, Rev. Henry Foxe of Kent. He has come to Norwich to stay with me for a little while and learn something of the trade of a bookseller.'

Hirons must have found this last statement extremely amusing as he burst out laughing, while at the same time reaching across to shake Nicholas's hand.

'Pleased to meet you, young sir,' he said, after he had recovered himself a little. 'Let me warn you, you won't learn much about bookselling from Foxe here, that I can promise you. He doesn't soil his hands with the shop since Mrs Crombie came along. She's the one who can tell you something about the business of selling books. Not Mr Ashmole Foxe.'

'I am going to leave him with Mrs Crombie as soon as we return,' Foxe said, seemingly unperturbed by this outburst. 'I have already explained to him the partnership she and I have. If you wish to be useful, Hirons, why don't you offer Cousin Nicholas the chance to have a look around your editorial offices and printing works. I daresay he's never seen how a newspaper is produced.'

'Indeed, I have not,' Nicholas said. 'I'm sure I would find it a fascinating process.'

'You're welcome to come on any day except Thursday and Friday,' Hirons said. 'Thursday's the day we finalise the copy and Friday we go to print. No one would have time on either day to show you around and you'd simply be in the way. Aside from then, I'll undertake to do the honours myself. It is indeed a fascinating process and you'll see it in no better light than you can in our works and offices.'

'You are greatly honoured, Nicholas,' Foxe said. 'The great editor rarely ventures so far from his desk at any time, save to come here, drink coffee, and pester me.'

'Speaking of pestering you, Foxe, what can you tell me about the death of this actor, Mr Chambers? I'm sure you're already up to your elbows in the matter.'

'In that, Hirons, you are mistaken,' Foxe said with dignity. 'I am having nothing to do with it. An unexplained death of this kind is a matter for the coroner, not for me.'

'Of course! I see now. It's Postgate, isn't it? You can't stand the man. Well, I have to say I agree with you there.'

'Whether I can stand Mr Postgate or not is irrelevant in this matter. So far as I know, the inquest has already been held, the death was judged to be from natural causes and there's an end of it.'

Hirons smiled. 'Quite wrong,' he said. 'That's what everyone expected, but it isn't what happened. The inquest was opened, the jury viewed the body, and evidence was taken on the identity of the cadaver. Then proceedings were at once adjourned, pending the outcome of a full medical examination. The inquest resumes this afternoon. Now, what do you say to that?'

'There must have been some doubt as to the cause of death. So much is clear. It is still nothing to do with me.'

'What about Mordifort then? Are you looking into that murder? A rich man is more in your line, I dare say.'

'The mayor has asked me to see what I can discover, so I attended the inquest yesterday; but so did you, I know, for I saw you at the front of the public benches. You therefore know as much at this stage as I do myself.'

Hirons, frustrated, now turned to Nicholas. 'I told you a moment ago, young sir, Foxe has all but abandoned the bookselling trade. All he ever does is wander into the shop, pass the time of day with Mrs Crombie for a few minutes, then wander out again. No, Mr Foxe spends all his time solving mysteries and chasing criminals. Now, here we have a bona fide mystery - a dead man who may well not have met his end from natural causes (though we don't know that for certain yet). It's also possible his death may, I stress "may", have been caused by a vengeful ghost, so some people are saying. Yet Mr Foxe says it has nothing to do with him and he has no interest in it. If I say I do not believe him, you will understand why.'

'My dear Hirons,' Foxe said, in a voice which came straight from the wastes and ice-fields of the Arctic. 'You are exaggerating your conversation in just the same way your newspaper exaggerates and invents the stories in most of its pages. I may indeed have assisted the mayor on two occasions in his role as a magistrate. I am doing so in the case of Mr Mordifort, as I have just told you. That is the sum total of my involvement. I cannot see it amounts to — what were your words? — ". . . spending all his time solving mysteries and chasing criminals".'

'I was wrong, I admit it,' Hirons said, unabashed. 'I forgot to mention the time you spend with your tailor, and dilly-dallying with actresses and other women. As for my newspaper, you won't find a more truthful one in the town. Now, since you say you have nothing to tell me, I will bid you both good day. I have things to do. The London papers will have arrived by now and those fools of sub-editors have no idea what it is worth considering for inclusion in our newspaper and what is not.'

With that, Mr Hirons rose and left them, while Nicholas stared after him, his mind a jumble of confused thoughts and impressions. This must surely rank as one of the strangest mornings he had spent, for it had already contained more surprises than he had ever encountered before. If his stay with Mr Foxe went on like this, he thought to himself, he would be a different person by the time he left.

'Pay Hirons no heed,' Foxe said to him. 'He delights in trying to worm information out of me. When he fails, he turns to his other game, which is to embarrass me if he can with exaggerated tales of my style of life. I was going to let you come to this gently, but since he has doubtless set your mind in a whirl I had best explain at once. I have never claimed to be a model of propriety or moral rectitude. I am — at least I was until recently — something of a dandy in my style of dress, although I have moderated my style lately. I am also known to associate — intimately — with various ladies, several of them actresses. I have no intention of changing that behaviour, though I promise not to compromise you by bringing any to my house during your stay with me. Your father, if he was aware of my behaviour, would be aghast and would tell you to leave my house on the instant. It is up to you to decide whether you can bear to stay. I am, I suppose you would say, a man of the world, though I would argue there are many, many men whose behaviour is much worse than mine. I cheat no one. I harm no one, if I can avoid it. No woman need fear affront from me, for I take my pleasure only with those who are eager to join me and do the same. You have already seen I give to the poor, since I am rich enough to do so. I am, in short, the most principled rake you will ever meet.'

Nicholas could not help but smile at this. It's true he was shocked by what Mr Foxe had told him. It was absolutely true his father would be appalled and launch into one of his sermons on the dreadful fate awaiting sinners in the next world. Yet it was also true he did not want to leave either Mr Foxe's house or this city of fascinations and surprises. Maybe it would, as his father would aver, put his immortal soul at risk, but he was determined to stick it out.

'I shall say nothing to my father of any of this, sir,' he said, 'you may be sure. Whether he knows, or guesses, you are a man most different in your ways to his I cannot say, but he sent me here and here I shall stay — at least for the present. I cannot deny what I have seen and heard this morning has shocked me, but that is mostly, I suspect, because I have been too long kept from the reality of this world in which we live. No, sir. I will not leave until my business is complete here or you send me on my way out of frustration at my ignorance.'

'Good man!' Foxe said. 'Now let's go back home.'

❧ 10 ❧

When they arrived back at his house, Foxe handed Nicholas over to Mrs Crombie, saying it was high time he began his education in how to become a bookseller, should this prove to be what he desired. But before he could escape to return to his library and peace, he was detained by Charlie, full of excitement over some gossip he had just heard in the bookstore.

'Let me tell you about it, master,' he began. 'It's murder!'

'What's murder?' Foxe said. 'Who?'

'The man at the theatre. The coroner's jury has found it was murder. People have been coming into the bookshop full of the tale. They say the medical evidence at the inquest proved it.'

'Did it?' Foxe said. 'So how was he murdered?'

'The jury was told he was hit over the head with something heavy, which broke his skull and killed him.'

Foxe was thoughtful about this. It seemed odd. If he'd been hit over the head with a heavy object, struck hard enough for the blow to kill him, there must have been some mark and the skin would have been broken through. Yet, as he recalled, Mrs Crombie said Postgate claimed there wasn't a mark on the man.

'Was anything else of interest said at the inquest?' Foxe asked the boy. 'Did anyone suggest why this actor was killed?'

'Not so as I've heard. It was just the jury said it was murder, based on the evidence from the doctor what examined him. Do you think the ghost did it? That's what people are saying.'

Foxe laughed. 'Ghosts are supposed to be insubstantial spirits, not creatures capable of carrying heavy objects about. I've never heard of a ghost being able to pick up a heavy object and use it to hit someone over the head. I suppose a ghost might be able to dislodge something which would fall, killing whoever it struck. If that were the case, surely the object would still have been lying by the dead man. The ghost wouldn't be able to lift it and put it away.'

Charlie could see the logic in this, but the ghost tale was more exciting than a human being with murderous intentions. 'Are you going to take up an investigation now, master?' he asked. He still hoped Foxe would get involved and draw him in as usual.

Foxe considered the position. Nothing had changed. Any action on his part would be taken to come from the original approach from Post-gate. On the other hand, Chambers' death had all the makings of a really intriguing mystery, exactly the sort of thing he had investigated several times before. He decided to stand firm.

'No,' Foxe said. 'Maybe others will look into the matter, but not me. There's probably quite a simple explanation. Actors are emotional creatures; feuds and hatreds between them are common, though they don't normally go as far as to kill one another.'

'Some people are saying it was Mr Edwards,' Charlie said. 'They say he and Mr Chambers hated one another. Done so for years, probably because Mr Edwards loved the actress what died and Mr Chambers was the one what started the fire.'

To Foxe, this seemed too neat; too like the plot of a cheap melodrama. If their hatred was so deep and had been so long lasting, why hadn't he heard about it before? The story had arisen only after Chambers was dead. There was another point too. How could killing Chambers produce any benefit for Edwards, save for revenge. They weren't in the same company; so far as Foxe knew, they didn't even play the same kinds of roles. Chambers' career was nearly finished after a long decline through heavy drinking. Edwards hadn't made a stellar success of his career, but he was a steady, workmanlike actor, who could be relied upon to fill a supporting role with no danger of the leading actor being upstaged. It was only if you assumed the rest of the story Postgate had spread about was true, that Edwards murdering Chambers made any sense.

It was just infuriating! In the normal way of things, he would have looked into this murder at once and found the answers by going to the playhouse and asking those who knew both men; or by going to the offices of the local newspapers and looking through the editions published at the time of the fire. The trouble was, either of those actions was bound to become known to Postgate. Damn the man! If he wasn't involved, it would be obvious what to do next. But as it was . . .

Foxe went back to his library in a foul mood.

His day grew no better. He found a letter waiting for him, written in curiously formed handwriting and sent by Mordifort's daughter, Mrs Dorothy Henson. It was brief and to the point and was clearly intended to cover her husband's response as well as hers.

'*My husband and I found your letter impertinent and thoughtless,*' she began. '*I cannot imagine why you thought it appropriate to request a meeting when my father's funeral has yet to take place. A person possessed of common tact and politeness would have waited until we had been allowed time to mourn. A person with sense would not have written in such a manner at all, nor attempted to interfere in that kind of manner.*

'*My father's death is no concern of yours or the mayor's, sir. Neither of you have any standing in this matter. If any prosecution is to be brought, it is the responsibility of the Mordifort family to bring it and no one else's.*

'*That being the case, there cannot be any occasion for you to question myself, my brother or my husband, as you suggest. Indeed, any attempt on your part to bother us with unwanted meddling in matters which do not concern you will be resisted in the most strenuous fashion.*'

That, as they say, was that. Foxe could not imagine a blunter or less courteous refusal. What was odd though was Mrs Henson had written it and not her husband, as head of their household. Maybe it was simply because, as Mordifort's daughter, she felt the refusal would have still more force coming from her. There was no response from the son,

Peter Mordifort, as yet. Maybe his sister's refusal to co-operate in any investigation was meant to stand for his response as well.

If none of the family were willing to answer questions, it would limit any enquiry to a substantial degree. If they demanded he and the mayor refrain from looking into the murder at all, that would most likely be the end of the affair, so far as they were concerned. Mordifort had been an important man in the city, a person with links to noble families such as the Townshends and the Walpoles. The mayor would never risk his future standing by upsetting such influential people as those; and if the mayor abandoned any further action, it would be foolish to press forward on his own. It was just . . . why respond with such anger to the letter he had sent? Surely the relatives of a murdered man would be eager to see the killer found and a prosecution brought against him? Yet . . . what had she written? . . . 'If any prosecution is to be brought, it is the responsibility of the Mordifort family to bring it.' That might almost imply bringing the murderer to justice was merely a possibility, not something they desired.

Foxe's curiosity was such he knew he would never be able to walk away from this puzzle and forget about it. He wouldn't be able to investigate openly, of course, but nothing would stop him from finding out all he could by more secret and devious means. He wasn't called Foxe for nothing!

❦

THAT NIGHT AT DINNER, NICHOLAS WAS FULL OF ENTHUSIASM FOR the way Mrs Crombie had been explaining the ins and outs of selling books.

'I'd never realised it was such a complicated matter, sir,' he said. 'I thought you just bought some books, put them on a shelf and waited for people to come in and buy. Instead, I find Mrs Crombie takes time to talk to the customers to find out how well they enjoy the books they're reading and what else they might find attractive. Even then, she doesn't hurry to order anything; not until she has either found a reasonable number of people interested in the same book, or someone has placed a firm order.'

'That's the sensible thing to do,' Foxe said. 'It's easy for people to tell you they'd like to read this or that — maybe even to buy it. Then, when you've spent the money in getting copies for your stock, they change their minds; someone lent them a copy, the fashion has changed, or the word is out that it isn't as good as people said. Often enough, they've forgotten about it and moved on to some other fad. You're left with books you can't sell. Books are far too expensive to do that too often, if you want to stay in business.'

'Mrs Crombie says listening to people, watching what they pick up and look at while they're in the bookshop, and encouraging them to talk is more important than a detailed knowledge of what books are available.'

'I'm not sure I'd go quite that far, despite Mrs Crombie's obvious success. There are times when you have to lead people — gently, of course — towards a decision you hope they'll be pleased with afterwards. There's no point in anyone telling you they'd like to read something, whether it's a title or a kind of book, which simply isn't available. Unless, that is, you're going to write them yourself.'

There was a long pause. Nicholas seemed to be making up his mind about something.

'I've been reluctant to mention this to anyone,' he said. 'If I tell you something important to me and ask you not to pass it on to my father, would you be willing to do that?'

Foxe didn't hesitate. 'Of course,' he said. 'It's not my job to report on you, even if I thought it might be useful, which I don't. If you tell me something in confidence, I won't pass it on to anybody, unless you tell me I may.'

'Very well. I've sometimes thought about writing. I would certainly like to try my hand at it. My hero is Mr Daniel Defoe, though the American, Mr Franklin, runs him a close second. What they write is so interesting, so broadening to the mind. I don't think I could write stories or novels, but I believe I would be able to write books that are interesting and useful, maybe exciting. I've always enjoyed reading about the history of our country, just as I've enjoyed books of travel and exploration in faraway lands. Sadly, I don't have the money to be able to travel myself, nor would my father ever allow it, so I expect this ambition to seek out new places and write about them afterwards will go the way of many things in this life. It will become something I would like to have done but was never able to attempt.'

'I wouldn't give up so easily, if I were you,' Foxe said. 'Now, to write as well as the people you've mentioned is not something you'll achieve without time spent learning the craft. Let me think about what you've told me. If you do decide you wish to make a living as an author, you'd better set aside all thoughts of riches or fame. It will be a long, hard road. The only alternative is to find a wealthy patron who will find you some means of earning a living while you write your book; and perhaps provide the finance to have your first one or two volumes printed and circulated. Either that or you must advertise for subscribers; people willing to pay a certain amount in advance to receive a copy of your book once it's finished and published.'

Nicholas winced at this. Still, Foxe thought, better to have a cold draft of realism now than to set out and suffer disappointment along the way.

'I have a practical suggestion for you,' Foxe continued. 'Use your time while you're here to look through the volumes in my library, in the bookstore, and in the circulating library. Find books on the topics you think might be of interest to you as an author. Read them all. Read them in detail too. Look at how they're put together, how the author has expressed themselves through their writing, what you think is interesting and what you think would have been better left out. There's no better way to learn to write than through reading the works of established writers; and no better place to find such works than in a bookstore, a circulating library, and the personal library of a bookseller.

'In the meantime, learn all you can from Mrs Crombie about the business of selling books. It's a poor author who gives no attention to how his book is going to find its way to those willing to buy it. If you understand what a bookseller looks for when he chooses his stock, you'll also understand the kind of books he'll never put on his shelves, because people won't buy them. Many people have written books which don't sell, since no bookseller is ever willing to stock them.'

Nicholas perked up at this suggestion, so Foxe now decided to venture a question of his own.

'Tell me, Nicholas. What have you heard about the inquest which was held on Mr Chambers, the actor killed at the White Swan Playhouse. Charlie came and told me the news that the coroner's jury had brought in a verdict of murder. Have you heard anything else?'

Sadly, for Mr Foxe, the answer was negative. Nicholas had been too wrapped up in Mrs Crombie's explanations to pay heed to anything else.

❦ 11 ❦

Foxe was late going into the bookshop the next morning. He'd slept poorly, his mind full of questions and theories about the two murders. By the time he'd gone into the dining room to take breakfast, he found Nicholas had finished his and returned to his lessons with Mrs Crombie. So, when he entered the shop some thirty minutes later, he was surprised to find Nicholas absent. Mrs Crombie was there, standing by the counter with Charlie alongside, but there was no sign of Nicholas. Perhaps he was upstairs in the circulating library, picking the brains of Miss Gravener, who was in charge there.

Before he could ask where Nicholas might be — indeed, before he could say 'good morning' — Charlie had rushed over to him, his face flushed with excitement.

'Have you heard the latest news, master,' he said. 'They're saying it's the ghost again.'

'What are you talking about, boy?' Foxe said. He was not in the best of tempers, while any mention of ghosts or the supernatural tended to irritate him at the best of times. 'Who is saying the ghost did what?'

'Mr Edwards,' Charlie said, unperturbed by his master's surly tone. 'He's been stabbed. On the stage too. Might be dead by now.'

Mrs Crombie intervened. 'What the boy is trying to tell you,' she said, 'is people have been coming in this morning with the tale that there was some sort of accident on stage last night at the White Swan Playhouse; an accident involving the character which Mr Edwards was playing.'

'What kind of an accident?' Foxe asked. 'Was the fellow badly hurt?'

'I do not know. Some say he was, others that his injury is comparatively minor. All I can tell you is it happened at a point in the play where his character was to be stabbed by one of the others. The trick dagger which should allow that to take place safely was either tampered with or another put in its place. People exaggerate, so it's hard to tell exactly the nature of his injuries. As for the involvement of the ghost, you may make of that what you will.'

Foxe didn't know what to make of it. It would be easy enough either to substitute a real dagger for the stage version, or to tamper with the stage dagger and turn it into a lethal weapon. But why Edwards? The rumour had been he was in some way mixed up in the killing of Chambers. If that were so, for someone to attack him made little sense. It suggested rather that both the men were targets of the same murderer. Had both been involved in the fire which broke out so long ago? He couldn't see any other link.

Mrs Crombie had the good sense to stay silent and give Mr Foxe time to sort out his thoughts. However, she hadn't reckoned with Charlie, ever eager to tell his master everything he knew as quickly as possible.

'It was while Mrs Halloran was here we heard about it,' he said, though what this had to do with the attack on Edwards or the ghost was beyond anybody's understanding.

Foxe became totally confused. 'Mrs Halloran?' he said. 'Was she the person who brought the news about Edwards?'

'Nah! Course not,' Charlie said. 'She came here with her two nieces.'

'Charlie! Get back to your work. Now! Stop bothering your master with your nonsense.' When Mrs Crombie spoke in that tone, Charlie knew better than to disobey her. He disappeared at once.

'Please tell me what is going on, Mrs Crombie,' Foxe said. 'One moment the boy is talking about an attack on an actor, the next he's going on about Mrs Halloran. I can't make head nor tail of it.'

'It's really quite simple,' Mrs Crombie replied. 'The rumours about Mr Edwards came from a number of people, which did not include Mrs Halloran. Her coming here is quite a separate matter. As it happens, you've only just missed her. As you know, she comes quite often, bringing her two nieces, Miss Maria and Miss Lucy. They ask to see the new novels which have come in, then they go upstairs to the library to return the last set of books they borrowed and obtain new ones. They had quite a pile of books between them by the end of their visit. I was going to send Charlie to carry their books home for them, but Mr Nicholas volunteered to do it instead. That's why he isn't here now. He's escorting them home.'

'So, Nicholas has gone back with them,' Foxe said.

'Yes. He said he would be delighted to escort them to carry their books. I saw no reason to prevent it. Indeed, I am in no position to stop him doing whatever he wishes.'

Foxe's expression revealed his thoughts. It said he suspected the young man of setting aside the serious matter of learning about book-selling, in favour of a pleasant walk through the city.

'Mrs Halloran also brought a message for you from her husband.' Mrs Crombie was now aware of the trouble hanging over Nicholas's head and sought to distract Foxe's attention. 'The alderman intends to pay you a visit today. He should be with you at around noon, if you will find it convenient.'

'Hmm? What? Oh yes. Quite convenient, I suppose. When do you expect young Nicholas to be back?'

'I couldn't say. It depends on whether Mrs Halloran invites him to stay a few moments to refresh himself; or if Alderman Halloran decides to show him over his library. You know how proud the alderman is of his book collection. Mrs Halloran and her nieces seemed to have taken quite a shine to the young man. He is exceed-ingly handsome, isn't he — and has such lovely manners.' Foxe was not the only one who could yield to the promptings of the devil within.

'When he deigns to return, send him in to me at once, if you please. He hasn't been sent here to wander around Norwich, displaying his fine manners to ladies. I dread to imagine what his father, the Rector, would make of such behaviour — or of me for allowing it. I can see I shall have to lay down some rules for the time he is here, or risk him disgracing himself.'

With that, Foxe turned and strode back into his house, leaving Mrs Crombie free to burst out laughing at his discomfiture.

What Mrs Crombie kept concealed was she too had 'taken a shine' to Mr Nicholas, as she now called him. Until Mrs Halloran had been ready to leave, she and Nicholas had withdrawn into the workroom to have a private conversation about Mr Foxe, his investigations, and his refusal to get involved in looking into the murder of Mr Lemuel Chambers at the White Swan.

The previous afternoon, when Nicholas had returned after going to the coffeehouse, the poor lad had been so bewildered and disorientated by all he had learned about Mr Foxe and his way of life, that he was unable for a time to turn his attention to anything else. Finding Mrs Crombie was an excellent listener, possessed of both intelligence and compassion, he had poured out his confusions and concerns to her.

'I can only too well imagine what my father would say to this,' he said. 'He would demand I return home at once.'

'And you do not want to go?'

'I do not. Do you think this is wicked of me, Mrs Crombie? I find myself under the roof of a man who tells me openly he is a rake and a philanderer, yet I am entirely unwilling to leave. Though I have been here but one day, there is something about this place which draws me to it.'

'My advice would be not to take what Mr Foxe has told you entirely seriously. I have worked with him for almost two years and have found him kind and appreciative and his behaviour towards me completely correct. He's no rake, Mr Nicholas, whatever he says. It's true he used to dress in a most extravagant manner at one time, but he has moderated his style of clothing considerably. He used to be notorious for keeping two sisters as his mistresses at one time—'

'Two sisters were *both* his mistresses?'

'The Catt sisters. One, Kitty, is an actress, now in London and possessed of considerable fame, as I hear. The other, Gracie, kept a bordello in the city.'

Nicholas groaned. 'He kept the madam of a bordello as a mistress.'

'It was an extremely luxurious and expensive bordello, I believe,' Mrs Crombie said. 'What's more, the Catt sisters came from a most respected local family. I never met them, but those who did have told me they were clever, accomplished people with fine manners and a good deal of common sense. What you must understand, Mr Nicholas, is that your cousin takes great pleasure in the company of women and sees no reason why he should not do so — provided the ladies concerned always express complete willingness to allow him the kind of intimate contact with them he most enjoys. I have never heard of him forcing himself on anyone, nor stooping to use his position as master in his house to cajole any of the servants to allow him to take liberties with them. How can I best explain it? Mr Foxe, I believe, thinks conventional ways of conducting relations are foolish. He therefore ignores them, relying instead on a strong sense of ethics to keep him from doing anyone wrong.'

She could see she was winning Nicholas over, though he obviously felt the need to find greater justification for ignoring the precepts his father had drummed into him.

'Are these two . . . ladies . . . you mentioned still in contact with Mr Foxe? Might they come to the house?'

'I mentioned Kitty is in London. Her sister went with her. I have no idea whether they will return or not. But let us not dwell on this any further. Mr Foxe's ways will not impinge on you, so you can ignore them if you wish to stay — as you say you do.'

Nicholas still looked dubious, but it was clear his mind was made up, so Mrs Crombie ventured to take another step in bringing him firmly into the Foxe household.

'Everyone in this house and shop thinks most highly of Mr Foxe. That is why we wish to help him at the present time, if we can. Has he mentioned to you about the murder?'

'The death of some rich merchant during a masked ball?'

'Not that one. The other murder. The one at the White Swan Playhouse.'

Since Nicholas seemed doubtful — so much had come upon him that morning he could no longer be clear what had and had not been mentioned — she explained the affair as briefly as she could, adding the knowledge that it was not definitely established as a case of murder. From there she explained about Mr Postgate and Mr Foxe's refusal to have anything to do with an investigation which involved such a loathsome man.

'Of course,' she went on, 'Mr Foxe is almost bound to get involved at some point, especially now there has been an attack on another actor at the same theatre. That's why we've decided to do what we can to prepare the ground by collecting information in advance of his becoming concerned with the deaths. What I wonder is whether you would be prepared to help us too.'

'Me?' Nicholas yelped. 'What could I do?'

'What we all do, which is to keep our eyes and ears open for anything useful. Charlie has enlisted the help of his friends amongst the street children. I am listening for gossip in the shop and the rest will do the same amongst the people they have dealings with in the course of their work. Mrs Halloran, the alderman's wife and her nieces are bound to come into the shop in the next day or so. What if I suggested you walked home with them to carry their books? Mrs Halloran is a most hospitable and kind lady and would be bound to invite you in. If she does not — which is unlikely — her nieces Miss Maria and Miss Lucy are certain to want to show you their uncle's fine library. Once you are inside, I'm sure you can improve your acquaintance to the point where they might mention things the alderman will have told them about these killings. He's a close confidante of the mayor and a magistrate besides.'

It took a little more persuasion, but Mrs Crombie succeeded in the end. That was why he was now absent at the Halloran's house in Colegate, and why he would not return for almost three hours.

As it turned out, no clandestine investigation was needed, since Foxe was about to become concerned in the deaths at the White Swan whether he wished to or not.

✣ 1 2 ✣

The bells of the great church of St Peter Mancroft were chiming noon as Alderman Halloran knocked on the front door of Foxe's house. Such punctuality was typical of the man. He liked to be precise and predictable in everything; the kind of person you could rely on to do whatever he had promised and deliver the goods you had ordered on the precise day you were expecting them. Much of his wealth and success as a merchant and factory owner had come from sticking to this simple rule of life.

Foxe welcomed him into his library and enquired what refreshment he would like to take. As usual at that time of day, Halloran chose a glass of cider and Molly was sent to fetch it. The two men then settled themselves comfortably in the padded leather chairs on either side of the fireplace.

Foxe looked at the alderman with some affection. Their relationship had begun formally, as customer and seller, but had evolved of late into something more relaxed and personal. You would never guess the alderman was such a power in the city. He was not an imposing figure. Rather ordinary in appearance, to tell the truth; his face now lined by age, though his eyes retained the liveliness of a younger man's. He had given up wearing a wig some while ago, so you could see his hair was almost completely grey. Everything he wore was well tailored and often made from the finest worsted, but of a conservative cut — nothing suggesting he was other than a bluff, down-to-earth merchant, conventional in manner, always polite, but managing nonetheless to convey the sense of a man with a strong sense of control and considerable firmness of purpose.

Halloran rarely wasted time on small talk. As soon as Molly had left after bringing the refreshments each had settled upon, he turned at once to the reasons for him coming that day.

'The mayor has received a letter from Mrs Henson, Mr Mordifort's daughter,' he said, 'telling him in the most forthright terms that neither he nor you should take any further interest in Mordifort's murder.'

'I had a similar letter,' Foxe replied. 'The wording came close to being insulting.'

'As did the one to the mayor. As you can imagine, he's angry, but if that's the way the family wish to proceed — an important family too with significant connections — he can hardly do other than agree. He therefore wishes you to drop your investigation at once.'

'As I shall, Halloran — at least openly.'

'What are you up to, Foxe? If these people find out you haven't done as they demand, they'll be bound to make trouble for you. Probably for the mayor too.'

'They won't find out, if I can help it. Tell me, are you at all bothered by this response from Mordifort's daughter? Does it seem what you might expect a grieving family member to write?'

Halloran frowned. 'When you put it like that—'

'There's no other way to put it. The mayor and I have been warned off without any assurance the family will undertake the kind of investigation needed to find the murderer. If this is in their mind, why not say so? If they wish to wait until the sharpest feelings of grief subside before seeking the culprit, why not allow us to proceed, but request us to share what we find? They could then take over and continue the process themselves, if they do not wish anyone else involved.'

'It does seem odd, doesn't it? I know the mayor isn't happy at the idea that delaying an investigation might well give the killer time to cover his tracks.'

'There's more to this than meets the eye, if you ask me,' Foxe said. 'If you're willing to help me, all you need to do now is tell the mayor I am doing as he asks. I'll use my own sources to see what else I can discover.'

'I'll do as you ask, Foxe, but I'm sure I can be more useful than that. At the least I can keep my wits about me and see what rumours come my way. I move in some of the same circles as Mordifort did and those people are bound to be talking about it and sharing what they know. At the least, they'll be concerned to know what will happen to Mordifort's various businesses. I imagine his son will inherit, but he's never shown the slightest interest in his father's commercial activities before. He'll probably sell out and live off the money.'

'I'll be delighted to have your help. I couldn't speak with Mordifort's competitors or associates without raising suspicion. You, I expect, would be seen as having a legitimate reason for curiosity. Is it settled then? We'll continue in secret and see what turns up?'

Alderman Halloran agreed and they shook hands on it. Foxe expected that would be the end of the business between them, but he was proved wrong.

'Did you go to the inquest on Mr Chambers, the actor?' the alderman said. Foxe shook his head. 'I thought not. I thought you might be interested to know what was not put forward in evidence. The coroner made sure only the facts needed to reach an appropriate verdict were brought out in court. "No point in supplying the scandalmongers with too much ammunition." That's what he said to me.'

'There was information left out?' Foxe said. 'All I heard was the jury brought in a verdict of wilful murder by person or persons unknown; and this was based on the evidence from the physician who had examined the body.'

'Quite correct. However, the man's death was far from straightforward. What the medical examiner found was the poor fellow's skull had been shattered by a heavy blow from above; driven in like an egg struck with a spoon. Even so, the skin on his scalp remained intact. The only way he could account for it was to assume the blow had come from something so soft and yielding that, although used with great force, it broke the bone yet failed to pierce the skin. The blow must also have come from virtually directly above. What do you make of his findings?'

'It sounds as if something heavy had been dropped onto Mr Chambers from a height. In almost all theatres, they use bags of sand as counterweights for raising and lowering scenery backdrops. Perhaps one of those was dropped on him?'

'That would make sense. However, his body was found in a small storeroom, not on or near the stage. Nor was any sandbag or other similar object found by the body.'

'Could he have been killed elsewhere and then dragged into the storeroom?'

'Again, that's the obvious inference. However, several witnesses said he had been seen about the theatre, alive and well, barely thirty minutes before his body was found. All this took place less than an hour and a half before the performance was due to begin. I have no great knowledge of what happens back-stage, but surely there must have been many people busy going about their business. To drag a dead body from one place to another at such a time would surely be to run a great risk of discovery. Mr Chambers was not a particularly small man, so it would have taken time and effort to drag him from wherever he was killed into the storeroom.'

Foxe thought about this for a moment. 'Did the medical examiner make any other suggestions?' he asked.

'None. The coroner asked him if a single person could have struck the blow. He said it could have been so, if the man who struck was standing behind him, though what weapon he might have used is unclear. The killer must also have been extremely tall — far taller than Chambers, who was at least of average height. Since the damage to his skull was so extensive, the blow must have come with considerable force. According to the examiner, his attacker was probably a giant: a tall, muscular fellow, capable of striking with great violence.'

'But a man?'

'I'd say it's impossible to imagine a woman of sufficient strength and size to commit this crime.'

'You say the body was found in a storeroom?' Foxe asked.

'Correct. A small, rather cramped room with a low ceiling; a place cluttered with all kinds of discarded and rarely used stage materials, sometimes used by the wardrobe mistress to store costumes not needed for the current performance.'

'I wonder how he came to be in there? It's not the sort of place you would expect an actor to go into,' Foxe said. A thought struck him. 'From what you said, he must have been found soon after he was killed.'

'All you say is true,' the alderman replied. 'The body was found by the wardrobe mistress. She said she'd gone into the storeroom to collect one of the unused costumes. She was repairing some garment needed for that evening and hoped to take a length of braid or something from elsewhere to save time in doing it. As soon as she went in, she came upon the body and raised the alarm.'

'There was no weapon by the body?'

'None.'

'It's all quite peculiar, isn't it?' Foxe said. 'Nothing adds up. Does anyone know whether Chambers was in the habit of going into that particular storeroom, or had been found there before?'

The older man shook his head. 'No one has any idea. There was no reason for him to go in there. By all rights, he should have been in his dressing room getting ready for the performance.'

Foxe tried another idea. 'I believe the man was a heavy drinker. You don't think he'd hidden a supply of alcohol in the room? He might have had an attack of nerves before going on stage and slipped away to take some Dutch courage without anybody seeing.'

'Not so far as I know. You understand everything I'm telling you I have learned only second-hand via the coroner. He interviewed the witnesses, either in court or before. I haven't spoken to any of them.'

Both men sat in silence for a while, mulling over the details and the problems they offered. This was just the kind of mystery which appealed to Foxe, full of complexities and impossible situations. Even so, his determination not to be seen helping Mr Postgate had not been overcome.

'It's all excessively intriguing, Halloran,' he said at length. 'Yet I see no reason why I should get involved. The constables will, I'm sure, have everything in hand.'

'I wish that was true,' Alderman Halloran replied. 'As you know, Foxe, our constables are not well-suited to more than dealing with fights or street robberies. No one wants the job, so the ones who find themselves pushed into it are neither much interested nor too clever. As the mayor and I see it, whatever is going on at the White Swan is both deliberate and well-planned. It may have something to do with past events, as the gossips claim, or which might be a distraction. No rational person could give credence to the nonsensical tale of murder by some vengeful ghost. The main point is this: this murder has caused enough interest amongst the people of the city to allow several leading citizens, opponents of the mayor both personally and politically, to begin demanding action and trying to characterise the mayor and his allies as complacent. I gather one of the most vocal has publicly declared His Worship to be unfit for the role of chief magistrate. He needs you, Foxe. The constables are never going to get to the bottom of this.'

Foxe couldn't help smiling. The mayor was a pompous fellow, full of his own importance and deeply attached to what he saw as his dignity and exalted position in the city. He would hate to be accused of incompetence; for someone important to brand him as complacent would be insupportable.

Halloran was still speaking. 'What the mayor needs is to show rapid progress in disentangling this affair — at least to understand the reason for the attack on Chambers and some firm ideas about the probable culprit.' He turned his head to look straight at Mr Foxe. 'You've heard about the second attack? The one on the other actor, Edwards?'

'I've heard something of it,' Foxe said carefully. 'I thought it was an accident on the stage, not an attack.'

'Then you thought wrongly,' the alderman said, his voice grim. I don't know the details — save that Edwards is still alive — but the mayor says it's clear the dagger had been tampered with. It was the kind where the blade should have retracted into the handle. It didn't, because a nail had been driven through to prevent it from doing so.

Here's the part which shows the cunning nature of whoever set this up. The blade was made of metal. It might have been blunt, but driven with sufficient force it could still pierce the skin. Whoever tampered with it had set the nail where it would leave sufficient space for most of the blade to retract as it was supposed to. Then, when the blade was stopped by the nail, enough would be left still protruding to cause significant hurt, but not enough to reach any vital organs.'

'What you say makes a significant difference,' Foxe said. 'I agree, there must be a clever mind behind all of this. The gossip going around was trying to set up Edwards as the murderer of Chambers, by claiming they hated one another. Now it sounds as if an unknown third party has a grudge against them both. If so, why kill Chambers and make sure only to wound Edwards? I can't see the point in that. Is he badly hurt?'

'Badly enough. He won't be acting again for many weeks, I believe.' By this point Alderman Halloran was tired of speculation. 'I'll get to the point, Foxe,' he said. 'The mayor and I want you to set aside your enmity with Mr Postgate and undertake an investigation. It's not for him, but for the good of the city. There's too much about this business that's unusual. Who's to say these two attacks will mark the end of it either? We need you, Foxe. We need you to find out what's going on and put a stop to it.'

'I don't know . . .'

'Please, Foxe. For my sake, if not for any other reason. His Worship is driving me insane with his complaining and dithering. Several ministers and leaders of churches in the city are already saying he was wrong to allow the playhouse at the White Swan to continue to engage companies and show plays. Such people believe all theatres bring unacceptable moral laxity and crime to the city. At the same time, the more sensible sort points out how the large number of theatres in this city adds to its reputation as a place of politeness and culture. Our mayor finds it hard to take a stand at the best of times — save, of course, on anything which pertains to his own dignity and status — and he's totally at sea on this issue. He has therefore instructed me to say he wants this matter cleared up as quickly as possible and is pinning his hopes on you taking an interest, given your deserved reputation for getting to the bottom of mysterious events speedily and with discretion.'

Mr Foxe had no choice but to yield to the inevitable and agree. He must be able to find some way of ascertaining what was going on without letting Postgate know what he was doing. *Two* clandestine investigations. Foxe could not have felt more excited.

❧ 13 ❧

Later the same day, Foxe called in to the bookshop and asked Nicholas and Mrs Crombie to join him in the workroom for a moment. Charlie, as he suspected, was already there, so it proved a good opportunity to tell all three of them that Alderman Halloran and the mayor had asked him to look into the events at the White Swan Playhouse.

'I've agreed to do so on the condition I shall be allowed to approach the investigation in my own way,' he said. 'What that means is I will be relying on your help still more than I have before. I include you in this, Cousin Nicholas, if you are willing.' Nicholas nodded vigorously. 'Good. As some of you know, I had already told that odious fellow Postgate, the manager of the playhouse at the White Swan, I had no intention of taking an interest in his problems. As far as I am concerned, my assertion still holds good. My investigation will therefore be carried out to some extent in secret. Mrs Crombie, I know you will be alert to gossip as usual. Charlie will enlist the eyes and ears of the street children. I'm not sure of your role yet, Cousin, but I'm sure I will find you one.'

Nicholas looked across at Mrs Crombie and smiled. 'I may already have found one, sir,' he said. 'Mrs Halloran and her nieces came to the shop this morning, as I gather they do often, to choose fresh books to borrow from the circulating library. Finding me there, Mrs Halloran naturally asked to be introduced, as did the young ladies who were with her. Almost at once, I found myself being interrogated by Miss Maria and Miss Lucy on my background, the place where I live and the reason for me being in Norwich. I assure you, it was a most thorough questioning, for they both have quick minds and were not content with generalisations or evasions. Their aunt was somewhat amused by the way I was treated, for so intent were those two young ladies on their questioning of me, they asked their aunt to choose suitable books for them and stayed in the shop, while she ascended to the circulating library. I assure you, sir, by the end of their interrogation no part of my life, opinions, and intentions had been left unexplored.'

'They rival yourself for curiosity, Mr Foxe,' Mrs Crombie said, laughing. 'The only difference is they are nearly shameless in finding out whatever they wish to know. I'm sure they would be more circumspect with an older person, but finding your cousin here closer to themselves in age, they plied him with questions until I felt I had to intervene to rescue him.'

'I was becoming a little flustered,' Nicholas admitted. 'Even when their aunt was ready to leave, Miss Maria and Miss Lucy were not finished with me and demanded that I accompany them back to their home. I think their aunt and uncle must indulge them a good deal, for no amount of protestation on my part that I was engaged in other matters would serve to obtain my release. There was nothing to be done but give in.'

'I was going to send young Charlie here to carry the ladies' books,' Mrs Crombie said. 'However, I found Mr Nicholas had been dragooned into doing it instead.'

Foxe couldn't help smiling. Halloran's two nieces possessed high spirits and lively minds. Their uncle and aunt doted on them, though their indulgence did not extend to accepting unbecoming behaviour. The two sisters might be allowed to step beyond the bounds of the strictest etiquette when in favoured households, but they were otherwise models of politeness and decorum.

However, Nicholas was continuing with his story and Foxe switched his attention back to what he was saying.

'I expected we would walk directly to their house and I could return at once, but it did not turn out that way. The two Misses Halloran were eager to show me as many of the sites of the city as they could and demanded we make several diversions for the purpose. Once we arrived, they further insisted on inviting me inside to show me their uncle's library. I gather, sir, you have been instrumental in helping him to build this magnificent collection. He allows his nieces free rein over his books, so they competed to show me what they considered the finest items and rarest volumes. They are both extremely taken with you, Cousin, as I soon learned, and hold you in the highest regard. Once we had finished in the library, they spent a good deal of time telling me of your exploits in the city and assuring me I was extremely fortunate to be able to spend time under your roof. It was a most convincing testimonial.'

'So, you are staying,' Foxe said. 'I feared our conversation and your experiences yesterday morning would send you hurrying back to Kent.'

'By no means,' Nicholas said. 'I had a most useful conversation with Mrs Crombie afterwards which helped settle my mind on several scores.'

Foxe glanced at his partner, but she refused to meet his eye. Since she had composed her features into an expression of angelic innocence, he was convinced she and his cousin had been up to some devilment. Well, doubtless it would be revealed in time.

'As you can imagine,' Nicholas went on, 'by now a considerable period had elapsed since I had arrived at the alderman's house; so much so that I was still in the house when the alderman himself returned from talking with you. There was then another round of introductions, more questions about my background and reasons for being here in Norwich, then a return visit to the library, in case any of the choicest volumes had been missed. I was at last about to leave when Mrs Halloran came in and insisted I should take some refreshment with them before doing so.

'It was during this time the alderman — a most kindly man, as I'm sure you will agree — said I should not be so cavalier in dismissing a career in the law, pointing out how lawyers undertake a wide range of activities, many of them far from the dull, paper-driven occupations I imagined. In support of this, he insisted on escorting me to the Mayor's Court, so he might introduce me to Mr Plumtree, the senior legal clerk there. Along the way, the alderman also suggested I should question Mr Plumtree on any new details that had arisen in the matter of the death at the White Swan Theatre, assuring me you had now agreed to open an investigation and would be most grateful for any further information which I discovered. I have therefore arranged with Mr Plumtree to return before I leave Norwich and settle on a date and time when he will be free to talk about his activities. Naturally, I did not wish to take up more of his time today, nor delay my return still longer. However, I thought it right to ask him if there was any fresh information about what had happened at the theatre. He said there was. I will be most happy to share it with you, if this is a convenient time.'

Foxe was disarmed and distracted by this narrative, as Mrs Crombie guessed he would be. Nicholas had played his part to perfection, in her estimation. He had avoided confessing that his visit to the alderman's house had been undertaken in large part to make an acquaintanceship which would be useful in looking into Mr Chambers' murder. He had also stimulated his cousin's curiosity to know what fresh information had come to light since the alderman's visit.

'Tell us all you know,' Foxe said. 'As I told you, I have agreed to see what I can discover for the mayor, but I have little idea where to start.'

After pausing to get his thoughts into the correct order, Nicholas began, explaining that most of what Mr Plumtree told him had to do with the other actor, Edwards. The man was seriously, but not gravely hurt, so Mr Plumtree had gone to his lodgings first thing to obtain his evidence at first hand. Mr Edwards claimed he had no idea who might wish to harm him, asserting he was one of the best-loved actors in the east of England. Mr Plumtree said he judged that to be merely a conventional response. He has, as yet, had no opportunity to speak to others to establish its correctness.

Foxe nodded. In the past, he'd encountered people with broken limbs and multiple bruises, each of whom claimed everyone expressed the greatest affection for them.

Mr Plumtree then asked if anyone might assume Edwards was involved in the killing of Chambers. The man's reply was unequivocal. At the time Chambers was attacked, Edwards claimed he was not in Norwich but in Lincoln, appearing at the playhouse there. He might well have been on stage at the time.

They all agreed this seemed to settle the matter of Edwards' supposed guilt. A lie would be too easily discovered. To come from Lincoln to Norwich and return would take at least two full days. If he were missing for that long, someone would have been bound to ask the reason. Mr Plumtree had been careful and thorough in his questioning, it seemed, and had reached the same conclusion.

Given the presumption of innocence, Plumtree had asked if Edwards knew why the gossips had so quickly fastened upon him for the role of Chambers' murderer. According to the tale being spread around about a malevolent ghost, he and Chambers were mortal enemies, both having been somehow involved in the fire and the deaths of the actress and her child.

'Mr Edwards claimed to be bemused about this,' Nicholas said. 'He said he'd played at the White Swan Playhouse many times over the years — and at other theatres in Norwich too — and had never heard stories of an unquiet spirit, either at the White Swan or anywhere else; certainly not one connected with the fire which damaged the White Swan Playhouse twenty years ago. As for the claim he and Chambers were mortal enemies, he dismissed it out of hand. He had not had any quarrel with Mr Chambers. It was a total fabrication. He admitted he had not greatly liked the other actor, but that was due mostly to the fellow's fondness for the bottle and the difficulties it could cause if you found yourself playing opposite him. Aside from that, the two had met from time to time, but only as all actors meet as the companies in which they are playing replace one another at particular venues.'

'I believe these stories are both of recent origin,' Foxe said, 'though why that should be, I have no idea. I wonder who spread them about? There is a mind behind this — a clever mind.'

'That's what Mr Plumtree thinks as well,' Nicholas said. 'He told me a nail had been driven through the handle of the knife which wounded Mr Edwards in such a way that the blade, made of blunt metal, would retract only in part, leaving about an inch and a half sticking out. Enough to pierce the flesh and cause a painful wound, but not enough to kill.'

'Yes,' Foxe said. 'Alderman Halloran told me the same. If it had been jammed completely, it might have gone in deep enough to kill.'

'Mr Edwards was wearing a thin, linen shirt at the time and the person who tampered with the knife must have known as much. If he'd been wearing, say, a coat — or any thick costume — the knife would only have bruised him. As it is, unless his wound festers, Mr Edwards will be fully recovered in a month or so.'

'I see it was still more cleverly prepared than I imagined,' Foxe said. 'Your Mr Plumtree has a quick brain, Nicholas.'

'I liked him,' the young man said simply. 'I was impressed by what I saw of his work. Magistrates, he told me, rarely do more than skim the outline of a case before it comes into court. They rely on men like him to write them a brief after considering all the evidence. He, as Clerk of the Court, advises the sitting magistrates on which questions ought to be asked and what might be an appropriate penalty, if the defendant is found guilty. It's a rash, or foolish, magistrate who goes against this advice. The clerk is trained in the law; the magistrate is not.'

They talked about Nicholas's news for a few minutes more, then returned to their normal activities. At no time had Foxe mentioned Mordifort's death and his proposed clandestine attempts to discover his murderer. To his mind, the fewer people who knew about that, the better.

❦ 14 ❦

Next morning, Foxe sat long over his breakfast, planning how best to approach an understanding of the strange events at the White Swan. There was no sign of Nicholas. He'd breakfasted earlier and was now back in the bookshop, being instructed by Mrs Crombie in the purchase and display of popular prints and caricatures.

Foxe had not forgotten his dislike of Postgate. He could imagine the look of smug satisfaction on the fellow's face if Foxe presented himself at the playhouse and began asking questions. Especially after he had declared so positively he would never do so. There had to be another way.

There was another reason for him to keep his distance too. If the killer feared detection, he might well lie low until all interest had died down — that is, if he had still more murders or attacks on his mind. It was also far from certain the murder had its roots in the past. From what Foxe knew so far, the current rumours linking the murder of Chambers to the death of the actress, Margaret Lindsay, all those years ago had started recently. People with little tolerance for uncertainty always sought an obvious — and suitably dramatic — explanation for events, but that didn't make it true. Why had the killer waited so many years to strike? Chambers had been in Norwich, and in that theatre, several times since the fire. It was only in the most recent years he had been absent, trying to rebuild his crumbling reputation and taking work wherever he could get it — which usually meant third-rate companies in remote areas. Why murder him now? What had happened to bring back emotion strong enough to provoke the impulse to kill? If he could discover the answer, it might offer clues which pointed to the killer.

The mantle-clock struck ten-thirty. Foxe was normally on his way to his favourite chair in the coffee-house by now. Today, his seat would stay empty. He had done enough thinking. It was time for action. Pushing back his chair, he rose and made his way across the hallway into his library and rang the bell for Molly, telling her to ask Mrs Crombie to send Charlie in to him as soon as possible.

Charlie Dillon had been finding jobs to let him eavesdrop on what Mrs Crombie was telling Nicholas. Whether or not Mr Foxe's cousin had any firm interest in becoming a bookseller. Charlie could imagine no better life. He'd set his hopes on one day having a bookshop of his own. He was therefore delighted by this opportunity for learning the ins and outs of the business. A proper acquaintance with the stock could come later, when his reading skills had improved. Nicholas's arrival had provided him with the chance to increase his knowledge. He did not intend to waste it. He was therefore less than enthusiastic when Mrs Crombie called him over and told him his master wanted him right away. He dawdled across the shop, still trying to hear the conversation between Mrs Crombie and Nicholas, until his sluggish progress was noticed and he was instructed to make haste or face the consequences.

It was obvious Foxe needed to know as much as possible about the movements of Chambers and Edwards since they came to Norwich. Since he couldn't ask at the playhouse himself without letting Postgate know what he was doing, he decided to use the sharp eyes of the street children. Many of them hung around the playhouse as the audiences arrived or left, taking the opportunity to beg or, just as likely, dip their hands into the pockets of the less wary, since crowds were the best setting for petty thieving. The older girls sold oranges and sweetmeats to the audience — sold themselves too, if the price was right. They had to be careful the manager didn't catch them. He didn't object to the trade, far from it. Their problem was that he considered he had a right to a substantial part of any money they made — or free 'entertainment' afterwards. Since he was both greedy and personally repulsive, none of the girls were keen to accept such a bargain. The timid ones plied their trade outside, away from the playhouse doors and the manager's prying eyes; the bold bargained rapidly over sales of their oranges, relying on sharp eyes and ears to spot him if he came close enough to see what they were about.

Foxe wasted no time in explaining to Charlie what was wanted. He'd undertaken similar tasks for his master several times before, so understood at once what he needed to do. Word of what Foxe wanted would be passed around amongst the street children within the next few hours.

'They could ask openly too, master,' Charlie said. 'Nothing suspicious in that, is there? With all the rumours about, it's reasonable they'd be curious.'

'Fair enough,' Foxe replied. 'Tell them to concentrate around the playhouse and make sure to include the doorkeeper. They shouldn't confine their interest to Mr Chambers and Mr Edwards only. I need to know about anyone unusual or suspicious seen hanging around the place. Will they know what these two actors look like? I've seen Mr Edwards on stage quite a few times. He's of medium height and thin build. His hair used to be sandy, but now it's mixed with grey and he wears it rather long. Oh yes, he's got a large nose and his eyes are rather close together. Not a handsome man, which has held his acting career back. Managers don't usually choose him to play the hero. Mr Chambers I hadn't seen for a long time, so I can't recall much about him.'

'Don't worry, master. The girls are familiar with all the actors, on-stage and off. They'll know what Mr Chambers looked like and can tell the others. Is that all?' He was desperate to get back to the shop to avoid missing more of Mrs Crombie's lesson than was necessary.

'I think so,' Foxe said. 'Off you go. Ah, I was going to—'

It was too late. Charlie was already out of the room and crossing the hallway at top speed.

Having set that part of his investigation in motion, Foxe felt justified in slipping away on his own to pursue enquiries into the matter of Mr Mordifort's murder. He had a contact at the Assembly House who would almost certainly have been present on the evening in question, since his tasks, as Master of Ceremonies, would cover all the arrangements: the layout of the rooms, the lighting, the dances, and the supper to be served midway. Frederick Shelwick and Foxe had been at the same school at one time, since Shelwick senior, like Foxe's father, was a prosperous shopkeeper in the city. Later, the family fell on hard times. The father somehow fell into the company of people more interested in fleecing him of whatever he had than helping him succeed. He took on a series of loans to expand his enterprises and found himself unable to keep up the repayments. In an amazingly short period, he had lost his shop, his house, and his respect in the city. It was more than he could cope with. One morning, he left the house alone, made his way into a secluded alleyway and cut his own throat.

When the news reached him, Foxe reacted at once. Charity would help the family over the worst times, but what they needed was some proper source of income to allow them to regain their self-respect. The Assembly House had just been completed at the time and Foxe managed to get Frederick Shelwick the post of butler there. The young man had worked hard and established a sound reputation with the customers and owners. When the first Master of Ceremonies left in the hope of a more glittering career in London, Frederick was the obvious choice. He and Foxe were not bosom friends by any means, but they stayed in touch and enjoyed their infrequent meetings.

Foxe couldn't help a feeling of pride as he walked towards the Assembly House. It had been built barely ten years before as a public venue for entertainments, the aldermen having obtained the lease of the site and the previous property on it from the Duke of Buckingham at an extremely modest annual rent. At once they commissioned Mr Thomas Ivory, a local man and the leading architect in the area, to undertake the necessary works. The result was a central section of two storeys, constructed in red brick, with the windows edged with pale stonework and the whole ensemble finished with a pediment at roof level and a fine and imposing doorway. This stood between projecting side wings of three stories, each coated with fine stucco. The sight of it was enough to make Foxe's heart sing. Like Mr Ivory's other great buildings, the Octagon Chapel and the Grand Concert Hall, it managed to enhance a city already noted for its gardens and many beautiful churches.

Foxe stopped for a moment to feast his eyes on the imposing mass of the main door, then turned aside to knock on a modest door in one of the wings. When he told the servant who opened it, he wanted to speak with 'my old friend Mr Shelwick', she hastened to admit him and lead the way to the neat room which was the great man's lair.

There followed the usual round of greetings and enquiries to be found whenever friends meet after a lengthy period of absence from one another's lives. Each asked of the other's health and prosperity, then swore never to leave it so long again before making an occasion to spend a little time together. That done, Foxe applied himself to the business in hand.

Frederick Shelwick had indeed been present on the occasion of the murder. He had been trying to lessen the crush which had built up in the doorway to the supper room, so had been within a few feet of Mordifort when he let out a sharp cry and fell backwards to the floor. Naturally, he had moved at once to try to bring assistance, only to see at a glance it was too late. The glazed eyes, fixed stare and twisted lips told their own story. It had hardly needed the two officious physicians who next pushed themselves forward to stand by the corpse to declare the man dead.

'Who was behind Mordifort when he cried out and fell?' Foxe asked. 'Could you see?'

'I was concentrating on trying to persuade a somewhat testy lady of advanced years there was no point in demanding others give way to her, since almost nobody could move,' Shelwick said. 'I only looked in Mordifort's direction when I heard him cry out. To be honest with you, the crush was so great I doubt if anyone could have been certain of their own position in the mêlée, let alone where others were standing.'

'I'm puzzled that he fell backwards. Since he was struck in the back, probably with some force, I would have expected him to be pushed forwards by the blow.'

'From what I saw, at the moment he fell he'd arched his back and had his left arm behind him, probably trying to discover what was causing him so much pain. I wouldn't say he fell either. As he cried out, several people started and tried to turn around to see what was going on. Since Mordifort had not yet reached the doorway itself when he was attacked, anyone ahead of him must have attempted to turn back the way they had come. My own guess is he was pushed over backwards by this process. Since his whole body was stiffened and his back arched, as I said, his body must have been rigid as it fell. Certainly, when I saw him, his posture was still stiff and elongated and his hand trapped under his back. I think that may be why the physicians stated so confidently he had died of a seizure of some kind. That's how he looked.'

'He didn't fall back against anyone?'

'No. He fell straight down to the ground, so far as I could see.'

'What about those who had been standing beside him?'

'They must have jumped out of the way.'

Foxe looked pensive. 'Yet it can only have taken a second or so for the man to fall.'

'I couldn't say. He almost reared up, thrusting his arm behind him, stayed in that posture for a moment or so, then fell — or was pushed — backwards onto the floor.'

'What happened then?'

'Pandemonium broke out. People shouting, women screaming and fainting, everyone close trying to move back and those further away leaning forward to get a better look.'

'Who first saw the blood?'

'I'm not certain. Probably several people at once. All I know is I heard someone call out, "Look! There's blood, lots of it". Naturally, that caused still more screaming and fainting. I had my hands full trying to cope with a room full of frantic guests. The man was dead, I was sure of that, so I left him to others to deal with. I was extremely glad I had a few moments after.'

'Why?' Foxe asked.

'That spitfire of a daughter of Mordifort's came rushing up and made a terrible scene, kneeling by the body in all the blood and calling down curses on just about everyone present.'

'Was she so upset then?'

'Upset? It isn't the word I would use. Angry, rather. Furious. I tried to help her to rise and she struck me in the face. No one could do anything with her. She knelt there in her cloak, shaking her fists at heaven and screeching like a Yarmouth fishwife.'

'In her cloak?'

'Oh yes. Mrs Henson had made something of an exhibition of herself barely five minutes before. What a family! First her brother, then her.'

'What did they do? I thought it was supposed to be a gathering of friends?'

'It all began when the dancing ended,' Shelwick said. 'Young Mordifort doesn't dance at all, of course. Too scholarly to indulge in such frivolous activities. I wonder he'd even come. Probably only did so because his father said he must be there. I'd noticed him once or twice during the evening, lurking on the side-lines and always on his own. It was supposed to be a masked ball, but he'd taken his mask off almost immediately. He wasn't trying to take part or mingle with his father's guests. His whole attitude spoke of boredom and disdain for the proceedings.

'His father must have noticed and gone over to remonstrate with him, because I heard raised voices and saw them close to the door leading out of the Assembly Room itself, both red in the face and yelling at the other. Young Mordifort then broke off and walked away, while his father shouted for him to come back and behave like a sensible human being. Those were his exact words. It can't have done any good, since I never saw the son again that evening.'

'What time was this?'

'About five minutes or so before the dancing ended. The orchestra was playing at full volume and people's feet were clattering on the floor. I imagine that, together with the general buzz of conversation, was enough to mask the row from most of those present. I just happened to be passing by.'

'You said Mrs Henson had also been involved in some upset.'

'A full-blown marital row! You know she's not what anyone would call an attractive lady? She arrived at the assembly wearing a gown which I can only describe as truly hideous. The bodice might have been acceptable on a woman of ample figure, I suppose, but all it did for her was accentuate the bony nature of her chest and her lack of anything which might be termed a bosom. Her hair was done up in such a way as to make her neck look longer and scrawnier than it is and her forearms poked out of the sleeves like little sticks. It wasn't at all surprising her husband had been taking his chance to feast his eyes on some real women when he could. There were some beauties there, Foxe! Fine complexions, fine figures, bosoms enough to make any gentleman long for the chance to rest his head — or his hands — on such plump pillows.'

'His wife caught him at it?'

'Couldn't have missed him. Nor did some of the ladies appear to object. I don't say he did anything improper, but his eyes were everywhere. My wife says it's little point flaunting what you have, if no one appreciates it. Some of those ladies were drawing plenty of appreciation, I can tell you; a good deal of it from Mr Alfred Henson.'

'What did she do?'

'When I saw them, she was already wearing her outdoor cloak and telling him she was going home. She told him he was a foul lecher and she would not demean herself any longer by remaining to be mocked by the other ladies. When he tried to calm her down, she actually spat in his face! It's true! I've never seen any woman do such a thing before, let alone a respectable lady, but she did. I half expected her to claw his eyes out, for if any woman could be described as a cat, Dorothy Henson could that evening.'

'Where was Alfred Henson afterwards, when the murder had taken place?'

'I've no idea. I didn't see him after the fracas I just mentioned. Either gone home or gone somewhere to pay for a little comfort and fun, I imagine. Having spent all evening feasting his eyes on female flesh, he probably wanted to get his hands on some. No chance of that from his wife!'

When Foxe was on the trail of a mystery, he ignored most other aspects of his life. Only when he was forced to come to a halt would he recall there were things waiting for him; maybe matters he should have dealt with some time before. Now, sitting back in his chair in his library and mulling over everything Frederick Shelwick had been able to tell him, he suddenly remembered he'd received a letter several days ago from his close friend, Captain Brock. Brock was presently in Italy, escorting Lady Julia Henfield on her Grand Tour. He'd written, both to bring news of the fact he and Lady Julia had decided to marry, and to remind Foxe it was time to ensure the managers of the wherry and shipping company, in which they were partners, paid over the annual dividends.

He had still to write a reply, or send congratulations on their forth-coming nuptials, which was scarcely how an old friend should be treated, let alone one as dear to him as Brock. He therefore decided to spend time first thing in the morning to write a suitable letter full of such local news as would be of interest to Brock and his lady. That done, he would visit his attorney and check up on the dividend payment Brock mentioned. If he wrote the bulk of his intended letter before he left the house, he would be able, on his return, to add a post-script confirming all had been done as Brock requested. That thought made him feel pleased with himself — a feeling that Foxe enjoyed a good deal more than most.

❧ 15 ❧

Next morning suiting action with intention, Foxe took pen and paper and began composing a suitable letter. It took him more than an hour. By the end, however, he felt reasonably content and so set aside the document to await his return after his visit to his attorney.

Mr John Morphew, Foxe's attorney, conducted his business from premises in King Street. It was a busy part of the city, since King Street marked the start of the road to London. It also stood right against the vast earthen mound on which stood Norwich's Castle. The crumbling walls and the mighty keep, erected at the orders of the first King William himself, towered high above the houses, like Dr Swift's hero in the land of the Lilliputians. While none of the other buildings could match the age of the castle, that part of the city still contained a good many houses and shops which dated from the time of Elizabeth or earlier. A few had been given a more modern front of brick and their roofs were now topped with pantiles, but there were others which still revealed their construction of oak beams, infilled with wattle and plaster, and retained roofs of good Norfolk reed.

Mr Morphew's house was one of the buildings of recent origin, a handsome, symmetrical property in the best classical style made from rose-coloured brick and pale limestone, its entrance marked by graceful columns and a pediment of plaster, with a decorative fanlight filled with fine glass above the main entrance door. Inside, all was arranged in a most gracious style, including mahogany furniture and pale plasterwork on the walls of the principal rooms, several fine paintings in oil, and Mr Morphew's growing collection of porcelain, bought from the East India Company and carried by their ships from far-off China.

Mr Foxe was an old and valued customer, so the attorney at once set all other work aside to attend to his needs. Morphew was maybe ten or so years older than Foxe, a man whose slow, deliberate speech and conservative style of dressing caused many to underestimate the quickness of his mind. The two men's relationship had progressed over the years of their acquaintanceship from that of customer and client to a warm friendship, based on shared interests and mutual trust. Today, one of those shared interests would hand Mr Foxe the greatest surprise he had encountered for many months.

The business which brought Foxe to visit Mr Morphew was soon concluded. The attorney agreed at once to speak personally with the managers of the shipping business, audit their accounts for the past six months and see the monies due to the two partners, Foxe and Brock, were paid in full. The amount due to Mr Foxe he would see credited to his account at Mr Gurney's bank as usual. Captain Brock's share would be dealt with according to the instructions he had left before departing for foreign shores.

The two men now moved from business to friendship. The attorney came out from behind his desk and he and Foxe sat themselves opposite one another on either side of the room's fireplace. There, a few logs were blazing merrily, for the wind outside was cold, despite the date on the calendar. Morphew rang for his clerk, told him to bring two glasses of good ale, offered Foxe his snuffbox and helped himself to a generous pinch for each nostril.

'I was beginning to become concerned about you,' Morphew said. 'You are normally as regular a patron of the theatre as I am, yet a good time has passed and I have not seen you there at all. I had decided this morning that if I did not see you tonight, I should send one of my servants round on the morrow to enquire after your well-being.'

'I have been somewhat unwell,' Foxe said, 'though it was nothing serious. A sore throat and a persistent cough. Both have now gone away, I am pleased to tell you. Because of my mild indisposition, the recent cold winds convinced me I would be better avoiding going out late in the day.'

'Did you consult a physician?'

'I did, though it brought me little benefit and lightened my purse a good deal.' They both laughed. Physicians were notorious for the high fees they charged and were widely ridiculed for the poor results obtained from their cures.

Having mentioned the theatre, one of the strongest ties between the two men, Morphew naturally went on to ask about events at the White Swan.

'I imagine you must've heard a good deal about the problems at the White Swan,' he said. 'Everything looks to be going wrong there at once. First the terrible murder of Mr Chambers, then the accident to poor Mr Edwards. Like you, I prefer the Grand Concert Hall — though I rather preferred its original name of the New Theatre — not just because of its better facilities, but because The Norwich Company of Comedians are resident there. To my mind, they must be one of the finest groups of theatrical artists in the whole of the country.'

'I agree with you entirely,' Foxe said. 'The best proof is they are able to engage many of the outstanding actors and actresses from the London stage to make guest performances. The decline of the White Swan is a matter for sadness though. It served this city well and provided at least an adequate playhouse long before Mr Ivory built his theatre at the Chapel Field.'

'Chambers would never have been accepted onto the stage at Mr Ivory's theatre,' Morphew said. 'The man was long past his best and even that was never good. His style of acting was too old-fashioned. To cap it all, he set about ruining what little talent he had with drink. Of course, he would not have been at the White Swan on this occasion, had it not been for the first misfortune which struck the company there.'

Foxe almost jumped out of his chair. 'The first misfortune . . .?' he said.

'Yes. Did you not hear of it? The major part Chambers took on was due to be played by Mr James Jagger, a fine young actor, full of promise. Unfortunately, he suffered an accident only four days before the company were due to open in Norwich and had to withdraw. The company's manager was forced to carry out a search in great haste to find a replacement; someone who knew the part and could step in at the last moment. The only one he could find was Mr Chambers. Not an ideal choice, you will agree. However, step in he did and, so I was told, made a reasonable job of it until he was struck down. They must have found some way of keeping him away from the drink.'

'So, this Mr James Jagger should have been playing Mr Chambers' part?' Foxe could still not quite believe it.

'That's right. I believe Mr Chambers only arrived in Norwich one day before the first performance. Despite all my reservations about him, I have to admit, to deliver a half-decent performance under those conditions was greatly to his credit.'

Foxe scarcely knew where to put himself. How could what Mr Morphew was telling him fit with what he and others had regarded as a carefully planned series of attacks? The murderer could not have known beforehand Chambers would be in the theatre. Did that mean he was not the intended target? Surely no one could mistake the middle-aged, drink-sodden Chambers for the young, highly-regarded Mr Jagger? What other assumptions he had made about events at the White Swan might prove erroneous? Perhaps the wounding of Mr Edwards was a spur of the moment decision; not the deliberate, carefully planned action it seemed on the surface.

'I'm surprised Postgate allowed Chambers into his theatre,' Morphew went on. 'He and Chambers had been rivals for the attentions of the same actress, sometime in the past, so people say, and Chambers proved the winner. Then there was the business over the fire, though that must be twenty years ago or more.'

'What business?' Foxe asked.

'I had just started taking an interest in the theatre around then,' Morphew said, 'though my father often berated me for neglecting my studies in favour of what he called "idle and frivolous" pursuits. I think he meant frivolous actresses, to be honest, though he was no mean hand at amorous games himself. You know about the fire, do you? Of course you do. There's all this nonsense flying around about vengeful ghosts, isn't there.'

'I was too young to know or care much about it at the time, so I would be glad to hear what you recall, Morphew.'

'Events turned out much better than they might have done, mostly due to a tremendous storm which broke over the city and produced a deluge to quench the flames. Nevertheless, there was a good deal of panic amongst the audience and the players as they tried to get out of the building. I can't recall all the details, but Postgate and Chambers, both young men at the time, got into a slanging match over what each had done that evening. Postgate claimed Chambers had run for his life, while he had stayed in the building to help others escape. Chambers denied running away and told anyone who would listen he had seen Postgate knock several ladies down in his haste to flee. He, on the other hand, had stood in the doorway, keeping it clear for the crowds to pass through.'

'Which one was right?'

'I don't think it could ever be proved either way. There was such a confusion and so many stories spread around, nobody was sure exactly what happened. I think the general opinion was Postgate, being the younger and less talented, was taken up with jealousy of Chambers for his greater success on stage and between the sheets. Being the kind of man he is, he seized an opportunity to defame Chambers more or less with impunity. Not that either was much more able than the other when it came to acting. As I recall, Chambers was eager, but wooden, while Postgate was too idle to learn his lines properly much of the time.'

It looked as if the supposed enmity between Chambers and Edwards, which Postgate had told Mrs Crombie about, was no more than a reflection of the man's own jealous dislike of Chambers. What else had he said that was untrue?

'Then there's the murder of Mr Mordifort,' Morphew continued. 'I imagine you'll be involved in trying to sort that out as well.'

'The family have forbidden any outsider to take an interest, including the mayor. They say they will deal with both investigation and prosecution, should any come about.'

'Have they? How peculiar. On second thoughts though, the family are all odd, so I shouldn't be surprised. Mr Edward Mordifort, who got himself murdered, was far from the most popular or best-regarded merchant in this city. Successful certainly, wildly successful maybe, but hot-headed and carrying a reputation for a good deal of sharp practice along the way. Peter, his son, is only interested in his antiquities and avoiding anything smacking of honest labour. I suppose he'll inherit all the businesses. If so, none of them will last long under his direction. Unlike his father, son Peter is the coldest fish you can imagine and as proud as Lucifer himself. Never married. Shows no interest in women. You can make of that what you will. To be honest, he shows no interest in anyone save himself.'

'What about the sister and her husband?'

'Mrs Dorothy Henson is like her brother, cold and arrogant. If, as is generally assumed, Alfred Henson married her for her money, he got a poor bargain. The woman looks like a wet stork in a gale and has the temper of a wasps nest poked with a stick. They say she rules the roost and I can believe it.'

'Do you know anything about Henson's business?'

'A ships' chandlery. In his father's day, it was a thriving concern. Since then, I don't really know. Henson never struck me as knowing or caring much about the mundane matter of running a business. His passion is shooting, I believe. He lives on the edge of the city in what he believes is too modest a house for a man of his importance. He stays there because it offers good access to meadows along the river where he can shoot snipe and duck and pretty much anything else which moves.'

'Can you think of anyone who might have wanted to kill Mordifort senior?'

'Not really. Plenty of people disliked him, but I wouldn't imagine any of them felt strongly enough to want to stick a knife in his back. Still, if the family have forbidden all outside interference, it doesn't really matter, does it? Either they will produce someone to face prosecution in their own time or the murder will remain unsolved. Nothing for you to do, Foxe, is there?'

Foxe went home from Mr Morphew's house with his mind in a whirl. He was so badly shaken by what he had heard during the afternoon he almost forgot to add the postscript to his letter to Brock and see it ready to be taken next morning to the Norwich to London carrier, who would deliver it to the Post Office in the capital to send on its way to Leghorn. What upset him most of all was his own carelessness and stupidity. He had stumbled into the middle of things rather than conducting proper investigations and dealing with events in their correct order. Now he had little choice but to go back to the beginning and start again.

❧ 16 ❧

'I see your nephew is not with you today.'

Foxe jumped. His thoughts had been many miles away, still struggling to adjust to the new reality of the events surrounding the death of Chambers and the attack on Edwards. He had come to the coffeehouse next morning expecting to be able to sit in peace and think things through for the twentieth or thirtieth time since he left his bed. Instead, much to his annoyance, he found himself being questioned by none other than Mr Sebastian Hirons, the editor of the Norfolk Intelligencer. If Hirons had sought him out, there must be something he wanted to know.

'My cousin's son,' Foxe said. 'I suppose you could say therefore he is my second cousin.'

'Well, whatever he is, where have you left him this morning?' Hirons was determined to start up a conversation.

'I left him in the bookstore with Mrs Crombie, if you must know, sir,' Foxe said, hoping the unaccustomed formality would persuade Hirons it was not a good time to pester him. It was not to be.

'Still pursuing the dream of becoming a bookseller, eh? He hasn't been to take up my offer to show him around the newspaper works and the editorial offices.'

'I'm sure he will come, once he has a moment,' Foxe said. 'It's a kind offer and will interest him greatly; although I do not believe he has any intention of entering so disreputable a business as the production of newspapers.'

Hirons roared with laughter. 'Disreputable? I should say it was not a bad profession, taken all in all. A good many booksellers have also been involved in the publishing of newspapers and pamphlets, have they not? Your own father, for one.'

'Oh, for goodness sake, Hirons,' Foxe snapped. 'Do sit down if you're going to. I cannot carry on a conversation with you looming over me. Ask what it is you want to ask me and leave me in peace.'

Foxe was feeling tetchy and had started the day feeling thoroughly out-of-sorts. He and Nicholas had sat long after dinner last night, discussing what he had discovered from Mr Morphew. Try as they might — and they tried hard - they could make little sense of either killing in the light of the fresh information. Even after he'd retired to bed, Foxe's mind kept him awake into the early hours. Now, to make matters still worse, he was going to be subjected to pointless questions from Hirons; questions he would almost certainly be unwilling, or unable, to answer.

'You're right,' Hirons said. 'There is something I wish to ask you. It's about what happened to Mr Edwards. I'm sure you know the answer. What I'm not sure is whether you will be prepared to give it to me.'

Foxe waited in silence. It was typical of Hirons to try to tempt him into an admission of knowledge before he knew what the subject-matter was.

'Nothing to say, eh?' Hirons pressed on. 'Very well. I want to know if what happened to Mr Edwards was an accident or deliberate.'

Foxe's mind had been running on at some speed while he was waiting for Hirons to get to the point. Instead of giving him an answer, therefore, Foxe took another approach.

'What about a trade?' he said. 'If I tell you the answer to your question, will you agree to tell me the answer to mine?'

'If there is to be a trade, I expect you'll make sure it's to your advantage. Suppose I say I will answer your question, if it is within my power to do so and not some matter I have agreed to keep confidential?'

'When it comes to you handing out information, I note you're most scrupulous about not disclosing matters you judge to be private. When I decline to tell you something, on the grounds that it's a private matter, you push me all the harder.'

'That's because I know what a tricky fellow you are, Foxe,' Hirons said. 'Whereas I am the essence of honesty and straightforwardness.'

'You?' Foxe said. 'You'd make a corkscrew look straight. Well? What do you say?'

'I told you already. If I agree to your trade, it will be subject to the conditions I set. You must be content with that.'

'No more than two questions each.'

'Agreed.'

'Right,' Foxe said. 'In earnest of our agreement, I will answer the question you have already asked first. What happened to Mr Edwards was certainly no accident. The trick dagger with which he had been stabbed had a nail driven through the handle to prevent the blade from retracting properly.'

'I thought as much! No accident, eh? So, who has it in for poor Mr Edwards?'

'If that's your second question, I cannot help you with it, since I do not know the answer myself.'

'It wasn't my question. Just a casual remark. This is the second one. How badly was the man hurt? Do you think it was an attempt at murder?'

'You have tried to slip in a third question and I agreed to answer only two. However, I'll be kind and allow both to stand. It was almost certainly not an attempt to kill him. The nail had been driven into the handle in such a way as to allow the blade to retract for most of its length into the handle. What was left to protrude was too short to have reached any vital organ. Nor, so far as I know, was the blade sharpened in any way. The other actor must have been playing his part with some vigour. When he stabbed Edwards, he not only bruised him severely, but struck hard enough for the shortened blade to pierce both cloth and skin and cause a nasty wound. Still, provided the cut doesn't fester, Edwards should make a full recovery.'

Hirons sat back to weigh over the matter in his mind. While he did so, Foxe considered again the two questions he intended to ask.

'Now it is my turn,' he said. 'My first question is this. What was the name of the company playing at the White Swan; the one Mr Chambers came to join?'

'The Suffolk and Norfolk Players,' Hirons told him. 'They're usually known as Hunter's Company after the name of their manager. Mr Franton Hunter runs a circuit across the south of this county and the north of Suffolk: places like Swaffham, Diss, Beccles, Bungay, and Lowestoft. I think they go to Great Yarmouth too. They only occasionally venture further north. They've been to Norwich once or twice recently, mostly because the White Swan finds it hard to attract companies of players to perform there these days. Mr Ivory's Grand Concert Hall has quite overshadowed it. I heard Hunter was hoping to obtain a week at King's Lynn, but that might have been only a rumour.'

'Thank you. Now my second question. I know your newspaper carries advertisements from local theatres, announcing the companies which are to perform and the plays they will present. Was any advertisement placed by the management of the White Swan to say their intended actor, Mr Jagger, had suffered an accident and would be replaced by Mr Chambers?'

'Do you recall on what day of the week this arrangement would have been finalised?' Hirons said.

'I do not know,' Foxe replied, 'although I do know Chambers did not arrive until late on either the Friday or the Saturday, when the company's programmes were due to commence on the following Monday night. All I was told aside from that was the arrangement was made at short notice. I took that to mean within two — or at the most three — days of his arrival.'

'In that case, I can give you an answer at once, without drawing on my memory. If we suppose he arrived on the Saturday, and the arrangement was not finalised until two days before, it means the management at the White Swan would not have been certain of his attendance until the Thursday. Even if we give them a little more time, I doubt they would have wished to insert a notice of the change of actor, until it was definite Chambers had reached Norwich. The man had a well-deserved reputation for being unreliable. No, given what you tell me, it's impossible any such notice should have appeared in my paper. We are, as you know, a weekly and we go to press on a Friday. Each edition is ready to be sold on the streets the following day — on Saturday. To place a fresh notice or advertisement on a page, rather than change one already there, would require the whole page to be reset by the printers — a task which would take several hours and one we would be unwilling to do at short notice, unless the matter was of major importance. I think you can be certain when my paper appeared that Saturday, it did not contain any information about Mr Chambers, whether he arrived in Norwich on that day or the day before.'

'Thank you,' Foxe said. 'You have spoken with admirable clarity. Those are my two questions.'

'I suppose it's no use me asking you why you want to know?' Hirons said.

Mr Foxe smiled. 'Question number four — and none whatsoever.'

'Well,' Hirons said, 'this at least proves you are now investigating the matter.'

'It proves nothing of the kind. I already answered the question the first time you raised it.'

'I hadn't realised you hated Mr Postgate so much.'

'Mr Postgate,' Foxe said, 'is a foul blot on the face of the earth. I would not lower myself to assist him in any way, not if he were dying in the gutter — which is his proper place. Our agreement is now concluded, Hirons, and it is time for me to leave. I will remind my second cousin of your offer.'

With those words, Foxe rose, took up his hat and cane and walked to the door, still annoyed that the peaceful thinking time he had sought had been denied him.

On leaving the coffeehouse, Foxe turned towards Gentleman's Walk, and spent some thirty minutes strolling up and down, past the Market Cross and back again, looking through the windows of certain expensive shops which lined this edge of the market, until he had at last walked off some of his bad temper. He could then have taken the shortest route home across the great Market Place, but that would have involved passing the fish market, an action which was best avoided, save on the coldest days of winter. Instead he turned southwards, past White Lion Lane and into the Hay Market, before striding purposefully along the south side of St Peter Mancroft church, thence into Swan Lane and the long Chapel Field Lane towards his home.

It was no use, he told himself as he walked along, he would have to seek out Mr Hunter, the manager of the Suffolk and Norfolk Players, and question him about the exact circumstances under which he had hired Chambers to replace the absent Mr Jagger. There was no other way forward, try as he might to find one. It had to be done — though he loathed the idea.

This odd reluctance stemmed from the fact that seeking out Mr Hunter must involve Foxe travelling away from the city, since Hunter's company of players had moved on some days ago, to be replaced by the company which included Mr Edwards. Not only did Foxe dislike being away from the comfort of his home, he had a strong aversion to suffering the many discomforts of travel in a public conveyance. However, since he possessed no carriage and horse of his own, nor any groom to take care of them and carry out the driving, he had no alternative.

The thought was enough to ruin the rest of his day.

⚜

To say he would seek out Mr Franton Hunter was one thing; to do it, quite another. Foxe had no clear idea of where Hunter and his company might have gone. He did recall Mr Morphew had said something about Mr Jagger being able to rejoin the company at its next venue, which was he thought, to be Dereham, but that was all. Foxe could not recall he had ever been to the town. If he had, which he thought unlikely, it had left no particular impression in his mind. He therefore went into his library and sought out his copy of the latest Norwich Directory, from which he learned Dereham was some twenty miles distant from the city along the route the stagecoach took to King's Lynn. To get there would require a journey of, say, two-and-a-half or three hours, allowing time for the coach to change horses at least once along the way. Being by nature a townsman and not at all drawn to the countryside, Foxe could scarcely recall the last time he had ventured that far outside his own city.

After this unpleasant discovery, he sat down and once again went over all the courses of action he now saw open to him, hoping to find some way in which he could avoid such an onerous journey. He failed. He did, however, reach the conclusion that going to Dereham was not something to be attempted without the assurance he would find Mr Hunter there when he arrived. The answer would be to send a letter with all speed to the gentleman, requesting a meeting at a convenient place and time. Only if he obtained a satisfactory response would he steel himself to set out on this epic and unwanted journey. He there-fore picked up the bell and told Molly to send Alfred to him at once, dispatching his manservant when he came to discover the quickest way his letter might reach the town of Dereham.

Of course, even when Foxe had completed his letter, his problems were not at an end. He had no idea where Mr Hunter might be lodg-ing; nor did he know the name of the playhouse where Hunter's Company were performing. In the end, he could think of no alterna-tive but to send the letter to Mr Hunter at 'the Dereham Playhouse — assuming Dereham had a building which went by such a name — and hope to catch him there.

In his letter, Foxe explained the Mayor of Norwich had asked him to look further into the circumstances surrounding Mr Chambers' death. He would thus be grateful for the favour of a personal interview on the matter, since he understood Mr Chambers to be a last-minute substitute and was curious to know how this came about. It was also of some importance to him to know precisely when Chambers was engaged, and the day — and if possible the time — when he arrived in Norwich.

By this time, Alfred had returned, bearing the news there was a regular carrier service to Dereham, departing early each morning. The man had promised to bear Mr Foxe's letter and see it delivered the moment he arrived, which would be by eleven or noon at the latest. With that Foxe had to be content. He took up the book he had been reading, rang for Molly again, and told her to bring him a pot of coffee and a piece of cake, if Mrs Whitbread had been baking. Fortunately, she had, and Foxe settled down to his reading with something approaching equanimity, if not actual pleasure.

Nicholas, of course, would have been delighted to go to Dereham on Mr Foxe's behalf, or almost anywhere else, but though the idea had occurred to him, Foxe had dismissed it. It was not that he had no faith in Nicholas to carry out instructions put to him; more that his thoughts on what questions should be asked of Mr Hunter were so vague and ill-informed he could not have communicated them to anyone else. So much depended on the answers Mr Hunter was able to give.

Everyone knew Chambers was unreliable and long past his prime. Was there really no one else who could have stepped in? In travelling companies in particular, it was not uncommon for actors to be expected to make themselves ready to take on any one of maybe twenty or thirty roles. Once they had set up in a town, one of the local nobility or gentry might well take it into his head to book the whole playhouse for an evening to entertain his family and friends. When that happened, the patron would expect to choose his own programme, regardless of the one offered to the general public on other nights, subject to some negotiation if his choice was particularly unusual. This was such a frequent occurrence that actors had to be prepared to step into a suitable role in almost any popular play of the time at a moment's notice.

It was difficult to believe Mr Hunter couldn't have found someone other than Chambers to fill in for Mr Jagger. Was there some other reason why Chambers had been chosen? Foxe needed to know if there was. Thanks to Hirons, he'd established Hunter couldn't have used a newspaper in the city to announce the substitution of actors. Yet that didn't preclude him having a handbill produced to that effect. When they were not needed for anything else, members of an acting company often dressed themselves in suitable costumes and went out into the streets to hand out playbills and notices of future attractions. Only the best and most famous actors and actresses of the day could fill a theatre on the strength of their names alone. For the rest, drumming up an audience was necessary and often laborious. The White Swan Playhouse had been in decline for some time. If it turned out the better-known Norwich Company of Comedians was playing at the same time at Mr Ivory's Grand Concert Hall, the older playhouse would be lucky to find itself half full. Travelling companies depended on the ticket receipts for their livelihood, since no theatre would pay them to put on a programme; nor were most actors and actresses paid, depending instead on so-called 'benefit evenings', when it was announced all the profits would be given to a particular actor. Of course, the playhouse still took a generous percentage, and actors had to be content with whatever was left after the costs of the evening and the playhouse's share had been deducted.

Unfortunately, all this was assumption. In some way, the information that Chambers was to take over Mr Jagger's part would almost certainly have been made public at least a day before the play opened. Would this have provided time enough for someone to plan Chambers' death? He had been killed towards the end of the run. That gave the murderer five days for his plan to be conceived and put into action — ample time, if the murder of Mr Chambers was all which was intended. What complicated matters was the subsequent incident involving Mr Edwards. Had he been selected by the killer to bear the blame for the murder? This made little sense. As things stood, there were no clues pointing to Mr Chambers' murderer at all. Why not leave things there? If a murder remains unsolved, what need is there to fix upon someone else as a scapegoat? Surely Mr Chambers was not murdered purely to bring Mr Edwards under suspicion, in the hope he would be convicted and executed? If this was the idea behind the crime, it had proved foolish, since Edwards could prove he hadn't been in the city at the time.

Foxe realised he had returned to the wearisome process of producing theories based on no evidence and alternatives based on nought but speculation. It was plain his actions in investigating this wretched affair would bring no credit upon him and he should have stuck to his refusal to get involved, whatever Halloran said.

❧ 17 ❧

Foxe's letter to Dereham was dispatched the following morning, which left him at a loose end until he received a reply. So far as he knew, Nicholas was still with Mrs Crombie, learning now about the means and benefits of running a circulating library. Given his peevishness about the young man's absence the other day, Foxe could hardly draw him away from such activity merely for the sake of his company. He therefore decided to go to his coffeehouse as usual, then take a walk to Alderman Halloran's house in Colegate and acquaint him with the facts as he now knew them. While the alderman would know all the mayor knew, neither could know about the last-minute nature of the engagement of Mr Chambers.

When Foxe reached the alderman's house, he found only Mrs Halloran at home. Her husband had gone to see the mayor, she told him, but would return quite soon. If he was willing to wait, she was sure he would be delighted by Mr Foxe's visit. He had only been saying to her at breakfast he wished to know how Foxe was getting on with his investigation.

Foxe was quite willing to wait. He liked Mrs Halloran and they chatted together amiably for a while. In enquiring whether Miss Maria and Miss Lucy were in the house, Foxe was told they had gone to his bookshop to persuade Mr Nicholas to escort them to the cathedral, having discovered he hadn't yet seen that magnificent building.

Foxe was not best pleased by this. Somehow Nicholas always seemed to find a reason to get away from what he should be doing to amuse himself.

Mrs Halloran, meanwhile, was explaining how nice it was for her nieces to have a suitable companion nearer to themselves in age; and how fortunate it had been Nicholas was able to escort them about the city.

'He is such an unaffected and intelligent young man,' she said. 'My husband and I both agree he is a wholly suitable companion for our nieces. Maria, in particular, has taken to him mightily, though Lucy is not far behind in her admiration. If they were older, I should reprove them both for the way they make eyes at him, but they mean nothing by it and he takes it all in good part.'

'They have gone to see the cathedral?' Foxe said.

'Indeed. Maria and Lucy are as proud of Norwich as if they had been born and bred here. They never tire of visiting suitable parts of the city, either to take in the air at the pleasure grounds and gardens, view what is on offer in the better shops, or enjoy the beauties of the churches and other buildings from the past. Ah, I believe that is my husband now. I will go and see.'

She had not reached the door before the alderman swept into the room, greeted Foxe warmly and led him off into the library where they might speak in private. There he sent for a pot of coffee and instructed Foxe to tell him at once of any new developments concerning the deaths of Mr Mordifort and Chambers. This Foxe did and had the pleasure of seeing the alderman was just as amazed by what Foxe had learned from Mr Morphew about the hiring of Chambers as he had been himself.

'The mayor will be most put out by this,' Halloran said. 'He is convinced Mr Edwards was behind the death of his fellow actor.'

'But how does he reconcile this with the attack on Edwards?'

'He sees that as proof of the man's guilt. To his mind, the care taken to make sure the knife was left in a condition where it would not kill, must mean Edwards staged the accident himself to draw away suspicion and send us off on a wild-goose chase.'

'My cousin Nicholas told me the mayor's legal clerk, Mr Plumtree has learned from Edwards he was in Lincoln at the time. What's more, he can prove it by many witnesses.'

Halloran laughed, saying the mayor was quite capable of believing any witnesses produced must have been coached by Mr Edwards in what to say. Maybe Halloran sensed he had gone too far in making this claim. He and the mayor were close friends and he would not have anyone believe the mayor was capable of such a gross dereliction of his duty as chief magistrate of the city.

'You realise I speak in jest, Foxe,' he said. 'I do not wish to malign the mayor. He would certainly not cling to beliefs refuted by plain facts. All I'm saying is that he would subject any witnesses produced by Edwards to close questioning. So, Foxe, what do you propose to do next?'

Foxe explained his plan to go to Dereham to catch up with Mr Hunter and the alderman approved it at once. He told Foxe he thought Dereham a rather ordinary town. Still, it was fortunate Hunter had not gone further afield, say to some grand place like Bury St Edmunds or Ipswich. Foxe certainly agreed with these latter sentiments, though he was hard put to admit any provincial town other than Norwich could possibly be considered grand.

'Anything relevant to the murder of Mr Mordifort?' the alderman asked. 'I assume you're still investigating that in secret. If not, I have something.'

'Nothing more than some useful background information on the characters of the other members of the family,' Foxe said. 'From what I've heard, Mr Mordifort's surviving children can have offered him little to boast about.'

'His surviving legitimate children, you mean. I believe he has two daughters born out of wedlock to different mothers. He was never especially faithful to his wife when she was alive. After her death, he cuckolded a good many of his friends and associates. I imagine he will have made some provision for both these extra daughters in his Will, though you could never be sure with Mordifort when it came to money. He might surprise you with a sudden gesture of open-handed generosity or appal you with some petty display of selfish greed.'

'Does he have — I mean, did he have at the time of his death — any special mistress? He'd need to make some provision for her as well.'

'I believe he did, though who it was I can't remember. He wasn't like you, Foxe, willing to show off his mistresses about the city. On the outside, he was the model of propriety, whatever else he did behind closed doors. His actions depended on what he wanted at the time. He'd spend money lavishly on things like his drive to become an alderman, if he thought it would get him what he wanted. For the rest, he demanded value for every penny he laid out. The kind of mistress who would have suited him couldn't have been extravagant or too demanding. A woman like that would have been sent on her way soon enough. My guess is you'd find his mistress to be a kind of surrogate wife, accommodating in bed and modest in her needs — this is, if you ever find who it was. He could be a secretive bugger.'

'You said you had some news about his death, I believe?' Foxe had long experience of how far from the point Alderman Halloran could stray unless kept on a tight leash.

'More about the consequences of his death. Last night was the regular meeting of the Mercantile Society. Have you heard of it? We're a group of the most important merchants and traders in Norwich, measured by the trade we do and the number of people we employ. At the moment, there are twelve members, though not all attend every meeting. The purpose of the society is to give members an opportunity to talk over anything likely to affect business in this city. Pushing your own business to the forefront is strictly prohibited, as is trying to wheedle out information to your own advantage. We stick to topics that have some impact on everyone and try to agree on a common course of action where it's justified by the public good.'

'All exceedingly laudable.'

'Stop laughing! You know as well as I do the real reason to get together is to have a good meal, drink several bottles of port and brandy and swap the gossip of the day. A good thing too, as it turned out. The word going around is Peter Mordifort had let it be known that he will put all his father's businesses up for sale the moment probate is granted on the man's Will.'

'What about his sister's share?'

'What share? I expect her father left her something, but she has no claim on anything more. Peter is the heir. It's odd though. Peter Mordifort and his sister have always been close to one another — insofar as either of them have ever displayed affection for anyone besides themselves. Maybe he reckons that wastrel of a husband of hers would soon get his hands on whatever she received, just as he did with her dowry.'

'So, Peter Mordifort will be a rich man.'

'Extremely rich. How long for remains to be seen. In the past, he's come up with all kinds of mad-brained ideas. Building a museum completely devoted to things dug up around this county, with a collection larger than the one Sir John Sloane left to the nation not so long ago. You know, the one that's now open to the public in Montague House in Bloomsbury. Then he wanted to finance a series of expeditions to the Holy Land to search for the treasure of Solomon's Temple, which he was sure was hidden in the Sinai Desert. His latest notion is to clear all the debris away from the ruins of Pompeii, remove any antiquities found there and bring them back to England where they can be made available for scholarly study. How he thinks he'll persuade the King of Naples to agree to this I cannot imagine.'

The two of them talked around Halloran's news for some time, but could reach no clear conclusion on its relevance to the murder. Aside from bringing Peter Mordifort his inheritance earlier than he could have expected, nothing else had changed. He had long been the sole heir and his father had never given any sign of wishing to divert the family fortune in any other direction; nor had Peter made any secret of his lack of interest in taking his father's place at the head of his many enterprises. Father and son might dislike one another, even hold the other in contempt, but there were no rumours of a split severe enough to change the details of the father's Will.

On his walk back home, Foxe found his thoughts veering between his plans for going to see Mr Hunter, assuming he could be found, and attempts to fit the information he now had about Edward Mordifort into a sensible pattern.

Foxe was greatly pleased to discover, later the next day, his letter had reached Mr Hunter successfully. Not only that, Mr Hunter had replied with similar haste, saying he would be delighted and honoured to talk with Mr Foxe, about whom he had heard a great deal during his short visit to Norwich and whose love of the theatre was well known to him.

However, he explained his company's period at the playhouse in Dereham had to be a brief one. The town lacked a sufficient population to provide an audience for a longer run. They were therefore departing the next day for Swaffham, another town in their usual circuit. He had obtained a full week's engagement at a playhouse there, with performances to start the day after their arrival. The heavy wagons which carried the company's wardrobe and equipment travelled at little more than a walking pace, so he could not expect them to arrive in much less than a full day. He would go ahead to see all was ready for them. They would remain in Swaffham for eight days, then depart again for King's Lynn. If Mr Foxe were able to make the journey to Swaffham or King's Lynn, he would be happy to receive him at either playhouse between noon and one o'clock on any day during their stay there.

This was a serious blow. Swaffham was, he discovered, thirty miles from Norwich, while King's Lynn was still further off — at least forty-five or fifty miles by his recollection. To Foxe, that seemed as far distant as Paris or Moscow.

However, since he could see no alternative, he dispatched Alfred at once to enquire about obtaining an inside seat for him as far as Swaffham on the next available stagecoach travelling from Norwich to Lynn. He was also to discover what accommodation might be found there when Foxe arrived. If possible, he would talk with Mr Hunter on the day he arrived, spend a single night in Swaffham and rejoin the stagecoach on its journey back to Norwich.

Alfred's task proving successful, Foxe found himself with an inside seat on the King's Lynn stage, leaving from the Angel at eight o'clock the next morning and due to arrive in Swaffham at noon.

❧ 18 ❧

The journey to Swaffham proved as bad, perhaps a good deal worse, than Mr Foxe had feared. The roads were rutted and uneven, so the body of the coach rocked and swayed like a ship caught in an Atlantic gale. If Foxe's fellow passengers had not all been of more than ample proportion, he might have been thrown to the floor of the coach several times. Instead, he spent the journey wedged next to the coach's side by a clearly prosperous attorney whose cleanliness did not match his obvious love for his food. As a result, Foxe emerged at Swaffham so cramped and twisted he could hardly walk from the coach into the Red Lion Inn when he arrived.

The good news was that he proved to be the only passenger to leave the coach at Swaffham, so had little difficulty in obtaining a private room for the night; though the price he was to be charged for the privilege was enough to convince him the innkeeper must be a most thorough rogue. Still, he paid it. The alternative would be to share a bed with whoever might happen along and that he could never countenance.

Swaffham's large market place, which stretched away on both sides from the inn where Foxe had taken his room, would have impressed most first-time visitors. Foxe, however, comparing it to the Great

Market in Norwich, thought it only tolerably large and the buildings about it, many of modern construction, no more than adequate to their purpose. Since the day was fine and the air surprisingly warm for the time of year, he might well have allowed himself an hour or so to look around the town and acquaint himself with some of what it might have to offer. Instead, he at once enquired of the landlord of the Red Lion where he might find the playhouse in which Mr Hunter's troop of players were due to perform and was delighted to discover it was situated close by. Mr Hunter was bound to be there, the landlord told him. The stage hands, aided by some locals, were setting up the stage scenery, a job which he knew Mr Hunter always supervised himself.

Stepping into the place which served as a theatre, Foxe found the building rather small, but otherwise suitable for its purpose. The stage was somewhat narrow, but deep enough to allow for the actors to move about easily. Best of all, it was not encumbered by boxes, as was the case in some older playhouses. Having boxes on the stage itself was annoying to the actors and often distracting to the rest of the audience. The wealthy patrons who hired them seemed to think being there gave them permission to call out comments to those on stage and bait any who were less than confident about their lines or moves. Worst of all, any young blades sitting there tried to flirt with the younger actresses or steal kisses as they passed.

In this playhouse, the boxes were set further back, to each side and somewhat higher than the bulk of the seating. The only other area was a balcony at the rear of the auditorium, sufficient to hold perhaps four or five rows of seating. The walls were painted and tolerably clean and the curtains to the stage, as usual of thick velvet, had no more than the expected number of tatters along their lower edges. All in all, it was a typical small playhouse in a provincial town, adequate, but not luxurious.

Mr Hunter was seated on one of the benches facing the stage, while various underlings ran backwards and forwards, erecting scenery and setting out props. The moment he saw Foxe enter, Mr Hunter guessed who he was and rose to his feet to welcome him warmly. He was delighted to make Mr Foxe's acquaintance, he said, and more than willing to assist in any way that he could.

Meeting him in the flesh, Foxe at once recalled seeing Mr Hunter on stage several times in the past. A competent actor, rather than a brilliant one; a man best suited to comic roles, since he greatly resembled Shakespeare's character Falstaff and had played that jolly old rogue on numerous occasions. On this day, dressed in old clothes and without any of the make-up or wigs he would've worn on stage, Hunter resembled nothing more than a prosperous local farmer.

After the normal pleasantries, Mr Hunter invited Foxe to take a seat on the bench beside him.

'I hope you will forgive me for asking you to sit with me here, sir,' he said, 'for I cannot leave the playhouse until I've satisfied myself all who work backstage during the performances know exactly what they must do and when they must do it. We cannot take many of our own people when we go on tour; only the few who are essential to us. For the rest, we rely on servants from the inns in whose buildings we perform or other local fellows. Most of them have never had anything to do with the theatre before; all are nervous and uncertain, and not a few possess less intelligence than you would find in sheep. They will ruin all if I do not sit here and coach them through every step, turning our performances into a shambles.'

'Yes,' Foxe said, 'to sit here will be fine. I do not have many questions. What I need to know most about are the circumstances in which you came to hire Mr Chambers. I believe it was to replace one of your company who was injured or sick — I am not sure which.'

'Injured. Mr Jagger tripped during a performance and hurt his ankle. How he did it, none of us can imagine, but there it was. The poor fellow could not walk. I had to find someone to take his part or cancel the performances altogether.'

'Was Mr Chambers the only person available?'

'More or less. The only person nearby — and the only one I was sure would know the part. I am well aware of his problems with drink, as you can imagine. Still, he assured me he would take himself in hand, at least for the period of his engagement, and was pathetically grateful for the opportunity. I believe he has had few engagements in recent times. Maybe he saw this as an opportunity to set himself on a path to convincing other managers to take a chance on hiring him.'

'Did he prove himself satisfactory?'

'He did. He was never — Idiot! Not there! The other side of the stage. Why would I need two doors next to one another? — much of an actor. Too old-fashioned in his style, too wooden and declamatory, and that was before he took to the bottle. However, to give him his due — The other side, I said, not at the front of the stage! — he made an enormous effort to stay sober and perform his role correctly and without causing problems for the other actors. It seems ironic his final few performances were the best he had produced for many years.'

Foxe was fascinated. Mr Hunter had the ability to break off his conversation, deliver an order or a rebuke, and resume at precisely the same point as if he had never interrupted himself at all.

'His death must've come as an enormous shock to you,' Foxe said.

'Yes and no. I never expected — If you put that chair there, somebody is bound to trip over it. Move it further back. A little more. Now, make a mark there on the stage with chalk, so you can put it in the right place the next time — that he would be murdered. Nothing like that. However, it was quite clear — That's the scenery for the burlesque. What we need is the scenery for the tragedy. If you can't tell the difference between the two, get someone who has a brain to help you — that poor Mr Chambers was greatly unsettled by something.'

'Something he had seen, or something which had been said to him?'

'I think it was the business about the ghost. The rumour began to go about — Don't just stand there with that stool, think where you need to put it. Not there! Think, man! Yes, there — within a day of our arrival. It was odd. I spoke to several people at the theatre. All agreed they had never heard such a story before. One or two knew about the fire all those years ago, but this was the first time it had been suggested the playhouse was haunted as a result.'

'How did Mr Chambers react to the story?'

'He struck me as being extremely upset — The other way up, man! Can't you see it's upside down? — I think he had a good idea who was spreading the rumour. Once I heard him say to one of the other actors that spreading a rumour like that was "only what he would've expected from the wretch". On another occasion, a day or so later, he told me he wished he had never come back to Norwich and would not have done so, if he had known — Don't just stand there. Go and fetch the next piece. We don't have all day — a certain person was still connected with the White Swan theatre. Then he assured me he would fulfil his engagement, as agreed, however hard this other person tried to force him out.'

'Did he say any more?'

'Not to me. But after his death, one of the actresses told me she believed — You can't just leave it there, can you? Anyone trying to make their entry will have to dance around it — he had started drinking again in secret. I asked her why she thought so. Her response was he must have been tipsy to say some of the things he did.'

'What did he say to give her that idea?' Foxe asked.

'He said if this other person could not be stopped in any other way, he would have to — Tom? Where's Tom? There you are. Show this lummox how to do it properly, will you? — reveal all he knew. Then the one who was persecuting him would soon come to regret his actions.'

'He never mentioned this person's name?'

'Not to my knowledge. He may have done to other people, though I doubt it. He seemed unwilling to divulge more than he had to. That was why the actress thought he had been drinking when he made those threats.'

'How long was this before he was killed? Can you recall?'

'About — No! No! No! I've told you a hundred times. You have it the wrong way up. I swear if you can't do any better, I'll ask the landlord if he can find someone in this town who would hire me a donkey to take your place! — twenty-four hours, I would say. Maybe less.'

Foxe longed to slip away and spend some time on his own, thinking through all he had learned. It turned many of his previous ideas on their heads. Yet there remained one matter he must explore further.

'Did Mr Chambers ever mention Mr Edwards?' he said. 'The rumour was there was some long-standing enmity between them.'

'Another oddity. I've never heard of either of them being in any way antagonistic to the other, and I've been in this business for twenty-five years and more. In answer to your specific question, Mr Edwards' name was never mentioned.'

Foxe could not have asked for anything more definitive. He therefore rose, thanked Mr Hunter profusely for his time and frankness, and left him to wrestle with his motley crew of amateur stagehands.

⚅⚄⚅

By now, Foxe was far too excited to sit still, so he was almost impelled to take a walk around the marketplace, hoping this exercise to his body would stimulate his brain. When he returned to the inn, he found, despite all his fears, the meal which was served to him surpassed his expectations; as did the bottle of claret he consumed with it. Indeed, by the time he climbed the stairs to his room, his thoughts about the town of Swaffham, like his notions about the death of Mr Chambers, had undergone considerable revision.

Settling himself in one of the comfortable chairs provided, Foxe intended to go over all he had learned. It was important to make sure he hadn't missed anything or jumped to conclusions not supported by the evidence. In moments, he fell asleep.

He was awoken about an hour later by a sharp knocking on the door, followed by the entrance of an extremely comely serving maid.

'I been sent to ask if you want your bed warming, sir,' she said, giving Foxe a shy smile and several sidelong glances. 'I got the warming pan just outside the door.'

Foxe considered her gravely. She had a fine figure and looked rather cleaner than a good many servants, even those in the better households. There was also a look in her eye which promised a good deal, if she could be persuaded to take part in what he now had in mind.

'I think I would definitely like my bed warmed,' he ventured, 'but you won't need a warming pan. How would it be if you slipped off your clothes and warmed it yourself?'

'Oh, sir,' the girl said, blushing prettily. 'Whatever makes you think I'd do such a thing?'

'I have . . . three shillings here says you might.'

'Is three shillings all you think my virtue be worth, sir? Three shillings?'

'Of course,' Foxe continued, emboldened now the girl had started bargaining. 'If you were to warm the bed all night, I could well consider it worth ten shillings — and another five to content your landlord he'd had his share.'

The maid — her name was Daisy — was amazed. This was a far more generous offer than she ever expected. On the occasions when she felt willing to suggest her services to gentlemen at the inn, she knew she would have to give a good half of what she earned to the landlord or lose her job. If this man was willing to pay her royally and give her what she could tell the landlord was his share, she'd better accept at once. She looked at Foxe again. A handsome enough gentleman too and quite young. Her usual fate was to bed with men old enough to be her father and not too lively either. There was also the fact it was far too long since she'd actually enjoyed a tumble. The local youths tended to be rough and thoughtless when it came to sexual matters. They took their own pleasure and gave no heed to yours.

'I just got to put the warming pan back in the kitchen, sir,' she said. 'You hold your horses an' I'll be back in no time. You did say ten shillings?'

'Ten for you and five for the landlord.'

'You'll get your money's worth, sir, I promise you.'

So will you, Foxe said to himself. I'll bet you rarely get treated as you should be. Let's see if we can make this night memorable for us both.

The combination of Daisy's eagerness to learn and Foxe's experience proved everything Foxe had hoped for. In the end, it was Daisy who begged for respite — and only after they'd both reached the desired culmination of their lovemaking for the third time. They snuggled into one another's arms, Daisy's head on Foxe's chest and his hand cupping one of her delightfully round, firm young breasts, and promptly fell asleep.

Foxe was awoken next morning by another serving maid — this one of such an acidulous and forbidding aspect he could not imagine anyone seeking to take advantage of her, however desperate he might be. Daisy must have woken earlier, since she was no longer beside him and the six half-crowns he had left for her on the cupboard by the bed had gone.

This second maidservant had brought him a bowl of hot water to wash and shave himself. As he stretched and prepared to leave his bed, once she was safely out of the room, she gave him a look of utter disdain and told him if he wished to catch the stagecoach back to Norwich, he should rise at once. Breakfast was ready downstairs and the coach was expected to arrive promptly at ten-thirty. After that, she left, closing the door behind her with a bang. Daisy must be either a sore trial to her, Foxe thought, or she was of the puritanical tendency. Whichever it might be, there was no chance the landlord would curb Daisy's activities by night so long as he was making money from them.

✢ 19 ✣

Foxe spent the journey back from Swaffham indulging in happy memories of his night-time exercise and congratulating himself on having solved the mystery of the murder of Mr Chambers. He imagined how Alderman Halloran, Mrs Crombie and even his cousin Nicholas would react when he told them: their amazement, the deep respect they would have for his powers of deduction, how they would marvel at the way he had fitted it altogether.

Of course, if he were being entirely honest, he would have to admit he should have suspected Postgate all along. He had long known him to be a man devoid of virtues or finer feelings; an obnoxious brute, who bullied anyone weaker than himself and cringed to anyone stronger. Postgate would get what he deserved — an appointment with the hangman — and Foxe would have triumphed over him at last.

Foxe was so intent on this orgy of self-congratulation he scarcely noticed the discomforts and jolting of the return journey. To be fair, this time the inside of the coach contained only him and two other passengers. Each of them had ample room to find the most comfortable position in which to settle themselves.

The faithful Alfred met him when he arrived and carried his bag, while Foxe stepped out briskly, whistling a little tune and smiling and nodding to everyone he met. The sun was shining, the breeze was gentle, the city of Norwich was humming with activity and Foxe was, by his own estimation, both the cleverest investigator and the most skilful lover in the county — perhaps even in England itself.

When they arrived, Foxe was tempted to rush at once into the shop to share his news with Mrs Crombie and Nicholas — assuming Nicholas was there — but decided to spend a little time getting everything in order in his mind. It would never do to stumble over a small detail while relating his solution. That would lessen its effect and thus the congratulations he might expect. He settled himself in his library to polish his story.

Unfortunately, while he was doing this the first seeds of doubt crept into his mind. Suppose he was correct that Postgate had spread the story about the ghost and the events of twenty years before to drive Mr Chambers away. Why choose a time that included whatever it was that was so much to his disadvantage? Until the arrival of Chambers, the fire at the White Swan, together with the death of the young actress and her child, had been almost forgotten. Why stir them up now? Especially if it might remind people of something so disreputable in your own past you would kill to keep it a secret.

Another doubt. He could understand why Postgate had killed Chambers; by uttering threats against him, Chambers had transformed himself from an irritant and a nuisance into a danger which must be removed at all costs. But why should he go on to fake the attack on Mr Edwards? There was no evidence Edwards knew anything. A rational murderer, having encompassed the death of his enemy, would allow the fuss to die down as quickly as possible. The affair of Mr Edwards nagged at him. He had little doubt it was Postgate who had rigged the dagger so that Edwards would be hurt. No one else had the same opportunity. It was the motive for doing so that puzzled him. If Edwards had been party to the secret from Postgate's past along with Chambers, wouldn't he have linked the death of Chambers to Postgate's need to be rid of him? The obvious course would be to go to the authorities and denounce Postgate as a murderer.

That all three men had known one another was obvious. They were part of the same profession, in which everybody knew everybody else.

Yet there was no evidence they had known one another intimately. Why should he assume, when Chambers hinted he knew who was spreading the rumours about the ghost and the death of the actress, that he meant Postgate?

By the time he went into dinner, Foxe had abandoned his earlier plan to reveal the answer to the mystery. To do so, he decided, could risk severe embarrassment.

Foxe and his young cousin chatted about unimportant matters during the meal, leaving more substantial discussion until later. When they were sitting with their brandy and cigars, Foxe began to tell Nicholas about his visit to Swaffham, trying to focus on his skills in teasing out important new evidence — and totally ignoring what he had been up to with the delectable Daisy. Throughout his story, he also carefully avoided suggesting what he had learned had solved the mystery. Despite this cautious approach, Foxe was delighted to find Nicholas was greatly impressed. Better still, the young man fell into the same error as Foxe.

'Now I understand!' Nicholas said, full of enthusiasm. 'You've solved it. It must have been Postgate who killed Mr Chambers to prevent him revealing this shameful secret in his past. He tried to drive Chambers away first; when he couldn't achieve that — and Chambers unwisely threatened to expose him — the only alternative was murder. Well done, Cousin!'

'Not so fast,' Foxe said. 'It's obvious Postgate must be mixed up in this somehow, but you've missed some important points.'

Foxe went on to make the very objections to Nicholas's theory he had made to his own. By the time he finished, the poor young man was deflated and embarrassed at his previous excitement. If he had known Foxe himself had fallen into the same error, he would have felt a good deal better. Naturally, Foxe admitted nothing of the kind. Eventually, seeing his cousin so cast down, even Foxe felt ashamed and came close to admitting he had made exactly the same mistake. However, his pride prevailed and he decided to change the subject instead.

'How did you spend your time while I was away?' he asked. 'Did you help Mrs Crombie in the shop?'

Nicholas hadn't done that, he explained. He decided Mrs Crombie should be left on her own for a few hours to get on with her work. Instead he'd gone to the Norfolk Intelligencer to take up Mr Hirons' offer to show him the editorial offices and the printing works. While he was there, he also decided to ask to see the editions from the time of the fire in the theatre. Until now, he had only heard of those events at second or third hand. The newspaper reports might include further details that had been overlooked.

Mr Hirons was delighted to see Nicholas and show him around. They had spent nearly two hours going through the whole process, from writing and editing individual stories to arranging everything on the page. He had even seen how advertisements brought to the offices were paid for and their position on the appropriate page decided. After that, Mr Hirons took him to the printing works and left him in the hands of his master printer. That gentleman proved an equally enthusiastic guide to the intricacies of typesetting, proofing, printing, and distribution of the final newspapers.

All this had lasted for so much of the day that looking at past editions covering the period of the fire almost slipped Nicholas's mind. Fortunately, he remembered when he returned to Mr Hirons' desk before thanking him and taking his leave.

He was not sure Mr Hirons really believed his explanation for looking at the old newspapers. Nevertheless, he said the appropriate editions should be available, calling one of his employees to take Nicholas to the shelves where they might be found. If Mr Foxe wished, Nicholas could tell him the whole story of the fire — at least as it was related in the Norfolk Intelligencer.

Foxe wasn't really that interested, but it would have been churlish to turn down Nicholas's offer. He therefore did what he could to express enthusiasm.

Nicholas began at once, explaining how the fire had broken out during the early part of the evening's performance. Although it was not yet dark, the link-men had prepared their torches ready for escorting theatregoers home, wrapping old rags around one end of a long stick to form the torch itself, soaking it in oil and tar so it would burn fiercely. Finally, they would stack them in an area to the side of the building. It was a convenient place for two reasons. It was not too far from the front of the building and so could be found easily in the dark. They only needed to walk close to the playhouse wall until they came upon it. It was also somewhat protected from any rain. The soaked rags on the ends of the torches would not have absorbed any water, being so heavily impregnated with oil and tar, but wet on the outside would make it harder to set them alight. Since they had been doing this for many months, if not years, the ground all about was heavily soaked with oil and tar from the rags. Most had also followed their usual practice of bringing a lantern with a lit candle inside, setting it on the ground near their stack. It was from this candle's flame they would light the torches when the time came.

The weather that day had been extremely hot and humid. People kept looking at the sky, anticipating the storm which must be brewing. By the time the evening performance commenced, the sky was a mass of heavy clouds. Some claimed they could hear thunder in the distance. Those who had come to the playhouse on foot feared they were likely to get a thorough wetting on their way home.

The storm began with a hot and gusty wind, which drove around the building, whipping up the dust and rubbish. Inside the theatre, the temperature was stifling and all available windows were opened in the hope of cooling air from outside. Backstage it was just as bad. The actors came off stage drenched in sweat and longing to remove their heavy costumes and greasy make-up. The moment any of them had finished their scenes in an item on the lengthy programme, they hurried back to the Green Room to strip off what they could and grab some respite before the next time on stage.

The Green Room where the principal actresses donned their costumes was on the first floor, behind the stage and the machinery which lifted the scenery up and down as it was needed. There too, the only window in the room had been opened wide, setting the scene for the tragedy which was about to unfold. It was so close and unpleasant that several of the actresses had taken the opportunity to slip outside at the rear of the building, hoping to find some relief there. The only one still in the room was Margaret Lindsay. She had stayed to watch over her baby, who was asleep in a cot placed close to the window. There was another cot and child in the room: that one belonged to

Margaret's maid. The two women had given birth within a week of one another and now took it in turns to tend to their infants. Margaret was alone because the maid, Maude Stebbings, had gone to relieve herself. The heat had given Margaret a headache, she told her maid, so she was going to lie down for a while on the day-bed that was right by the open window.

No one knew for certain how or why the stack of torches caught fire. Perhaps a lantern was blown over by the wind and the candle fell out, igniting the tar and oil on the ground. Perhaps a spark blew from a neighbouring chimney and caught in the piles of rubbish. Whatever the cause, in moments the whole stack of torches was ablaze, belching out thick, acrid smoke and sending flames up the wall of the playhouse towards the thatch above. Blazing tar dripped from the torches onto the ground, where it set the piles of rubbish alight in earnest, producing more smoke.

The violent gusts which preceded the approaching storm took this column of smoke and flame and drove it through the open window into the room where Margaret Lindsay must, by this time, have fallen asleep. Parts of the lath-and-plaster wall of the building where the torches stood also caught fire, sending yet more smoke in through the open window above.

The whole playhouse would have been burnt down had it not been for the prompt action of some waiting grooms. Smelling the smoke, they ran to discover the source of the fire, then fetched pitchforks and other implements to pull the blazing torches away from the building into the yard where they might burn themselves out. At the same time, the storm finally broke, producing a torrential downpour of rain which extinguished the greater part of the flames.

According to the newspaper reports, two of the younger, less experienced actors heard the commotion and left the Green Room, which the lesser male actors shared, to find out what was going on. Seeing fire had broken out below, they naturally ran to escape from the building.

One of these two became the hero of the evening. While his colleague ran ahead, down the stairs towards the back of the stage and outside, he paused and looked through the partially open door of the actresses' room to make sure no one was inside. This simple act of thoughtfulness saved two lives, for there, lying right beside the doorway, he saw a young woman, obviously overcome by the smoke still pouring through the open window. Without any hesitation, he seized her under her armpits and dragged her into the corridor, then went back inside in case there should be others. It was almost too dark to see through the smoke. But when his foot struck something that cried out, he bent to find a baby lying there. The woman he had rescued must have been carrying the child when she fell.

Snatching up the infant, he took it into the corridor as well and shut the door behind him. He told the inquest it seemed obvious to him at the time that no one else could have survived in that room. The greater danger would come from setting up a through draught that would draw more flames and smoke into the body of the building. Alerted by his shouts, others now rushed up the stairs and helped carry the woman and child to safety.

'Did the newspaper give any names?' Foxe asked. 'This young hero might be someone worth speaking to.'

'Nothing easier,' Nicholas said, smiling broadly. 'It was a Mr Christopher Edwards, an eighteen-year-old stagehand and occasional actor.'

'Edwards! So, he was there at the time. Who did he rescue, did it give the woman's name as well?'

'Maude Stebbings, maid to the actress who died, Margaret Lindsay. Each of these women had an illegitimate child, as I mentioned already; one a boy and the other a girl. Margaret's boy died in the fire. Maude Stebbings' baby daughter, the one she had been carrying out when she collapsed, survived.'

'Edwards saved two lives, while his friend, whoever that was, ran off to save himself.'

'One report also mentioned another man who, it claimed, had been seen to leave the actresses' room a few minutes before. However, no one came forward and the coroner suggested that report was in error. Do you think there was someone?"

'Lots of young men try to gain admittance to the actresses' Green Room,' Foxe said. He didn't say how often he'd done it himself. 'If there was, I expect we'll never know his identity.'

'But to run out and leave two women and two babies behind . . .'

Foxe sat up straight, his eyes blazing, then relaxed. He had no evidence Postgate had been at the playhouse that night. It was only his instant prejudice that made him suspect he might have been the missing man. It was just the kind of thing he would do, of course. Still, no sense in jumping to more conclusions without proof to back them up.

'You've done an excellent job, Cousin Nicholas,' Foxe said. There was real warmth in his voice. 'I congratulate you. The way you have recounted the events of that evening made me feel as if I was there myself. However, from our viewpoint in unravelling Chambers' death, it doesn't advance matters much. If it had been arson, or the result of some other deliberate act, it might have given us a reason: that is, if someone held Chambers responsible. As it is, it's plain it was an accident, terrible though the outcome was. The link-men shouldn't have stacked their torches in the way they did, nor left lanterns with burning candles in them so close by, but that's being wise after the event. Wooden buildings like the White Swan Playhouse are always prone to fire. Had it not been for the providential downpour which prevented it spreading and then put it out, the whole place would have burned to the ground. There would certainly have been more deaths. Imagine the panic and chaos as hundreds of people fought to get out of the blazing building.'

They talked around what he been learned for a while longer, then left it — no nearer than before to understanding how the new information that had been discovered was to be fitted into a pattern — if such a pattern existed. That was the problem, Foxe explained. They now had a good deal of information, but no idea if any of it was relevant to Chambers' death or the attack on Edwards. Without being able to understand why the murder or the attack took place, it was almost impossible to decide how the events of the past might relate to recent happenings. By the time they parted to go to their respective rooms, all their earlier enthusiasm had been lost.

🎋 20 🎋

It was a downhearted Mr Foxe who went through to the bookstore the next morning to acquaint Mrs Crombie with the results of his visit to Swaffham. For all his efforts, he felt he was no further forward. Indeed, he was beginning to believe that the mystery might never be solved.

Mrs Crombie tried to look on the bright side. 'You shouldn't be so downhearted, Mr Foxe,' she said. 'You haven't been working on this investigation for long. You've also been doing so by indirect means, since you don't wish to go to the playhouse or ask your questions openly. I can understand your reasons, but it surely must make the whole process a good deal more difficult.'

Foxe agreed it did. On the other hand, he didn't believe anyone at the playhouse would be able to give him better information then he had obtained already. The mayor's clerk, Mr Plumtree, had interviewed a number of people without finding anything pointing to who was behind the murder of Mr Chambers or the attack on Mr Edwards.

'If this had been a simple matter, your skills wouldn't have been needed,' Mrs Crombie said. 'I'm sure Mr Plumtree would have come to the answer himself and seen the malefactor brought before the mayor's court. It is precisely because the actions of this murderer are shrouded in such darkness the mayor has sought your help.'

Foxe looked at her closely, but could see no signs of flattery. Of course, what she said was undoubtedly true. He had never been involved in investigating straightforward activities, nor would he wish to be.

'Perhaps you're right,' he said. 'It is just that I feel so frustrated. Every time I think I have made a breakthrough, it disappears. All the way back from Swaffham, I was certain Mr Postgate was the murderer. Now I'm far from sure he is; and if he did kill Mr Chambers, I can see no way of bringing a sound case against him. There's simply no evidence sufficient to convince a judge and jury.'

'What about the events surrounding the fire when the young actress was killed? I don't mean the story about the vengeful ghost. Were any of these men involved in the event in such a way as to invite violence against them — twenty years later too?'

'The only one I know about so far is Mr Edwards — and he was the hero of the hour for saving the life of a young woman and her baby. You'd hardly take revenge for that. Chambers may well have been there. He was probably a fairly established actor by then, since he was five or more years older than Edwards. Postgate? I have no idea. I'm hoping to be able to speak to Mr Edwards — presuming he's still in Norwich — and ask him.'

'I'm sure you'll find the answer, Mr Foxe,' Mrs Crombie said. 'You always do. I've never seen you beaten yet.'

Thanks to her faith in him, Foxe started to feel a good deal better. He'd been dreading the idea of seeking out Alderman Halloran to report on progress. Now he could see a way of giving a more positive report, while still stressing the difficulty of the whole matter. Much had been disclosed which had not been known before. It hadn't provided the answer, but it was still useful, if only to rule out some theories. Perhaps he should forego his daily visit to the coffeehouse and visit Alderman Halloran. If Charlie could be spared, he would send him ahead to make sure the alderman was willing to receive him.

Foxe glanced around the shop. It was still early, but one or two customers had arrived already. More would follow as ladies ventured out to take the air and meet friends and acquaintances. The circulating library was already becoming a favoured place for the wives and daughters of merchants and the better class of tradesman to meet and gossip, under the cloak of returning or choosing reading material. Maybe the world was not such a bad place after all.

That was when he noticed Nicholas was not present. Where was he this time? Surely he had not deserted his post yet again? If he had, it was time to have a severe word with him. Nicholas's father hadn't sent him to Norwich to fritter away his time.

Mrs Crombie must have noticed the direction of his glance and the change of expression, for she offered an immediate explanation.

'If you are looking for Mr Nicholas,' she said, 'he asked if he might absent himself today to visit Mr Plumtree. As you know, Mr Plumtree offered to spend time showing Mr Nicholas the kind of work he undertakes in his branch of the legal profession. A messenger came this morning, just after the shop was opened, to say Mr Plumtree was unexpectedly at leisure, due to a particular case in the court being postponed. If the notice were not too short, he would be delighted to spend the day as he had promised. Mr Nicholas asked me what he should do and I said I thought he should accept. I didn't think you would mind. After all, he has come to Norwich to reach a final decision on his way in this world. I know he was greatly impressed by Mr Plumtree, as well as by discovering that lawyers could be involved in more than drawing up Wills, leases and indentures.'

There was no way Foxe could disagree. Nicholas might also find out something useful while talking to Mr Plumtree, just as he had done when he spent time with Mr Hirons in the newspaper offices. The lad had a sharp mind and was by no means lacking in initiative.

Mrs Crombie had not finished. 'I hope you will not think it presumptuous of me to say this, Mr Foxe,' she went on, 'but to my mind Mr Nicholas is unsuited to life as a bookseller — or a tradesman of any kind. He is too much like you. He thrives on challenges, variety and excitement. He's done his best to show enthusiasm for what we're doing in this shop and what we've achieved, but I can see his heart isn't in it. I'm sure you can understand that.' She paused. 'May I speak frankly?'

Foxe was intrigued. 'Of course,' he said.

'When I came here, it was clear to me your heart was not in running this business either, Mr Foxe. Your father must have loved this place. Until I suggested one or two changes, everything about the business dated from the time when he was the owner. Aside from buying and selling rare books to discerning collectors — a business in which you clearly excel and where you have established extensive knowledge — the bookshop had been, if you will pardon my saying so, almost entirely neglected.'

'You're quite right, Mrs Crombie,' Foxe said. 'My father loved this shop, although, towards the end of his life, it made up only a small part of his mercantile activities. He was a clever and practical man, far more practical than I am in many respects, and also a prudent one. As I may have told you, my mother died when I was born, so I never knew her. My father was determined he should deal with me as he believed she would have done. He was always kind towards me, tried to be interested in all my activities and, I have to admit, somewhat indulgent of my many whims. I believe he had also set himself to ensure I should not want in this world, whatever I decided to do with my life.

'The money he made from his printing works, his newspapers and this shop, he invested in loans and property in and around this city; property that would bring in substantial rents as well as increase in value over the years. In this, he was as successful as he had been in all his business activities. When he died, far too young, I determined to try to live up to his achievements to the best of my ability.'

'As I am sure you have,' Mrs Crombie said. She was intrigued by what Foxe was saying. She'd never before heard him speak so openly about himself and his life.

'I hope so. I soon discovered I'd inherited my father's talent in the matter of investing. He left me a substantial portfolio of loans and properties, which I've increased more than threefold in the time I've had charge of them. I could easily live from my rents and other income alone if I wished. Yet the desire to create more wealth took hold of me. Not for its own sake — I am no miser, piling up gold to no purpose. What holds me in its grip is the sense of achievement. The businesses which I own or have financed provide employment to a good many people in this city. I have also been able to indulge myself in a number of philanthropic ventures. I met Captain Brock by making him a loan to expand the shipping business he'd started. His friendship is most dear to me, Mrs Crombie, and I would happily sacrifice every penny I've invested in his business to retain it.'

By now, Mrs Crombie was completely enthralled. She had known the bare facts of Foxe's various activities before — well, most of them — but she had never realised he pursued them with such passion.

'The business in rare books it is just a kind of hobby,' Foxe went on, 'though a profitable one. For the rest of the time, I make loans and buy and sell property. This bookshop, I am afraid, has never attracted me as much as it should have done.'

Mrs Crombie now ventured a comment. 'I wonder you have not sold it then,' she said. 'What has caused you to retain the ownership of an asset which brought you little?'

'Sentiment. I told you my father loved this place. It would have broken his heart to see it pass out of the family. You've done me a great service in coming here and transforming the shop as you have. Should there be another life after this one, and should I meet my father again, I feel I will now be able to look him in the eye and report that I have done my best with all of his ventures, not just some of them. Fortunately, he sold the printing works and the newspaper before he died. Those were of least interest to me. They would also have proved the most onerous to retain and the hardest to find someone to run on my behalf.'

'I'm sure your father would be very proud of you,' Mrs Crombie said. 'But if the business of loans and property is of such great interest to you, I wonder why you have not opened a bank.'

The plain fact was Foxe had never thought of doing such a thing. Now Mrs Crombie had mentioned it, he wondered why the idea had not crossed his mind before.

'I never thought of it,' he said. Then he laughed. 'Can you see me as a grave-faced banker, Mrs Crombie?'

'Perhaps not grave-faced,' she said, joining in his laughter. 'Prosperous, yes. Adventurous, still more. Still, we're drifting away from the point. What I wished to tell you was Nicholas is not suited, to my mind, to make his living through the world of business. I believe he understands this. He would probably already have returned home, were it not for the fact that the idea of doing so appals him.'

'How so?' Foxe said.

'He's convinced if he doesn't settle firmly on a different future, his father will renew the pressure on him to enter the church. He also thinks his father wishes him to leave because he has a new wife in the offing.'

'He's probably right on both counts. From what Cousin Nicholas has told me, she is not far from his own age. Few older men with young wives would relish having a potential rival for affection in the house.'

'Your cousin is also worried about his aunt's situation. He believes she's wretched now, but can see no way to alleviate her distress.'

'I wonder he has spoken to you so freely, Mrs Crombie,' Foxe said. 'These are, as I judge, all family matters.'

'Do not be angry with him, Mr Foxe. He misses a mother sorely and has been bearing this load alone for long enough. He found in me a sympathetic ear and the willingness to listen without judgement or comment. I think you know I am no tittle-tattle. If I mentioned this to you, it is because it affects you directly and you are a member of his family. I would assuredly not breathe a word of it to anyone else.'

'I have never doubted your discretion, Mrs Crombie. I was just somewhat startled. If I am angry with anyone, it is with myself. I see now I have been so wrapped up in my own concerns I have left my Cousin Nicholas without the support he needs. Far from being annoyed by what you have told me, I feel gratitude you've been willing to fulfil a role which I neglected.'

'You are being far too hard on yourself once again,' Mrs Crombie said. 'You cannot do everything.'

'I could — and should — certainly do something. I too have been worrying about my Cousin Harriet. Not as much as young Nicholas, I admit, but enough that I've already begun to form a plan to release her from her problems and will now accelerate the matter.'

They were still talking when Mrs Crombie's cousin, Eleanor, who assisted her in the shop, came into the workroom bringing the news that Mrs Halloran was in the shop, asking for either Mr Foxe or Mrs Crombie. Naturally, Foxe went out at once.

Mrs Halloran wasted no time in getting to the point of her visit. 'I was talking to a friend of mine recently,' she told Foxe. 'She wasn't at Mordifort's masked ball herself, but several of her friends went. One of them, a Mrs Delaware, was a witness to the argument between Mr and Mrs Henson and said it was most embarrassing. According to her report to my friend, Mrs Henson rushed off to get her cloak and it looked as if she was going to leave right away. Mrs Delaware was therefore quite surprised when she saw Mrs Henson walking towards her a few moments later, obviously going back into the supper room.'

'Did she see what she was going to do?'

'No. However, she did speak a few words to Mrs Henson as she passed. Mrs Henson told her she was going to tell her father she was leaving. It was soon after that the murder took place, so in the general chaos Mrs Delaware didn't see Mrs Henson again until she was kneeling by the body of her father, raining down curses on whoever had killed him.'

'Did your friend tell you whether this Mrs Delaware had seen Mr Peter Mordifort at all? Around that time, I mean.' Foxe asked.

'Apparently everyone thought he'd already gone home,' Mrs Halloran replied. 'He's well known for being a most unsociable person. I think most of the guests were surprised he had attended at all. Now I must be on my way, or I shall be late arriving at Lady Bastwood's weekly morning salon. She's most particular about timing, you know. If anyone arrives after the appointed time, she becomes something of a martinet on the subject. On the other hand, she's an extremely generous hostess and attracts many of the best minds in Norwich to the discussions she holds, men and ladies. I'm surprised she hasn't invited you.'

'My mind is far from being of the best, Mrs Halloran, I assure you. Sometimes I wonder if it works at all.'

21

While Foxe and Mrs Halloran were talking, Charlie was at the back gate to Foxe's garden, listening to a small group of disreputable-looking street-children. They'd come to report what they and their friends had discovered about the movements of Mr Chambers and Mr Edwards. It was not much.

Chambers, they said, hardly left the playhouse during the first part of his time in Norwich, save to go to his lodgings in the evening. Once inside, he had remained there too. Only in the last two days had he been seen leaving the playhouse during the day. Two of the girls saw him early in the afternoon and described his behaviour as furtive. He'd slipped out through a back door and disappeared quickly into one of the alleys nearby.

At first, they thought he was going to visit a woman. But when one of them ventured up the alley a little way, she found the entrance to a low-class grog-shop. Abstaining from alcohol had finally got too much for Chambers. Either he was going to the grog-shop to drink, or he was buying smuggled Genever spirits to take back to the theatre.

Edwards had not been at the playhouse long before he suffered his supposed accident, so none of them had seen a great deal of him. All they could report of interest was he had left the playhouse on two days, early in the afternoon, and headed off around St Peter Mancroft church. They had seen no reason to follow him, so they could not be certain where he was going. However, there was a general agreement amongst them that it was probably to a Molly-house. Edwards was well known to have a taste for boys and young men. On previous visits both to the White Swan and The Grand Concert Hall, he was known to have frequented Molly-houses.

None of the children had noticed any strangers hanging around the theatre. There had only been the normal crowd of young men trying to get into the actresses' Green Room or waiting for them when they emerged after the evening performance. No more than that.

Although this was disappointing in its way, Charlie hurried to report to his master. Foxe listened and thought it progress of a kind, if not what he would have liked. At least it proved the murder must have been inside the theatre. He told Charlie to thank the children and gave him twelve pennies to be shared out amongst them.

'I've told them to come at once, if there is anything they think they should tell me,' Charlie said. 'I mean anything new or unusual happening.'

Foxe nodded his head in approval. 'To be honest, Charlie, we could do with all the new information we can get. I'm sure there's a pattern behind this, even if I can't yet see it. By the way, did any of them say anything about Mr Postgate?'

'They all hate him,' Charlie said, 'especially the girls. He's cruel and mean. If he gets one of them on her own, it's up with her skirts and out with his — beg pardon, master, but you know what I mean.'

Foxe did. 'He's violent with them?'

'Takes what he wants, when he wants it, how he wants it, and never pays a penny. They all stay away from him if they can.'

'Just the girls?'

'Mostly, as I hear it. Though one or two say he's been known to do the same with some of the boys, if they're pretty enough.'

Foxe now had another good reason to hate Postgate. The street-children were not angels. Many of the girls made their living by selling themselves to men. But it was quite another thing for Postgate to treat them as if they were dirt under his feet. By God, if he could have his way—

These dark thoughts were interrupted by the entrance of Mrs Crombie.

'Excuse me, Mr Foxe,' she said, 'but I need Charlie a moment. There's a young . . . woman, I suppose you'd say . . . standing right by the door to the shop and peering inside. From the way she's dressed, and her general dirtiness, I think she must be one of the street-children.'

Charlie darted forward, full of indignation. 'I've told them not to do that!' he said. 'If they want me, they're to come to the back of the building, where none of the customers can see them, slip through the gate and come down to the kitchen door. Flo or Molly then come and find me. Leave it to me, master. I'll give her the rough edge of my tongue.'

Foxe put out his hand and took hold of Charlie's arm. 'Wait a minute,' he said. 'I'm sure they all know this. Why would one of them decide to break your rules?'

'It would have to be something real important,' Charlie said. 'So important they had to get to me right away.'

'A moment ago, you told me you'd instructed them to let you know at once if anything new or different happened in the theatre. Might it be something of that nature?'

Charlie thought it might, though his anger was not fully abated.

'Very well,' Foxe said. 'Go out quickly now and tell whoever it is to go around the back in the normal way. Then come back through here and let me know. I'll go out to the back and speak to this girl myself.'

'Are you sure you want to do that, master? It'll be one of the whores. You don't want to run the risk of anyone seeing you talking to someone of that kind outside your back gate.'

'It's happened before,' Foxe said, smiling. 'Don't worry about me, Charlie. Just go to the door as quick as you can, so the girl doesn't alarm Mrs Crombie's customers. I'll give you a few moments, then I'll make my way out into the yard and go to the back gate.'

The girl Foxe found waiting for him when he got there was a poor, half-starved little thing, dressed in the kind of ragged finery many of the cheap whores used. She told him her name was Rosie and she had run all the way from the White Swan to bring him the latest news.

'Rosie Rabbit they calls me, Mister,' she said. 'On account of they says I look like a skinned rabbit when I got me clothes off. I've come to tell you that evil bugger Postgate is dead.'

'Dead? Are you sure?'

'Sure as I'm standing here, Mister. Dead as a door nail — and good riddance, if you asks me and a good many of us girls.'

'Do you know how this happened?' Foxe asked her.

She did not, only that his body had been found in the theatre. How he died she didn't know. For her, it was enough a man she feared and hated would no longer be able to force himself on her whenever he wished.

Foxe had one more question.

'Has the constable been sent for?' Rosie nodded her head. 'Very well. You did the right thing in coming here so quickly. I'll tell Charlie and make sure he doesn't scold you. Now, here's a sixpence for your trouble.'

'Cor! A whole sixpence! An' you didn't even feel under me skirt.'

With that admission, and probably fearing Foxe might change his mind and take his money back, she dashed off.

Foxe went back into the house in something of a daze, forgetting to go through to the shop to tell Mrs Crombie and Charlie what all the fuss had been about. By the time he remembered, they'd heard it anyway, for the whole area was buzzing with the news. Not just another death at the White Swan, but a body found in the same room, so the gossips claimed. Could it be the ghost after all? Even some of those who had dismissed the possibility out-of-hand before were less sure of themselves.

Once more Foxe set out for Alderman Halloran's house to tell him the news and see if he could throw any light on possible reasons for this additional killing. The alderman was away at the mayor's house when he arrived, but Mrs Halloran said he was expected back soon. The mayor had sent a servant to ask him to call on an important matter, but that was of little significance. Her husband received such a summons two or three times each week and it was rarely caused by more than the mayor's habitual anxious pessimism.

Sure enough, Foxe had not been in the house for more than five minutes before they heard the alderman had arrived home again.

'Foxe!' the alderman said when he saw his visitor. 'Do you have the Second Sight or something? I was about to send one of my servants to ask you to call when he told me you were here already. I presume you've heard about Postgate of the White Swan? A message reached the mayor when I was with him. He wasn't best pleased with your efforts so far, I can tell you. Wants these murders brought to an end, not more of them. Now, read this. The mayor gave it to me. He received it this morning. It's the latest oddity in the murder of Mordifort.' He handed Foxe a single piece of paper which had been folded and sealed.

A single glance at the peculiar handwriting told Foxe whom it had come from. After the usual salutation, Dorothy Henson had written in her typically terse, blunt style. She said the family had arranged for their father to be buried in the parish church yard of the village where he was born and the interment would take place that afternoon. There would therefore be no requirement for the civic funeral the mayor had offered. They were grateful for the honour, but did not believe their father would have wished to be buried with so much ceremony.

'What do you think of her message?' Halloran said. 'I'm not even sure which village they mean. Neither the mayor nor anyone else I know was invited to the funeral. It's almost as if they wish to get him safely in the ground and forgotten as quickly as possible.'

'That's precisely what they do want,' Foxe said. 'I'm sure of it. What I'm not sure of is why they want it so.'

'Do you think the daughter is embarrassed by the fact her father was murdered?'

'Heaven knows. Don't you think it's strange she's always the one who writes?'

'In any other family, I would. In this one . . . she's the elder of the two siblings, of course, so maybe that makes a difference. She's also by far the stronger of the two. Her brother never seems to stir himself for anything. She probably knows he wouldn't think to send a reply to the mayor's offer of a civic funeral. All Peter Mordifort's interested in are his precious antiquities.'

'Her handwriting's odd, isn't it?'

'I suppose it is,' Halloran said. 'I've seen writing like that before . . . can't remember where though. The whole Mordifort family is peculiar. I told you how secretive Mordifort was about everything, both his life and his business affairs. I suspect some of what he did to build up his business included actions he wouldn't want anyone to know about. He wasn't always fair or scrupulous in his transactions. The ends justified the means, so far as Mr Edward Mordifort was concerned.'

The two sat in silence for a while, then the alderman gave a great sigh.

'I can't see my way through any of this, Foxe. You don't think these killings are linked, do you? A homicidal maniac on the loose?'

'It would be most unlikely. I don't imagine Mordifort was a patron of our theatres any more than Chambers, Edwards or now Postgate enjoyed hospitality at Mordifort's house.'

'What we need is something to show an opening — a clear way forward. We don't need more bodies and more puzzles to go with them.'

'You mentioned Mordifort's business dealings, Halloran. Can you find out what he'd been up to in that part of his life of late? It occurs to me we've rather neglected the possibility that his death is linked to some shady dealings at his brewery or maltings. Aside from marvelling at their oddity, I can't see there's much more to be learned by concentrating on his family . . . no, I'm wrong there too. The son-in-law, Alfred Henson. It's easy to forget about him. You told me he's a ship's chandler and not much of a businessman. Is there anything else to be discovered about him?'

'Well done, Foxe! Knew you'd put your finger on what we're missing. I'll get onto both those matters as soon as possible. Some of my friends amongst the city's merchants and tradespeople are bound to be able to provide some useful information. What are you going to do next?'

'My cousin, Nicholas, has been spending today with Mr Plumtree. I'll wait to hear if he has anything new to report on either murder. I was going to say I could go to the White Swan and ask my questions openly now Postgate's dead. On reflection, I think that might not be such a good idea. Everything points to the murderer of Chambers and Postgate — assuming it's the same person, which I think it must be — as someone closely connected with the White Swan Playhouse. Our best hope is to convince the murderer he's got away with his crimes. If he relaxes his guard, he may make a mistake which will give us a vital clue.'

❧ 22 ❧

Nicholas was still with Mr Plumtree when a constable arrived with the news of Postgate's murder. He thought there might be a flurry of action, but Plumtree explained that unexplained deaths did not become the business of the magistrate until after an inquest had been held and the cause of each one legally determined. He would inform the mayor at once, but no more at this stage. For the present, the matter rested in the hands of Mr Brindley, the coroner, who would arrange for an inquest to take place as soon as possible. Mr Brindley would probably arrange for a medical examination to help determine how Postgate came to meet his death. All the evidence would be laid before a jury and they would give their verdict after due consideration. It was a time-honoured system and worked well enough. Finding Nicholas had never attended an inquest, Mr Plumtree suggested he might find the process of interest, quite apart from its connection to the earlier death at the same theatre.

Just before leaving Mr Plumtree's office, word had come that the inquest would be held at ten o'clock in the morning, on the day after next, to allow time for the medical examiner to complete his work.

Since Mr Brindley anticipated a large number of people might wish to attend, he would set up his court at the White Swan Playhouse.

'If you agree, Cousin, I would like to attend,' Nicholas said to Foxe that evening. 'I have found many aspects of the criminal law interest me and it would be good to see the process through from start to finish.'

'We'll go together,' Foxe replied. 'It will be the simplest way to learn the basic details. Any information which does not come out at the inquest, I can probably discover from Alderman Halloran afterwards. I sent Alfred to the landlord at the White Swan to enquire if he knew whether Mr Edwards was still at his lodgings. If so, Alfred was to take my card there and ask whether it would be possible for me to speak with Mr Edwards tomorrow morning. I believe that has now been arranged. We can set Postgate aside until after the inquest.'

'It's a shame you were forbidden to investigate Mr Mordifort's death,' Nicholas said. 'We might have spent some time on the matter in the interim. Mr Plumtree told me at least one thing which might have been of assistance.'

'Did he?' Foxe said, trying to sound casual about it. 'What was it?'

'Two things really, I suppose. He said he'd heard gossip amongst the city's lawyers that Mr Mordifort must have taken his legal business away from his usual attorney. It seems he hadn't consulted him on anything of importance for many weeks.'

'Perhaps he had no need of legal advice or documents.'

'Maybe. Yet Mr Plumtree said Mr Mordifort was usually in the way of needing some legal document or other most weeks. He had extensive business interests, you see, as well as a good many loans and bonds outstanding, especially to publicans. According to Mr Plumtree, that was how Mr Mordifort had obtained most of his tied houses. He would encourage an independent publican to take out a loan from him to improve his inn or add extra space, using the business as security. When the man fell behind on his repayments, as most did at some time or another, Mr Mordifort was ruthless in seizing the business for himself.'

'I'd heard his business methods were doubtful,' Foxe said. 'This shows just how far he was prepared to go to climb upwards on the backs of others. What was the other thing you said Mr Plumtree told you?'

'He didn't know where the rumour came from, but it was being said Mr Mordifort had been talking confidentially to the trustees of a number of major charities in the city about possible donations.'

'It doesn't sound like Mordifort, does it? Not based on what I've been told of the man. I wonder what he was up to?'

'As I said, it's a shame you haven't been allowed to investigate. Who knows what you could have found out.'

'Who knows indeed,' Foxe said. 'Yes, it is a shame.'

⊗⅍⊗

EARLY THE NEXT MORNING, FOXE MADE HIS WAY TO THE LODGING-house where he'd been told he would find Mr Edwards. The building was much as he expected; constructed of wood and wattle-and-daub with a thatched roof in urgent need of replacement. In its day, probably some two hundred years earlier, it must have been a substantial home, but the intervening years had not treated it kindly. The lime wash and plaster had come away in several places, exposing the wooden laths beneath, while the main wooden beams had lost most of the tar which had once protected them from the weather. The only advantage it seemed to offer was its proximity to the White Swan Play-house and The Grand Concert Hall.

The lodging-housekeeper was also exactly what anyone familiar with theatrical lodging would have predicted. A short, substantial woman past middle-age and running to fat. From her clothing and gaudy make-up, she had most likely been part of an acting company herself in her youth, perhaps in burlesque roles or as a singer. She didn't have the look of someone who might have been cast in a tragedy. Still, she was cheerful enough and didn't greet Foxe with the kind of grovelling obsequiousness he had expected.

'I been waiting for you, sir,' she said, when she answered his knock on the door. 'Mr Edwards said to send you straight up to his room. He's on the first floor, right-hand side. We gets all the theatrical folk here. It's close to where they're working, see. Easy for them to get back late at night without risking too many dark alleys. I does my best for 'em, poor lambs, but most on 'em can't afford to pay for what you'd call proper decent lodgings, can they? Mr Edwards 'as got me best room, now. Very comfortable that one is, though I says it 'as shouldn't. Unless you're famous, acting's a hard life. On the move, week after week, and precious little reward. I knows. Did it myself for nigh on twenty-five years, I did. Best in burlesques and comedies, I was. Not a bad acrobat either, though you wouldn't think of it to look at me now. That's what age does to you. Turn right at the top of the stairs, sir, and it's the door facing you.'

Foxe thanked her and stepped inside, to be greeted at once by a smell compounded of decay, human sweat, urine, mice, and stale food. How did people live here? Such carpet as was left on the stairs was worn into holes and the bannister wobbled so much he determined not to touch it again for fear it would fall off. Up one flight of rickety stairs, turn around ninety degrees on a half-landing and up another flight. Then along a short landing over the stairwell and the door was in front of him.

'It's the one in front of you,' the landlady called up from below. 'Walk straight in. He's not to get out of bed unless he has to, so the 'pothecary says.'

Foxe found Edwards lying propped up in bed in a room whose furnishing and fittings could best be described as basic. Still, it seemed slightly cleaner than the average room in a cheap lodging house of this type, so what the lodging-keeper said about it being her best room was likely true.

Edwards looked a far cry from the dashing presence he tried to cultivate on the stage. He appeared weary and wretched, his face decorated with several days' growth of beard, his night-shirt none too clean and even dirtier nightcap on his head. It was plain he hadn't risen from amongst the grubby sheets and threadbare blankets more than he was forced to do. Foxe supposed the landlady was looking after him. If so, she hadn't been to empty his chamber pot for some time. The smell of it caught at your throat.

'I'm sorry to bring you to this wretched place, Mr Foxe,' Edwards said, 'but the man who's been treating me says I mustn't get up until my wound has scabbed over fully. Take the chair to the left. Mrs Trull claims it's the best one in the house, not that any of them are worth a shilling. I understand you want to ask me about poor Lemuel Chambers. Why are you interested in him, may I ask?'

'I'm assisting the mayor in his capacity as chief magistrate for this city,' Foxe explained. 'There are too many strange events taking place at the White Swan. You've heard Mr Postgate is dead?'

'Mrs Trull came bursting in with the news this morning. I assume he was murdered too, like Lemuel.'

'I don't know yet. The inquest isn't until tomorrow morning. I also want to ask you about the fire which took place at the same playhouse some twenty years ago. I gather you were something of a hero on that occasion.'

'Surely you don't believe all the story about the ghost, do you? Margaret Lindsay has been dead and gone many years. Why should her spirit be walking now? Besides, no one killed her or her child. The whole thing was an accident.'

Foxe shook his head. 'No, I agree the ghost story is hogwash. Yet there is something about those events which interests me, if only the fact they may provide a link between those who have been attacked in the last few weeks. That is, if you, Mr Chambers and Mr Postgate were all present on the night of the fire.'

'I can set your mind at rest on that point right away,' Edwards said. 'The three of us were certainly there. Postgate and I had just started out in the theatre, working mostly as stagehands with occasional walk-on parts carrying spears and the like. It was a red-letter day when we got a single line of our own. As I recall, the reason I was upstairs was I'd gone back to the Green Room to put on the costume for my single appearance that night. Postgate was in the room when I arrived. He'd done his one minute of acting a few minutes before I was due to go on stage, so was getting out of his costume as I was getting into mine. We started to walk back along the corridor together. That was when I smelled the smoke.'

'Yes,' Foxe said, 'The newspaper report mentioned you had a colleague with you when you rescued the maid servant.'

'It's not quite correct,' Edwards said. 'As soon as I told Postgate the playhouse must be on fire, he took to his heels and ran. That was the last I saw of him for the evening. I was tempted to run too. I don't know what made me open the door into the actresses' Green Room. When I did, the place was full of thick smoke. If the maidservant hadn't been lying right by the door, I would never have seen her.'

'Yet you went back for the baby. What made you do so?'

'The maidservant, I suppose. She was gasping for breath, coughing and wheezing terribly, but even so she managed to croak out something about an infant; her infant, as I supposed. One or two other people had come upstairs by then to make sure no one was left in those rooms, so I told them to look after her and tried to go back into the Green Room.'

'The newspaper report said you did go back.'

'I suppose that's true, but I didn't get far past the door. The smoke was truly terrible. No one could have lasted in there more than a few moments. You couldn't see either. If I hadn't stumbled over the child, I would never have found it. As it was, I snatched it up and got out again as quickly as I could. By the time I did, I was in almost as bad a state as the maidservant had been.'

'You shut the door of the room behind you?'

'I did. There was no sense in letting all the smoke billow into the rest of the building. It was chaotic enough as it was. The performance was still in progress when word of the fire spread amongst the audience. As you can imagine, they panicked and tried to get out as quickly as they could, swiftly followed by those who'd been on stage. What with the shouting and screaming and coughing, it was total bedlam. Don't be misled by the fact the final damage wasn't too great. That was entirely due to the storm. Had the rain not come pouring down when it did, I'm sure the whole building would have gone up in flames.'

'You said Mr Chambers was there that evening as well.'

'Yes. Lemuel was five or six years older than Postgate and myself. By then, he was something of an established actor, at least in more minor and supporting roles. The poor fellow never got to take on leading parts, then or later. Not good enough, you see. Acting was changing. At one time, it was all about striking heroic poses and declaiming your lines loudly enough to be heard over the noise from the gallery. Little more than that. Then Mr Garrick and Mr Barry came along. After them, acting had to be more emotional and subtle. Lemuel simply couldn't manage it. It wasn't his style. He tried, of course, but it wasn't long before none of the major companies would look at him. That was when he started drinking.'

'Mr Hunter told me he'd only taken on Mr Chambers because it was an emergency.'

'I'm not surprised. I don't think Lemuel had worked more than a few weeks in the previous year. He must have known it was time to pull himself together and stop drinking so much. Maybe he would have succeeded. He knew all the usual parts, so he could have made himself useful, at least in some of the minor touring companies. Now we'll never know.'

'Do you know where he was at the time of the fire twenty years ago?' Foxe asked.

'I'm pretty sure he was onstage. Downstairs anyway. If he wasn't onstage at the time, he would have been waiting in the wings to go on. He was playing a role in the burlesque the company was performing when the fire broke out. They almost always finished the evening with a burlesque. So far as I know, he didn't have any more costume changes. I certainly never saw him go back upstairs.'

'You and Postgate were upstairs in the actors' Green Room — or, to be accurate, on your way downstairs when the fire broke out. Chambers was either onstage or waiting in the wings. Have I got that right?'

'You have. That's exactly where we were. We all got out too. I didn't see Chambers after the fire, but I heard him come up to his room in the lodging house. Postgate and I were sharing a room and his was next door to ours.'

'Can you think of anything which happened on the evening of the fire to explain why the three of you have been attacked?'

'Nothing at all, either then or thereafter. I have no idea who would want to kill poor Lemuel, any more than I can think why anyone would want to kill me.'

'And Postgate?'

'Not Postgate either, though he was never a popular person. I gather he's got even worse over the years. He's the only one of the three of us whom I could possibly imagine doing something bad enough to cause someone to want to kill him. But what it was, if it ever existed, I have no notion. I would just about call Lemuel Chambers a friend of mine, though I hadn't seen him for perhaps five years past. Josiah Postgate wasn't anyone's friend. Too selfish, too sly, too treacherous. Too fond of women too. Most of them weren't keen on him though, so I gather he sometimes tried to take what none would offer him willingly. He could have paid for it, of course. Anyway, I did know he was now house manager at the White Swan Theatre, here in Norwich. If Lemuel was a poor actor, Josiah Postgate was a terrible one. He soon dropped the idea of going on stage and made a life for himself working behind the scenes instead. To be honest, I didn't expect to see much of him during this run. As an actor, nearly all my dealings are with the manager of our own company, not the person in charge of the theatre where we're playing. You could be sure I wouldn't seek Postgate out either.'

There didn't seem much more to learn, so Foxe thanked Mr Edwards, wished him well for the future and made his way back down the stairs and out into the fresh air. The whole business had taken less than half an hour, but it was time well spent.

❧ 2 3 ❧

Foxe and Nicholas got to the playhouse for the inquest in good
time the next morning to be sure of securing seats close to the
front, from where they could hear everything which was said.
The coroner's court had been set up on the stage. It looked as if a play
was about to take place and the chairs and tables were part of the
scenery. Mr Brindley, the coroner, would be in the centre, his clerk
would sit beside him and whoever was giving evidence would sit to his
left. On the right were the chairs on which the jury would settle themselves. The public would sit on the benches which formed the theatre's
stalls.

Mr Tobias Brindley, the coroner, once a well-known attorney in the
town but now retired, opened the proceedings promptly at ten o'clock.
The jury had been sworn in the day before and had viewed the body at
that time, so the hearing began with evidence of identity given by
Henry Raven, the landlord of the White Swan.

After him, a wiry little man by the name of Gabriel Plover was
called to the stand. He spoke so quietly, and with such a strong
Norwich accent, Mr Brindley had to keep asking him to repeat what
he had said. It therefore took an inordinate amount of time to discover
Plover was employed as a carpenter at the playhouse and had found

the body, which had been lying, face down, in a store room behind the stage — the same room in which Mr Chambers' body had been found. Asked why he had looked into the room, which he had already said was rarely used, Plover explained the door was open. This had excited his curiosity and caused him to look inside in case something had been taken.

'Not but what anybody would 'ave to be out of their mind like to take anything from in there,' Plover told the coroner. 'Nothin' but rubbish, that is. Bits of ol' scenery, painted cloths, that kind of stuff. If you took it all, you'd not get more'n sixpence for it. That's right enough, that is. Mebbe not even sixpence.'

Mr Brindley tried to get back to the point by asking where in the room the body had been lying.

'Right there!' Plover said.

'What I meant,' Mr Brindley said, rolling his eyes and sighing, 'was whereabouts in the room. Was it on the floor, for example?'

'No, it weren't.'

Brindley tried again. 'So where was it? Answer the question, man!'

'I did, so don't you go getting' all uppity with me. You asks me if it were on the floor and I said it weren't. That's answering the question, that is, or I'm a Dutchman.'

Mr Brindley banged his gavel down hard in his frustration, making everyone jump. 'I'll have you keep a civil tongue in your head, Plover. This is my court and I'll see things done properly. Any more of your impudence and you'll be sentenced to the lock-up for a week to learn to mind your manners when dealing with your betters. Now, I'll ask you for the last time. Whereabouts in the room was the body? Describe exactly what you saw.'

'If'n you'd said that in the first place . . .' Plover muttered. Seeing the look on Mr Brindley's face, he decided, wisely, to add no more in that vein. 'That body were lying face-down on a pile of ol' painted cloths, on the far side of the room from the door.'

'Thank you,' Brindley said. 'You may stand down.'

At last came the stage in the proceedings everyone had been waiting for. Mr Brindley called Mr Barnabas Leggett, physician and surgeon, to take the stand and give his evidence. Mr Leggett had carried out the medical examination on the body and would now report his findings.

Mr Leggett must have carried out this duty many times, for he seemed to know the procedure almost better than Mr Brindley did. As a result, his evidence was brisk and to the point. Mr Josiah Postgate, he said, died as a result of a single blow to the head, delivered with considerable force, probably from above and behind. His skull had been crushed and death would have been instantaneous. The skin, however, had not been broken.

'What is your opinion on the nature of the weapon, Mr Leggett?' the coroner asked. 'It appears odd the man's skull was so badly damaged without the skin being broken.'

'The dead man was not wearing a wig,' Mr Leggett replied. 'If he had been, that might have accounted for it. As it was, I can offer only one suggestion. I judge he was struck by something heavy wrapped in thick coverings; something like an iron bar with several layers of cloth wrapped around it. However, while this is a reasonable hypothesis, it does raise another question. The cloth would have absorbed part of the force of the blow. To do the damage it did, therefore, the blow must have been delivered with a surprising degree of force.'

'Are you suggesting it was done other than by human hand?' Mr Brindley was obviously thinking of the story of the ghost.

'No, I am not suggesting anything of the kind', Leggett replied angrily. 'What I am suggesting is the person who delivered this blow may have been unusually strong. If Mr Postgate had been standing up at the time, his assailant must also have been well above the average height, since the blow was delivered more or less from directly above. To say more would be to enter the realms of conjecture.'

This evidence was so similar to the evidence delivered at the inquest on Mr Chambers that the whole court was now buzzing with excitement. The coroner had to bang his gavel several times to restore order.

Mr Leggett had no more to add, so he was told he could stand down and Mr Brindley turned to address the jury.

'The purpose of this court is to confirm the identity of the deceased and enquire, so far as is possible, into the circumstances surrounding his death. That includes the cause of death, if it can be established. You, members of the jury, are charged with reaching a verdict on how this man died. In this case, both accident and suicide can be ruled out. It is plain it was an unlawful death. If you believe death was brought about without intention, you may return a verdict of manslaughter. I see nothing to support such a notion. If you think Mr Josiah Postgate was murdered, that should be your verdict. No evidence has been offered to suggest who the murderer might be, so it is not possible to bring in a verdict naming any particular person. I therefore suggest to you that you bring in a verdict of murder by person or persons unknown. Do you wish to retire to consider your verdict in private?'

The jurymen conferred amongst themselves for a few moments, then their foreman stood and returned the verdict the coroner had suggested. With that, the court was closed.

'No surprises there,' Foxe said to Nicholas.

'What about the cause of death? Wasn't that a surprise? This fellow Postgate has been killed in the same way as Chambers.'

'And by the same person, I would say. I would have found it more surprising had it been proved he died in a different manner; something that would've suggested a different person was responsible for this murder. For two actors to have died, murdered, within seven days of one another, in the same city and in the same theatre, without the two murders being connected, surely stretches credibility beyond breaking point. The only question still open in my mind is whether both were killed for the same reason. Somehow, I doubt it. Yet, since I cannot find a reason in either case, my doubts must remain unresolved.'

'When you put it that way—'

'There's no other way to put it. Find the reason and we'll be most of the way towards finding the killer. I thought, at one time, it was something to do with the death of the actress and her baby in the fire. Perhaps someone believed Chambers and Postgate were responsible and decided to take revenge — though why they should have waited twenty years is beyond my understanding. However, we know those two deaths were due to an unfortunate accident. Although I have established Postgate and Chambers were both there at the time, neither of them bear any responsibility.'

'You haven't mentioned Mr Edwards,' Nicholas said. 'Doesn't his affair make three attacks, even if only two of them resulted in death? He was present at the fire too.'

'The attack on Edwards clearly has nothing to do with the two murders,' Foxe said. 'That's been plain almost from the start. You're also forgetting, whoever set that up — and the answer there is easy as well — had no intention of killing Edwards, merely of driving him away from Norwich. Let us forget Mr Edwards for the moment. What we require is a person who hated Chambers and Postgate enough to murder them both, together with sufficient reason for him to do it. If Mr Leggett is correct, all we need to do next is search Norwich for an immensely strong giant. Easy enough, don't you think?'

By any reasonable estimation, the events of the inquest should have provided enough drama for one day. However, as the old saying goes, it never rains but it pours. When Foxe and Nicholas returned home, they found a message waiting from Alderman Halloran. Foxe read it out.

'Heard this morning Mordifort recently sold his brewery and maltings. The deal was concluded two days before he was killed and the purchase price paid over in full in bills drawn on Hackett and Sons Bank. The purchaser was asked to keep the sale secret until Mordifort could announce it himself and in his own time. That's typical of the man and his mania for secrecy.

'The deal came to light late yesterday afternoon when the executors sent word to the brewery to set up an audit and inventory for the purposes of probate. No one knows what has happened to the money.'

'What do you make of it?' Foxe asked Nicholas. 'Mordifort's brewery business alone would have been worth a good deal of money. With the maltings, the amount paid over by the purchaser must have been substantial. I wish the alderman had been more precise in explaining what he meant by saying no one knows where the money has gone.'

'You would have to pass those bills through a bank, wouldn't you? Unless you endorsed them to someone else and used them for a purchase at the same time.'

'A whisper reached me about Mordifort making a large purchase of property,' Foxe said. 'Maybe you're right and he used the bills — or some of them — to complete the purchase. But what property? Why the devil did the man have to be so keen on hiding his actions from everyone else?'

'Would he make such a large change in his circumstances without informing his son?'

'We don't know he didn't. On the other hand, his son showed no interest in any of his father's business ventures, so they say. Oh, to hell with the whole family! A more exasperating, peculiar, mad-brained, cross-grained bunch of people I cannot imagine!'

'It's a good job you aren't investigating their actions connected with the murder, isn't it?'

'It is indeed.'

෨෯

FOXE SPENT THE AFTERNOON IN HIS LIBRARY, TRYING TO MAKE SOME sense of all he had heard. On the matter of the murders at the White Swan, he had to admit defeat. He'd tried every way he could think of to fit events, past and present, into a pattern which would show him what he needed to do next and came up with nothing. Unless some new facts emerged, he could go no further. The only part of the mystery he was sure about was the attack on Edwards. Perhaps he should set it aside and focus instead on the murder of Mordifort.

It is often when he had given up on a problem and turned to something else that Foxe had his best ideas. During dinner, he had a sudden thought which promised a way forward. To Nicholas's great surprise, Foxe set down his cutlery, grinned like an ape and posed him a question.

'What is the most common element in the plot of a melodrama, Cousin Nicholas?'

'I do not know, Cousin. My father disapproves of the theatre on principal. The inquest the other day was the first time I have ever stepped inside such a place.'

'A sad gap in your education, if I may say so. Once this business is over, I shall take steps to fill it. I will tell you the answer then. It is mistaken identity. Mark it well. Add the unintended consequences of actions and you have the entire course of ninety-nine in every hundred of the melodramas which grace our stages.'

'If you say so.'

'I do say so and you should mark it well, especially if you ever consider a future in the criminal law. When those who commit crimes set out their plans, they often draw on things they have seen or heard. Not in their normal lives, you understand. Even the most hardened criminal doesn't spend more than a small proportion of his time carrying out his crimes. What they plan needs to be special, unexpected, mysterious and hard to detect. That way, they hope to avoid being caught. It's my experience many criminals are devotees of the theatre. Some go there to commit their crimes — pickpockets, cutpurses and the like — others for simple recreation. Either way, they are constantly exposed to melodramas. When they come to plan their crimes — and, still more, their alibis — they cannot help using elements from these melodramas. Tragedies end badly, which is not what they want for their criminal endeavours. Farces are one constant failure from beginning to end, as we watch all involved make fools of themselves. That leaves melodrama; full of danger, excitement and suspense, but almost always with a happy ending. The ideal pattern to copy.'

Nicholas began to wonder how much strong drink his cousin had taken before dinner began. Foxe's next remark convinced him it must have been a good deal.

'I think it's time I bought myself a carriage; say one with two horses to pull it. If I am to spend more time travelling outside the city — as I did in this case — it would be more convenient and save Alfred the trouble of hiring transportation every time. I'll also need a groom, of course. Someone to look after everything and do the driving — though I could learn how to do some of it myself, given time. Charlie lives in part of the stables behind this house, but there should be sufficient space for a groom to have a bedroom separate from his. The carriage house and stable is completely empty.'

'A carriage,' Nicholas said.

'Perhaps something like a gig or a curricle. Not a phaeton. Our roads aren't really suitable. Definitely something which doesn't need more than a pair of horses though. No room in the old stables for more. Too pretentious too. I tell you what, I'll consult the Earl of Pentelow next time I see him. He must have several carriages and is bound to have some idea what might suit me best. What do you think?'

Poor Nicholas was too bewildered by this time to think of a reply.

24

Foxe planned to speak with Alderman Halloran the next day, but once again his plans were overtaken by events. Mistress Tabby, the Cunning Woman, sent one of the street children with a message, asking Foxe to call on her as soon as it might be possible, since there was someone it was vital he should meet. Foxe was reluctant to go. It was many years since he and Mistress Tabby had met in person. There was too much history between them; too much pain and resentment, at least on Foxe's side of things; too many memories of the dark time when his father's sudden death left him alone and rudderless in the world.

Still, her message sounded urgent and he was sure she wouldn't have asked for a meeting if it wasn't about something of real significance. There was also the fact that she lived on the same side of the River Wensum as the alderman, though not in such luxurious surroundings, and he could combine answering her summons with his intended visit to the alderman's house in Colegate. To still refuse to go in such circumstances would be childish.

He found her in her garden, which was what he expected on any day free from rain, snow or the most bitter winds. Bart was nearby, digging over some ground in preparation for planting, while Mistress Tabby was gathering herbs for drying.

'Good morning,' Foxe began. 'I trust I find you well.'

'Indeed, you do, Ashmole,' she replied, straightening from her task. 'I was afraid you might not come. It's been a long time, hasn't it? I wouldn't have put you to this trouble, but this isn't something that can be done any other way. I can see from your face that you haven't forgiven me yet. I wish you would. I did love your father, you know. I simply couldn't bear to see you on the road to wrecking the business he'd spent his life creating.'

'You gave me no credit for sense, Tabby. It's true I neglected the shop, but I was never much of a bookseller. I tripled the value of his other investments in as many years.'

'How could I know that? All I saw was the son of the man I loved strutting about the city like a London dandy and spending money on all sides. I had to try to bring you to your senses.'

'You hurt me badly. If it comes to apportioning blame, I hated to see you getting mixed up in what seemed — and still feels to me — mere superstition and nonsense for the gullible. You're a fine herbalist, Tabby. You don't need the charms and spells or whatever.'

'Many of my patients do, Ashmole. What you call superstition is what persuades them to follow my instructions to the letter.'

'And second sight! You can't believe in that, surely?'

'Do not grave physicians need to maintain the notion they have special powers?' She paused, her expression downcast. 'Can't we be friends again?' she said softly. 'It's all in the past now and I know your father would be proud of you and what you've done.'

Foxe hesitated, then gave in. 'You do a great deal of good in this city,' he said, 'especially amongst the poor. And you were right. I did make something of a fool of myself in my expensive clothes and eagerness to flout convention. I suppose I was angry at losing my father and quite unsure what to do with my life. I haven't changed that much, you know, though nowadays I try to appear less outrageous.'

'I'm glad to hear it,' Tabby said. 'What would the ladies of Norwich do without you to excite and shock them? May we be friends again, please, Ashmole dear?'

'Yes. Let us be friends, Tabby. Here's my hand on it.'

They shook hands solemnly.

'If I told you I expected you would need to pick my brains at some point, would you ascribe that knowledge to my magical powers? I hope not. It wouldn't be true. I know you're investigating the murders at the White Swan and I would either have to entice you here or send you a long letter about it. Still, it's the murder of Mr Mordifort that concerns me at present and which demands quick action on your part. Will you come inside and take some coffee — arriving at this time must mean you haven't been to the coffeehouse as usual — or do you fear I will serve you a potion to turn you into a frog?'

'Now you're laughing at me, Tabby,' Foxe said. 'A moment ago, you accused me of dressing myself in frippery to disguise what lies within. I see now you're doing the same thing with your spells and talismans rather than lace and silver thread.'

Mistress Tabby called out to Bart to continue what he was doing, then clean out the fowls' run and collect any eggs, and Foxe followed her into the house.

'Let me get the White Swan business out of the way first,' she said, after the coffee was made and poured out. 'You need to seek out Slippery Joe. His knowledge of everything to do with the theatre in Norwich stretches back thirty and more years. Joe was doorman at several theatres in the city until his legs began to fail him. Now he lives with one of his daughters in a small cottage just beyond St Martin's Gate. It's a good distance to go on foot, but not too far in a carriage. I've written down exact directions on this paper. Slippery Joe is sure to be at home. He can't walk more than a few paces these days.'

Foxe thanked her and was about to ask her to tell him more about this former doorman with the strange name when she hurried on.

'You will probably not believe what I am going to tell you now,' she told him, 'but I'll do it anyway. Something keeps telling me that we aren't yet done with death. Two people may have died, but I fear that a third is to follow them. It's a death I don't think you can prevent, Ashmole dear, whatever you do. Hopefully you can put an end to the killing at that point. It all depends on you. Please go and see Slippery Joe soon. I'll send word that you're coming.'

She got up, collected the coffee things together and set them to one side to be washed.

'Now to the vital matter which made me call you to see me. I've been attending a young woman who lives very near here. She's enceinte with her first child, has no mother to advise her, and is anxious about the birth that is now very close. Her name is — or rather was — Henrietta Stoke and she's been Edward Mordifort's mistress for almost two years. You must go to see her right away and hear what she has to tell you. Be gentle, my dear. The poor woman is terrified as well as prostrate with grief. Mr Mordifort married her in secret barely a week before he was murdered. Now she doesn't know what to do. I said you would be able to advise her. If you come to the gate in my garden, I'll point out the house to you.'

Foxe's brain was already plunging ahead. 'I'll go this instant,' he said. 'Will you do something for me while I'm inside talking to this lady? Send Bart in haste to find a good number of the street children and tell them to wait for me to come out. I'm going to need their help. Now which house is it?'

An unremarkable house it was, though built of fine brick and obviously in good order. Foxe knocked and was greeted by a neatly dressed maidservant, who showed Foxe to the parlour, where she told him her mistress was waiting for him. On the way, Foxe looked around him. There was nothing grand or imposing about the interior or furnishings, yet all spoke of a quiet good taste, backed up by careful tending and household management. Whatever else this lady was, she knew how to keep a comfortable and gracious home.

Miss Henrietta Stoke — or rather, Mrs Henrietta Mordifort now — proved to be a handsome woman of perhaps two or three and twenty years, her hair dark and her complexion good. What her figure was like it was impossible to say, since her belly was swollen to such a proportion Foxe wondered if she might not be bearing twins. He refused refreshment with the excuse that he had come from drinking Mistress Tabby's coffee and seated himself where the lady of the house indicated.

Even if Tabby hadn't warned him, Foxe would have been aware at once of the need to offer comfort as well as advice. Mrs Mordifort —

for so he must think of her — was plainly in dire need of reassurance. Her skin showed a sickly pallor and she could not keep her hands still a moment, for all her efforts to confine them to her lap. He also guessed she didn't know where to begin her tale, for she had hardly spoken other than to proffer the conventional greeting to a visiting stranger.

'Mistress Tabby has told me something of your situation, Mrs Mordifort,' Foxe began. He saw the use of her new name had already gone some way to convincing her he was a friend. 'Let me begin by offering you my deepest sympathy on your loss. I will not presume to offer the conventional platitudes people use on such occasions. Mistress Tabby says you wish to seek my advice on your best course of action from this time forwards. Please believe me when I say I will offer you every help I can.'

Her story wasn't complicated. She'd been brought up in the modestly prosperous household of a mercer, an only child who was given the best education her parents could afford. Sadly, both her parents died in quick succession when she was still but twelve years old and she was sent to live with an uncle, who owned a tailor's and haberdasher's business. He had six children of his own, so there was no more money to keep her at school. Instead, she began to help in his shop. That was her life and would have remained so had Mr Mordifort not come in to buy some trifle about two years before. She had served him, he was attentive to her and before long he found various reasons to keep returning. She'd abandoned hope of a suitable marriage, since she had no dowry, so when he offered to make her his mistress and set her up in the house they were now within, she accepted with little hesitation. For the most part it had turned out well. He had treated her kindly, requiring little more than a comfortable place in which to relax, with regular, but undemanding, excursions to her bedroom. It had been a great surprise when, on telling him she was expecting his child, he had at once asked her to marry him.

The ceremony had taken place in a church in Great Yarmouth in conditions of some secrecy, why he had not explained. Only the two of them and the necessary witnesses had been present, aside from the parson. That had been eight days before he was murdered.

'He gave me a sealed paper packet to keep safe,' she told Foxe. 'It is on the table behind you. With it went a note of the name and address of a lawyer in Yarmouth. That is there as well. I was not to open the packet, just keep it safely hidden. Only if something happened to him was I to take it personally and at once to the lawyer. He would know what to do with it. It grieves me that I haven't been able to do as my dear Edward asked, but you will understand that to travel in my present condition is impossible. Indeed, Mistress Tabby has forbidden it.'

'She is wise to do so, I'm sure,' Foxe said. 'Do you wish me to take it on your behalf?'

'Mistress Tabby says you are an honest man, Mr Foxe, and I trust her judgement implicitly in such matters. Do you believe that is the right thing to do?'

Foxe took a few moments to think. 'It really depends what is in the packet,' he says. 'I know your husband asked you not to open it, but he could not have anticipated what was going to happen to him. With your permission, I would like to take the packet to the house of a good friend of mine, Alderman Halloran. It's close by and I have arranged to see him there today on another matter. With him as witness, I will open it, consider what's best to do in the light of the contents and return to tell you what I propose. Will that be acceptable?'

'I think so. I can understand it's impossible for you to know what the right course of action may be without seeing what is inside. Very well, Mr Foxe. I will trust you and the alderman to advise me. Several days have elapsed since my husband . . . met his end. To journey to Great Yarmouth must take at least another full day. Better to know right away whether the need for haste is now passed.'

When Foxe emerged from the house, the paper packet buttoned safely into his pocket, he found no fewer than eight of the street children waiting for him. They gathered around him at once to know what they must do.

'Keep a close eye on the house I have just left,' he told them. 'Let no one in or out until I return. It's essential you do this, so don't hesitate to use whatever means you can, to keep the lady inside safe. I shall not be gone long, but I dare not leave her without protection.'

Though some of them probably didn't understand all his words,

Foxe's manner was sufficient to let all know what was expected of them. As he hurried away, he looked back and saw them standing in a huddle, agreeing their plans, then scattering into smaller groups. Three of the younger ones squatted in the road playing some game with small stones, while the older boys lounged against a wall opposite Mrs Mordifort's house. The two older girls began walking up and down as if they were plying for trade. Foxe smiled to himself. Nothing would get past them. His belief was strengthened into certainty when he noticed Bart walking towards them.

⁂

ALL THE WAY TO ALDERMAN HALLORAN'S HOUSE, FOXE FELT MORE and more uneasy about leaving Mrs Mordifort in that house alone. Even the street children couldn't keep watch over her all day and all night. He assumed Tabby was acting as her midwife as well as confidante, so he decided he must persuade the young woman to move into Tabby's home, at least until her child was born; if Tabby would have her, that was.

When Foxe was ushered in to see Alderman Halloran, he found him standing in his library with his back to the fireplace, adopting a pose that became second nature to him during the winter. On that day, with no fire burning in the grate, it looked as if he wasn't sure what to do with himself and had gone to the hearth in the hope that he might find inspiration there.

'What have you been up to, Foxe?' Halloran said at once. 'I expected you before this. Will you take some refreshment?' While he was still speaking, his butler brought in a tray with a choice of ale or cider.

'Best Herefordshire cider,' the alderman said. 'None of the feeble stuff they produce around here.'

They both chose cider and Foxe expressed his appreciation of the fine quality on offer. Then, at last, they got down to business.

'I'm afraid something has happened that must take precedence over what we proposed for this afternoon, Halloran. I'll bring you up-to-date on all I've discovered at another time. What matters now is speed.'

With that, he brought the paper packet from his pocket and explained what it was and how he had come by it as succinctly as he could. As he did so, the alderman's expression changed from amazement to concern to anger.

'Let's open that packet at once and waste no more time,' he said. 'I quite agree that the young woman is in danger and we've had enough killings. As soon as we know what it contains, you'd better hurry back to her and get her away.'

Foxe broke the seal, opened the packet and took out the two sheets of paper inside. 'My God!' he said. 'It's Mordifort's Will!'

'His Will? You mean a new one?'

'Dated three weeks ago. He was planning all this, Halloran, probably ever since he asked that young woman to marry him, if not before. Let me see . . . mmm . . . yes, that's the motive that makes sense of his murder.'

'What is it?'

'Money, of course. Money! By this Will, Peter Mordifort gets just two thousand pounds and the injunction to find some employment instead of sponging from others. The daughter gets an annuity of two hundred and fifty a year. All the rest goes to his new wife and her child. If the child is a boy, she gets a third outright and must hold the rest in trust for him until he reaches his majority. If it's a girl, she has the same amount and another third is to be held as the girl's dowry. The remaining third is to be split between various charities. See for yourself.'

The alderman waved the paper away. 'I believe you, Foxe. I believe you. Do you think this is the original Will?'

'It looks that way. I expect the lawyer named on this other sheet of paper, the one in Yarmouth, has a copy, but these look like original signatures.'

'Who are named as executors?'

'Mr James Hanock, Sir Theodore Gimblet, and Mr Hezekiah Ransford.'

'All sound men and honest ones. Here's what I suggest we do. You

hurry back to get Mrs Mordifort to safety and I'll take this Will immediately to the mayor. Once he's seen it and can vouch for its contents,
no one will be able to contest it or claim it's been forged. Then, with
the mayor alongside me, if he'll come, I'll take it to whichever of these
executors I can find first. Once it's in their hands, they can get in
touch with the Yarmouth lawyer. What do you think?'

'I think it's an excellent plan, especially involving the mayor. Since
you and he are both Justices of the Peace, your evidence would be
unimpeachable. Right, I'll be off!'

Foxe returned to Mrs Mordifort's home to find the street children
in a state of high excitement. Almost as soon as Foxe had gone, a man
had come up the street, counting the houses, then tried to peer in
through the windows of the one Foxe had told them to keep an eye on.

'Bart wanted to bash 'im right away,' said their spokesman, a young
tough Foxe knew to be a cutpurse. 'We tells 'im to wait a bit, 'cos we've
got a better idea, right? While this cove's peekin' through the winders,
Sid and I does our normal act. I snips the cove's purse, making sure 'e
feels me, like, and Sid runs off as fast as 'e knows 'ow. 'Course, the
stupid git runs yelling' after Sid, leaving me wiv 'is purse. Do I 'ave to
give it back?'

Foxe smiled. 'Not this time, Jack. I never heard you say you'd got it,
did I?'

The boy's grin could have lit up a whole street after dark. 'I'd better
let Mabel tell you what happened a'ter,' he said. 'She an' Alice done
the rest.'

What they'd done was position themselves a little way down the
street, where Sid could make sure to run close past them. By this time,
the lad was enjoying himself, slowing up just enough to make sure the
man made a final effort to catch him. As he did so, Alice stuck out her
foot and Mabel gave the man 'a smartish kick up 'is arse', as she
described it. He sprawled full-length in all the mud and filth of the
street, still going so fast he slid maybe six or eight feet along on
his face.

'Gor!' Mabel laughed 'That were a rare sight, that were! All 'is front
was drippin' wiv mud an' shit. 'E'd got it in 'is mouth too! Didn't 'ang

around after that, I can tell you. Limped away the way 'e come. We wuz laughin' so much we near shit ourselves an' all!'

'Did anyone know him?' Foxe asked. 'What did he look like?'

'Natty dresser,' one said. 'Looked like a bookie.'

'Tall? Short?'

'We can do better'n that, Mr Foxe,' Mabel said. 'When 'e got 'isself up, 'e left this bit o' paper lyin' on the ground. Must've fallen out of 'is pocket. There's writin' on it.'

Foxe looked at the piece of paper she gave him. It was, in fact, a letter; an extremely explicit love letter to 'Alfie' from someone calling herself — or conceivably himself — 'Cuddles'. It was addressed on the back to Mr Alfred Henson.

What was Henson up to? Extortion? Trying to take Mordifort's place and get his hands on any money coming to Henrietta? Neither was likely. Though he'd found Mordifort's secret mistress, he couldn't know about the new Will. The more Foxe thought about it, the more he thought Henson must have been spying on the couple well before the murder took place, looking for some way to turn his discovery into cash. The man was always short of money. The real question was whether he'd told his wife what he had discovered. Probably not. Those two hated one another. Henson would want to keep any profit for himself.

It didn't take Foxe long to explain to Mrs Mordifort what he and Alderman Halloran proposed to do, nor for her to agree without reservation.

'What about his children?' she said. 'Won't they be terribly upset? I know he didn't like either of them, but to cut them almost entirely out of his Will seems dreadfully harsh.'

'I wouldn't spare any tears for them, Mrs Mordifort. I'm going to ask you most earnestly to come with me to Mistress Tabby's. We'll ask her to take you in, at least until your baby is born and I can bring this matter to a conclusion. You mustn't stay here. It isn't safe.'

'Do you really think my husband's children will seek to do me harm, Mr Foxe?'

'I do. I left some . . . friends to watch over you while I was away.

They tell me a man came and started trying to see in through the front windows of this house. They scared him off, but I'm sure he'll be back.'

'Won't I bring danger on Mistress Tabby?'

'With Bart to look after the two of you? Hardly. It would take several strong men to get past him.'

As Foxe expected, Mistress Tabby accepted Henrietta Mordifort into her household at once and without any protest, especially after Foxe told her about Henson and the way the street children had driven him off.

'Bart will make sure we're safe, Ashmole,' she said. 'You can trust him with that. Does all this mean what I think it does?'

'The only question in my mind is which one of them did it,' Foxe said. 'Maybe it was both of them. I just wish I knew how they found out what their father was planning. That's the only weak link in the case against them. Now I must go back to Colegate and see what Alderman Halloran has been doing. Maybe he'll have an idea how to find the answer to my question.'

Alderman Halloran did. 'Why not start by going to Mordifort's house and questioning the servants?' he said. 'The mayor asked you to look into this murder and he only just told me to say that still stands. We know now Peter Mordifort isn't the heir, so he can't keep you away, as he could before. Without his father's money and businesses, he'll have no influence in the city either, so the mayor doesn't give a jot about his wishes anyway. To bring you up-to-date, the mayor and I found two of the executors of that Will right away. Both of them live close by here, you see. I left the mayor with the second one, waiting for the first to join them after he'd collected the third. I came back here because I guessed you'd come to tell me whether Mrs Mordifort was safely hidden away.'

'She's safe enough,' Foxe said. 'Your idea is a good one. Do you know where Mordifort's house is?'

'Some way off, I'm afraid. Better leave it to the morning. Come here again first thing and I'll take you in my carriage.'

✤ 25 ✤

'I'm almost the last one here, gentlemen,' the man who answered the door to them said. 'My job is to supervise the removal of all the furnishings and fittings for sale. There are also two maidservants to keep the place clean and tidy so prospective buyers can look it over. All the others were dismissed with a week's notice. Some of them had served the Mordifort family for years! It wasn't right, was it?'

'Your new master is selling everything?' Foxe said.

'Down to the linens, sir. He came here the day before yesterday, told the others to get out and told me everything has to be sold.'

'And you were . . . are . . .?'

'Amos Hampnet, sir. Butler here for nigh on fifteen years and a footman before then.'

'My name is Foxe. I need some information and I'm sure you can help me. This is Alderman Halloran. The mayor has asked us to look into the death of your former master, Edward Mordifort.'

'Someone needs to, if you'll pardon me saying so, sir. The old master wasn't an easy man to work for, but he was fair, I'll give him that. Didn't deserve to die the way he did.'

'Your new master, Mr Peter. Did he get on well with his father?'

'Not him! They were always at one another's throats.' Any remaining loyalty the butler had to the family had clearly been destroyed by the treatment the servants had been given and he was eager to say his piece. 'Why, only a day or so before the master's murder I heard them going at it, hammer and tongs.'

'Do you know what the row was about?'

'Money, I imagine. The master made his son an allowance, but it was never enough for him. He wouldn't work though. Not even in the family firm. Claimed his "antiquarian interests" — whatever they were — had to take precedence. His sister was almost as bad, though in her case it's her useless fool of a husband who wastes all their money. I think the master had reached breaking point.'

'What makes you say so?'

'I heard him shout he was going to cut both of them out of his Will and leave all his money to charity. "Then you'll have to earn your living or starve!" he said. He had no time for people sitting around with books or drooling over old bits of pots dug up from the ground.'

'What about his daughter?'

'I've heard him tell her he didn't care whether she was desperate to marry that wastrel Henson or just find someone willing to roger her. She chose him and she'd have to put up with him. He was tired of keeping her. That was her husband's job, not his.'

'Not a harmonious family,' Foxe said. 'I assume Peter Mordifort didn't still live here.'

'Got his own house over the water. Magdalen Street, I believe.'

Foxe turned to the alderman, who had been silent since they arrived, his expression becoming ever darker as the butler proceeded. 'That's our destination, Halloran. As quick as we can, I think. I have a nasty feeling our murderer guesses we're onto him and is going to try to remove anyone who might provide us with conclusive evidence.'

As they left, Foxe handed the former butler half a guinea and told him to do nothing about selling the house contents until he heard positively from his master's executors. Next, he and Halloran hurried out to the alderman's carriage and headed for Magdalen Street as fast as they could. Along under the walls of the old castle they clattered, down into Tombland, past the cathedral and over Fye Bridge. There they pulled up while the coachman enquired where Peter Mordifort lived.

The house they were directed to sat in the mouth of a small court off the street. Quite a modest affair, it appeared. Peter Mordifort's allowance obviously didn't stretch to anything better than what must once have been the home of a family of weavers. The long windows in the upper story showed where the looms had been set up to catch as much light as possible. As their carriage pulled up they found another ahead of them; a small gig with a single horse.

'Henson's gig,' the alderman said. 'I've seen it several times before.'

He expected Foxe to knock on the door at once, but his companion had other ideas. He stepped down from the carriage, put his fingers to his mouth and produced a series of long, piercing whistles.

'It's a poor wager,' he said to Halloran. 'Still, it's better than nothing. The street children don't often go over the water. Still, you never know. Let's wait just a moment in case someone has heard me.'

'Street children?' Halloran was bemused.

'We're going to need help. My hope is to send one to fetch at least one constable — two would be better. Ah! My luck's good today. Here's Harry . . . and Gaiters too! Excellent.'

Two filthy, disreputable boys of about twelve ran up to Foxe, panting hard. In a moment, he'd given them their instructions and backed his words up with a few coppers for each. Like magic, the boys disappeared in to the crowd.

'Now we'll go in, Halloran, but take care. These are desperate people, believe me.'

Foxe went up to the door and beat on it with both fists, producing a thunderous booming. When there was no immediate response, he picked up a large cobble from the street and beat on it again. This time, the door opened and a housemaid peeped timidly out. Foxe at once flung the door open and dashed past her, with an astonished alderman bringing up the rear. Dorothy Henson was standing in the hallway with her back to a door opposite.

'What is the meaning of this outrage!' she screeched. 'Banging on the door and forcing your way in. I'll have the law—'

The rest of her words, whatever they were going to be, were cut off by the unmistakable sound of a gunshot from the room behind her. Foxe bounded across the hall, thrust the protesting woman out of his way and tore open the door, shouting to Halloran to grab hold of Mrs Henson and stop her running off.

The sight which greeted them proved they were too late. Peter Mordifort was standing in the middle of the room, a small pistol still in his hand. At his feet lay the body of Alfred Henson. There was a neat hole in his right temple and the room reeked of the smell of black powder.

'Bring the woman in here!' Foxe barked. 'Let her see what her brother has done for her.'

'For her?' Peter Mordifort said. 'Oh no. Not for her. For myself. This snivelling creature tried to blackmail me—twice. I knew if I didn't put an end to him, I'd never be free. Now you've spoiled my splendid method of avoiding the blame, Foxe, interfering bastard that you are! Ah, and that old fool Halloran as well. It's all over for me then. Such a nice plan too. The wastrel brother-in-law making one last plea for help, before staging what he planned to be an empty threat of suicide. He used this pistol, which I had carefully left visible on my desk. How sad that it was loaded. What a tragedy! Put it to his head, pulled the trigger, expected no more than a snap, and sends himself into eternity instead. Rather elegant, don't you think?'

He walked back to his desk and laid the pistol down.

'He'd found your father's mistress,' Foxe said.

'Yes, and thought I'd pay him to keep quiet. What a fool! I didn't care about some trollop my father had been bedding. Her kind can be bought off; and, if not, there's always another way, isn't there? No matter now. I told him to forget about any more money, now or in the future.' He turned away from Foxe towards his sister, still held tightly by an embarrassed Halloran. 'You'll never guess what he said to me, dear sister. He told me he'd seen you stab your father. Watched from the doorway. He thought I'd pay him to save you from the noose.'

'Be silent!' Dorothy screamed. 'Can't you see what you're doing?'

'I'm taking you with me, my dear. You don't think I'd go to the gallows bearing the blame for what you did, do you? Noble brother saves sister from ignominy and death? Oh no, I'll make sure you hang too. We were in this together, remember?'

Dorothy let out a wail and thrashed wildly, almost escaping Halloran's grip. Whether she wanted to run or scratch her brother's eyes out wasn't clear.

Peter Mordifort turned back to Foxe. He clearly saw him as the principal witness to his confession. 'I laughed in his face at first. Why should I care if my elder sister took all the blame? She's bullied and pestered me long enough. Having all the money and being free from her constant complaints seemed like paradise. Of course, it didn't take me many moments to work out that if she was tried for murder, I would be bound to be implicated. I was the heir, not her. Anything she was left in my father's Will would be her husband's. We'd planned to get rid of Henson anyway in due course. My sister hated him, of course. Why she married him beats me.'

'He's lying!' Dorothy yelled. 'I'm innocent. I couldn't have killed my father. I wasn't there in the room.'

'But you were,' Foxe said to her. 'We have a witness who saw you. You told her you were going to tell your father you were leaving.'

'Mrs Delaware!'

'Exactly. You had your cloak on at the time too; ideal for concealing the knife you had in your left hand. Of course, you were born left-handed, weren't you? I imagine, since you would have been compelled to use your right hand as you grew up, either hand is just as useful to you now.'

'Oh yes,' Peter interrupted. 'Quite ambidextrous, I assure you. Her left arm and hand are as strong as her right ones. Maybe stronger.'

Foxe ignored him. 'You guessed your father would have stayed behind in the room to allow his guests to go into dinner first, so you stepped up behind him, staying just a little to his right, and thrust the dagger into his back with your left hand as hard as you could, making sure your cloak hid your action from anyone who might notice. Afterwards you slipped out in the confusion, ready to make your dramatic re-entry as the grieving daughter. You even made sure to kneel down in your father's blood, didn't you? That would account for any splashes which might have reached you when you stabbed him.'

'Neat, wasn't it?' Peter said. 'I'd gone, so I couldn't be blamed. All part of the plan, you know. Besides, who suspects a woman of murder by stabbing? Poisoning, yes, but not stabbing. Most don't have the strength — or a sufficiently vicious nature. Dorothy's a big, strong girl though, and, as I said, her left arm is probably stronger than the right one. She was to kill our father; I would kill her husband later — just as I did. Afterwards we would split the money and he wouldn't be able to claim any of her share.'

'There wouldn't have been any money,' Foxe said. 'Your father made another Will in secret. We found it and it's now with his executors. You and your sister are left with only small bequests. You see, you were wrong to ignore the mistress. She is quite a sensible and well brought up lady, who also happens to be about to bear your father's child. He was hoping for a son, of course — and a better one than last time — so he married her, also in secret — only days before you two murdered him. Most of his wealth goes to her and his unborn child; the rest to various charities.'

For a moment, Peter Mordifort seemed stunned by the news, then he threw back his head and broke into raucous laughter.

'So, it was all for nothing in the end!' he said when he regained his breath. 'Almost poetic, isn't it?'

At that moment, the door of the room in which they were standing opened wider and one of the constables poked his head inside.

'Ah! You are 'ere, alderman,' he said. 'Some liddle guttersnipe said you was. Mr Foxe too, I sees. What was it you wanted, sir?'

'Take this woman from me, Constable,' Halloran said with evident relief. 'Watch out for her. She's a vicious beast. Are you on your own?'

'No, your worship. I got Constable Knipe with me. Out there in the 'all.'

'Call him in and let him take Mr Mordifort here. You're to see they're both safely put in the lock-up — separate cells, mind! I'll arrange with the mayor to hold a hearing as soon as possible, so they can be remanded to the castle gaol to be tried at the next assizes. Keep them close! They've murdered two people between them. I'll tell my coachman to take you in the carriage. I can walk to my house from here.'

As the brother and sister were led away, Halloran turned to Foxe in disbelief. 'I would never have believed those two capable of such wickedness, Foxe. Patricide! They'll both hang for such a foul crime, that I'm sure. Without your brains, they'd probably have got away with it. What put you onto them?'

'It started with the handwriting on Dorothy Henson's letter's. You said yourself you'd seen a similar style of hand from someone who was left-handed, and it had to be a left-handed person who stabbed Edward Mordifort. They also made a bad mistake in losing their nerve sufficiently to try to prevent any investigation of their father's death. Innocent children would have been only too happy for any help in finding their father's murderer. The final proof came in their father's new Will. You don't cut your existing children off with paltry bequests, even if you do intend to marry again, unless relations have reached the very lowest level. It was clear from the start we'd never find the murderer, if it proved to be one of the other guests. Too many of them and nothing to point towards any one. The other alternative was one of his three close family: Peter, Dorothy, and her husband. The only question was which one of them.'

'You've done splendidly as usual,' Halloran said when Foxe had finished. 'I don't know how you managed to nose all this out. The mayor will be delighted. He's faced a good deal of criticism from his enemies and political opponents for being inactive. Not that they could have done any better, mind you. Now he'll be able to deal with them with much greater confidence. What are you going to do now? Take a rest?'

'There's still the business at the White Swan to be cleared up,' Foxe said. 'Tomorrow I'm going to visit an old man who lives with his daughter beyond St Martin's Gate; down the Coslany Road, a little way outside the walls. I'm hoping he'll be able to tell me something to make sense of why Chambers and Postgate have been murdered.'

'And Edwards attacked.'

'No, I understand all about that. It's related, of course, but still a sideshow. It's the two murders I'm interested in now. Once I know why, I'm pretty sure I'll know who. The murderer's still out there and I don't want to put him on his guard. It's when he makes mistakes we'll have the best chance to catch him. He's already made one bad mistake. Unfortunately, it's not been sufficient to give him away.'

'What mistake was it?'

'Killing Postgate now. We've been able to rule Edwards out as a murderer, though the real murderer doesn't know that. The other obvious candidate as the killer of Chambers was Postgate. With him dead and in the same way as Chambers, it's obvious another person is to blame. We can also be sure it's someone connected with the theatre; someone with easy access behind-the-scenes, who can move about unnoticed and who lured his victims into the storeroom. There can't be many people who fit all those requirements.'

'Do you think you're close?'

'Not as close as I'd like to be, but a good deal closer than I was. The man I'm going to visit tomorrow was once doorman at several of the city's theatres, including the White Swan. That's why I'm hoping he'll be able to tell me something to give me a clue to the real reason behind the two murders.'

'And you think you know all about the attack on Edwards? It's got to fit into the pattern as well, hasn't it?'

'I have the answer there already. The only thing I'm missing is what caused the attack on Edwards to take place now. Please don't press me any further on the point. Until I have the missing piece, I might still be proved wrong. I'm vain enough not to want to run the risk of having to eat my words later. If my reasoning is correct, the attack on Edwards is a completely separate matter from the two murders, as I said before.'

'Astonishing!' the alderman murmured. He sat for a moment trying to puzzle it all out himself, before giving up and returning to Foxe's narrative. 'So far as I can see, such evidence as there is backs up what you've told me — concerning the two murders anyway. I'll have to be content with that. You've told me what you're going to do tomorrow — to see this old doorman. What comes afterwards?'

'It depends very much on what he tells me. The problem is this. I can see a good many of the gaps in my knowledge. What I can't see are all the things I don't know, because I don't know that I don't know them.'

'What? Don't follow you, Foxe.'

'It's one thing to be aware there is something you'd like to know but haven't yet discovered. It's quite another to be ignorant that you need to know it anyway. What I'm trying to say is I can see the gaps which need to be filled in my present picture of events. The trouble is I suspect my picture is defective; I'm seeing only part of the true picture. Exactly how much of the rest of the picture is missing, I don't know. I don't even know if it is truly missing. All I understand is, when I'm able to fill in all the gaps I'm aware of, the completed version of events still won't be adequate.

'For example, there's the business of the fire twenty years ago. I keep being brought back to it. Yet, try as I may, I can't see how — or if — it's relevant to recent events. The deaths at the time were accidental, a consequence of the fire. Besides, two decades have passed, and most people have forgotten about it. Why should it suddenly be the cause of two murders so long afterwards? Especially when it turns out Chambers was not meant to be in Norwich at all, until Mr Jagger hurt himself — which was an accident too.'

'Please don't go any further, Foxe. My head is aching as it is. Give me a good, plain highway robbery any day. You know where you stand with that. This business sounds more like a melodrama than reality.'

The effect those words had on Foxe was scarcely believable. He gave a start of such severity you would think someone had poked a pin into him, then stared into the far distance for a full two minutes, before slapping himself hard on the thigh and crying out, 'Of course! A melodrama. Why didn't I think of that? It's taken place in the theatre, after all.'

He shook the alderman warmly by the hand.

'Thank you! Thank you! You've just given me an enormous clue. Now, if you'll forgive me, I must take my leave right away. I have a great deal to do. You're not planning to be away from the city at all, are you?'

A perplexed Alderman Halloran said he was not.

'Splendid! Please tell the mayor this. If things go well, I will be asking the City Swordbearer and some of the sergeants to get themselves ready to make another arrest on his behalf. Maybe within days.' And with those words, Foxe was gone.

❧ 26 ❧

When he got home, Foxe said little to anyone about the solving of Mordifort's murder. They'd hear about it soon enough; his mind was already running ahead to the problem of the White Swan killings. Time enough when it was done with to add in the details his household would doubtless demand. For the moment, he needed to put all that from his mind and concentrate on finding the last few pieces to complete the pattern and explain the other murders.

It was plain throughout dinner Foxe was brooding over some matter. Nicholas was becoming used to his cousin's tendency to withdraw into himself when he had something complex to think over. He therefore stayed quiet, waiting until Foxe chose to speak. It proved to be a long wait. Eventually, Foxe sighed and shook his head, though whether from puzzlement or frustration was not at once clear.

'I have been telling myself that much of my confusion over the business at the White Swan arose from denying myself the chance to question those who work at the theatre,' he said. 'I was wrong. I'm sure few of those there today could have added anything useful. The only person who could have made things clearer is dead anyway.'

'Who's that?' Nicholas asked.

'Postgate. I don't believe he intended events to turn out as they did, but he clearly had a hand in them. Of course, he'd never have told me anything, even if I'd asked him. Now, thanks to Mistress Tabby, I have another opportunity to discover at least some of the elements of this wretched business which elude me at present. It's too far to walk, of course. Alfred will have to get me a carriage.'

Foxe's remarks weren't usually so cryptic, nor his manner so distracted. It was becoming clear to Nicholas his cousin was talking to himself as much as to him. At last, after another lengthy pause, the young man ventured to pose one tentative query.

'Are you going outside the city again?'

'Tomorrow. I'm going to visit an old man who lives with his daughter about half a mile beyond St Martin's Gate. I'm told if you drive down the Coslany Road you can't miss the place.'

That was it. No explanation of who this person was or why Foxe was going there. Nothing.

His young cousin's disappointment must have impinged on Foxe's consciousness, for he tried to make some amends.

'I cannot ask you to come with me, Nicholas,' he said. 'I suspect the presence of another unfamiliar face will impede conversation. It's imperative this fellow tells me all he knows, so I can't risk it. Don't be downcast. If I'm successful, Mr Plumtree will be kept busy enough and I'm sure he'll let you observe. If you have no better employment tomorrow, ask Charlie to show you something more of the city.'

Then, after another pause, Foxe added an instruction which made Nicholas more confused than ever.

'Better still, there is something important you can do for me after all. See if you can find advertisements or playbills for the productions at the White Swan over the past three or four months, say. Look for anything — tragedy, farce, melodrama, anything at all — some programme which included a ghost in the plot. If you don't find it, try a little further back. I'm almost sure it's there somewhere.'

'A ghost?'

'Exactly! It's just a theory, of course.'

Nicholas, being now completely in the dark and so torn between pride and embarrassment, decided to say nothing further. Maybe Mrs Crombie would be able to enlighten him, he told himself. Maybe not.

※

WHEN FOXE REACHED SLIPPERY JOE'S COTTAGE THE NEXT DAY, HE found the old man sitting on a bench near his front door. He and his cottage presented a picture which any painter of romantic scenes might have gone a long way to find. The house was built with oak beams, with wattle-and-daub between them and a roof of Norfolk reed, which reached down almost to the ground in places, so much had its weight caused the frames of the roof to bend and sag. With the luxuriance growth of garden flowers rising up from the garden below, and the thick covering of moss on the roof itself, the whole place looked more like a verdant hillside than a work of man. Its occupier appeared, if anything, still older and more weather-beaten than the cottage he sat in front of. He was very short, rather stout, and he had such a luxuriant growth of white beard and whiskers, most of his face was obscured. Two sharp button eyes peered out at Foxe from amidst the tangle and his skin, in the few places it could be seen, was so lined and coloured by sun and alcohol he could have stood as model for a pixie or one of the fairy folk of rural legends.

He greeted Foxe gravely, apologised for not getting up, only his legs could no longer bear him, and invited his visitor to sit on a bench set to his left, out of the sun. Meanwhile, his daughter, who must herself have been at least sixty, fussed around him constantly, completing his sentences, criticising and correcting what he said, and apologising when she thought his words might be inappropriate to polite company.

Thanks to the daughter's constant interventions, her father's deafness and tendency to ramble, his thick Norfolk accent, and the slowness of his thoughts, it took a considerable time for Foxe to obtain the information he wanted. Slippery Joe turned out to be eighty-six years old — nearly eighty-seven, his daughter interjected — and had left off work in the theatres of Norwich some twelve years before. That answered one question right away: the reason why Foxe hadn't recognised the man. Foxe would have been only just seventeen years old at the time and had not started to frequent the theatres. As to the man's nickname, he turned out to be neither slippery in a dishonest way nor especially cunning. He had been called Slippery Joe for no other reason than his real name was Joseph Slipper.

'I'm Mary Slipper,' his daughter added at this point. 'Never married, y'see. Looked after me dad for more'n thirty years now, I 'ave, ever since mam died. Of course, we ain't always lived in this 'ere cottage. In the city most of the time. Came 'ere when dad gave up 'is work. He can't walk much at all now, y'see, so I helps 'im come outside where 'e can sit and see the folk going by. When the weather's warm, that is. When it's cold—'

She would have gone on to tell Foxe their whole life story, had he not interrupted to ask if Joe had ever worked at the White Swan Playhouse.

'Course I did!' said Joe. 'That's why you be 'ere, bain't it? Got a message from the Cunning Woman, young Tabby. You're the one what's lookin' into these murders. I were door keeper at the Swan for nigh on twenty years, so I expect you wants to know about the fire. Can't be anythin' more recent, 'cos I stopped work an' that a good while ago now.'

Foxe agreed he did and Joe launched at once into an account of the night. Stripped of the digressions, interruptions from Mary, corrections and re-corrections, it amounted to little more than a repetition of what Foxe already knew. Joe had been at the stage door at the side of the playhouse building when the fire broke out. He wasn't even aware of it until people started running past, urging him to save himself. The audience and the actors who had been on stage ran out through the front of the theatre. The only people who passed him after that were Postgate — running as if the hounds of hell were after him, according to Joe — and later, Edwards and the actress's maid, carrying her baby.

'I stuck at my post,' Joe said proudly, 'like a reg'lar soldier. No desertin' for Joe Slipper. Not even if the 'ole place was to go up in flames. When the rain came an' the fire was put out, the rest o' those silly buggers looked right fools.'

'Dad!' his daughter protested. 'Fancy usin' that kind o' talk afore a gentleman!'

'Reckon 'e's 'eard worse,' her father said. 'I'm a plain man an' I uses plain speech.'

Foxe tried to get things back to what happened on the night of the fire. 'Did you know those two, Postgate and Edwards?' he asked.

'Aye, o' course I did. An' Chambers with 'em. Kind of a gang, them three were. A wild bunch too, mind. The Mohocks we used to call 'em, after they gangs in London a time back. All us up to some kind o' mischief. Chambers was the leader. He was older than t'other two. He and Postgate were mad after women. Edwards tried to pretend 'e were, but we all knew 'e was one of they sodomites.'

'Father! I won't tell 'e again. Don't use words like that in front of the nice gentleman,' Mary said. 'Tain't polite.'

'What should I call 'em then?' her father protested. 'Pansies? Mollies? Shirt-lifters? You said I wasn't to say buggers.'

This scandalised his daughter so much she struck him lightly on the arm. 'Behave yourself! I never bin so embarrassed—'

Foxe intervened yet again to get things back on track. Did Joe know whether the actress who died, Margaret Lindsay, had any dealings with The Mohocks?

'Not 'er! The men she allowed to pleasure 'er 'ad to be better class'n 'im. Full of ambition was our Maggie. Saw 'erself marrying some lord and joinin' 'igh society. Chambers and Postgate was always sniffin' around 'er, but she kept 'em at arm's length. No, 'twas her maid, Maude, Chambers was sleepin' with. I don't know about Postgate. Reckon neither on 'em fancied 'im. Not many women as did.'

'I understand both the actress and the maid got themselves with child at about the same time,' Foxe said. 'Do you know who the fathers were?'

'I'd say Chambers was the father o' Maude's child. She was pretty gone on 'im at the time. She used to let almost any man who'd pay lift up her skirts 'til she met Chambers. Then 'twas different. Maggie's child? Can't 'elp you there. There was always a crowd o' young blades 'anging round 'er. Could 'ave been any on 'em. Don't expect she knew 'erself.'

'Maude and her child were rescued and Maggie's baby died along-side her?'

'No, you got that wrong, Mister. Maude was rescued along with Maggie's daughter. It were Maude's baby, the boy, who died.'

The old man's words hit Foxe like a bolt of lightning. There it was! Foxe knew one of the two had given birth to a baby boy, and thought it was Margaret Lindsay. But if it had been the other way around . . .

'Are you sure?' he asked Joe.

'Sure as I'm sitting 'ere. Maggie was real miserable she 'ad a girl. If she'd 'ad a boy, she was going to pick on whatever of 'er lovers she thought was the wealthiest and try to convince 'im 'e was the father. That way she'd 'ope to get 'im to marry 'er. Never would 'ave worked with just a daughter. I did 'ear she tried to persuade 'er maid to agree to swap the babies, but Maude wouldn't 'ave it. 'Course, if she thought Chambers would marry 'er along of 'er bearing 'is son, she was well wide o' the mark. She might 'ave doted on him, but there was no way 'e was going to tie himself to anybody, let alone a trollop like 'er.'

Foxe pressed on with his questions, though there wasn't much else to learn. The trio of Chambers, Postgate, and Edwards had broken up after the fire. Chambers went to London to seek his fortune, where he failed to find it and consoled himself by turning to drink. Edwards managed to get a place in a provincial touring company and had been doing similar kinds of acting ever since. Postgate, finally admitting he had no talent for acting, made a life in stage management.

'Postgate's first job was at the Red Lion,' Joe said. 'They never 'ad much of a playhouse, so the people who worked there was allus leavin'. Old Sam Nunn was landlord at the time. God! That'n were up to more tricks than a wagon load o' monkeys! You won't believe what 'e did whenever a play was 'aving a bad run and the audiences was thin.'

Foxe was about to cut him off, when he decided the old man didn't often have someone new to talk to. It would be a kindness to let him tell at least one or two of his stories. Afterwards, he was very glad he'd let Joe ramble on.

'It was like this, see. Sam reckoned people love nothing' more'n scandal. Give 'em a sniff o' scandal or excitement and they all comes rushin' to take a look. So that's what 'e did. If there weren't any real scandal, he upped an' invented some. Even persuaded the actors and actresses to go along with it. Most of them was only paid a small share o' the profits, so they wanted a full 'ouse as much as 'e did.'

The essence of Sam Nunn's idea was to spread a rumour in the city which suggested something startling or suggestive was happening — or was going to happen — in his theatre. He might spread a rumour one of the actors was having an affair with a pretty young actress, despite his wife being part of the same company. Most touring companies were based on an extended family, so this was easy to set up. Most of the plays performed at the Red Lion were comedies, often based on star-crossed lovers, it wasn't hard to find a scene in which the actor and the young actress would be on stage, expressing their love for one another. Primed by the landlord, these two would take their onstage love-making a good deal further than was strictly necessary. The actor's wife would either stand in the wings, shouting insults at the pair, or rush on stage and drive them apart.

A variation involved spreading a rumour that two of the actors were at daggers drawn, usually because they were fighting over one of the actresses. It would then be suggested the management were at great pains to keep them apart, but their respective parts in the play meant this could not be extended to cover their time on stage. Fight scenes were common enough to allow for the two actors concerned to pretend to attack one another in earnest. The first night they did this, they'd take care to go no further than menacing looks and gestures. As the rumour spread, neither would be content until they came to blows. You could be almost certain the theatre would be full for the following performance, as people hoped to see a full-scale fight break out on stage.

'That Sam should 'ave bin a playwright 'isself,' Joe said, wheezing with laughter. 'You never knew what 'e'd come up with next. One time, 'e put the rumour about some trickster was planning to substitute real weapons for the fake ones they used on stage. Seems he hated one of the actors and 'oped to see 'im injured. Another time, 'e spread the idea around that the playwright, putting together a scene involving witches, saved 'isself time an' effort by borrowing magical words and phrases from an ol' book. Trouble was, old book was what they calls a grimmer' — Grimoire, Foxe translated for himself, a book of spells - 'so what 'e'd writ down was the genuine article. Said in the right way an' when the phase of the moon was just right, the spells would work. You couldn't 'ardly get into the theatre the next night, nor the night after that. Nothing happened, o' course, so Sam simply explained the moon 'adn't bin quite right, or the actresses 'adn't said them words in the proper way. Come along the next night, and you don't know what you might see.'

Joe was laughing so much at this point he made himself cough and his daughter scolded him for being a silly old man and wasting the nice gentleman's time. Foxe assured her he was fascinated — and this time he meant it.

So many of Foxe's ideas had now been confirmed he didn't think he could take much more. He was almost desperate to get back to his house, sit in his library and set it all straight in his mind. That done, he would go to see Halloran yet again and ask him to obtain the mayor's permission to arrest the murderer. As luck would have it, Mary Slipper gave him exactly the excuse he needed by telling her father he was not to tire himself too much, nor bore their distinguished visitor with any more of his old stories.

So much for Foxe's plans. Soon after he arrived back at his house, the rest of his day was thrown into complete confusion and he found himself having to deal with another crisis.

❧ 27 ❧

Mrs Crombie brought the news, hurrying through from the bookshop to tell Foxe someone had just told her one of the young actresses at The Grand Concert Hall was boasting that she was the lost child of Margaret Lindsay who had died in the fire twenty years ago at the White Swan. According to her, she had been rescued, unbeknownst to most people, by 'a kind gentleman' who, knowing her mother had died, took her home and brought her up as his own daughter.

'The stupid, little, addlepated fool! God damn all actors and actresses and their mutton-headed ambition! Ah, please forgive me Mrs Crombie. That was an unpardonable thing to say in the presence of a lady. I can only offer you my most abject apologies.'

'You're upset, Mr Foxe. Let's say no more about it. But could what this actress says be true?'

'No, it's impossible. I've learned today that Margaret Lindsay's daughter did indeed survive the fire but wasn't brought up by any kind gentleman. Nor is she this young actress. Both those are certain facts. I'm almost certain I know where she is and who she's living with. This ass of a girl is trying to cash in on the talk going around the city about Margaret Lindsay; trying to suggest that she's the daughter of an actress who's suddenly become famous. A good many actors and actresses are members of a kind of theatrical dynasty, like the Kemble family. Having family connections can be an excellent way to get a start in the profession. In this young woman's case, there are no living connections, but she's hoping to suggest to actors and managers she has inherited talent. Blockhead! She's going to get herself hurt, if only she knew it. I just hope there's time for me to get to her before our murderer does.'

'Do you mean that?' Mrs Crombie was astonished.

'I do, I'm afraid. Please excuse me. I need to get to The Grand Concert Hall as quickly as I can. You don't happen to know the name of this foolhardy young actress, do you?'

'The person who came into the shop called her Lizzie Aggs.'

'Lizzie Aggs. Not much of a name for an actress. I suppose she thinks Lizzie Lindsay will sound much better.'

Foxe reached The Grand Concert Hall in less than fifteen minutes. Preparation for the evening's performance was in full swing and there were people rushing about everywhere. Fortunately, Foxe was well known to the theatre manager, Mr Samuel Garrod, who was more than willing to find time to talk with such a wealthy and generous patron. He sent at once to tell Lizzie Aggs to join them, expressing his own view about what she was doing.

'She's just a feather brain, Mr Foxe, who's filled her head with dreams of being a famous actress. It won't happen. She hasn't got the talent. The company has only taken her on because she looks good, she can sing a bit and she's shameless enough to give the men in the gallery a good look at her abundant charms. Somehow, she's convinced herself that making this ridiculous claim is going to give her career a boost. To be honest, I don't think she'll last much longer on the stage. There are plenty of other young women where she came from — and some of them can act.'

'I'm afraid she's going to get herself hurt,' Foxe said.

Garrod frowned. 'Is this about the business at the White Swan? I was sorry to hear about Chambers. As for Postgate, I'm surprised somebody hasn't done for him before now. I told Studwell, who's land-lord there, he shouldn't give Postgate the job. Ignored me, of course, pig-headed idiot. Not only has Postgate upset a good many of the servants and stagehands there, especially the female ones, he can't organise a good programme. Their audiences had been falling steadily before. Recently, thanks to Postgate, they've been declining yet faster. I happen to know he'd been told the current programme — that's the one that's just finished with the company from Lincoln — was almost his last chance. If takings didn't improve, he'd be dismissed. Of course, with all this talk of ghosts and the like, the place has probably been packed out.'

They were interrupted by the sudden arrival of Mr Kenwood Knight, the leading actor and manager of the stage company performing that day. He was half in and half out of his costume and looked like a nobleman of olden days who'd fallen on hard times and borrowed clothes from his servant. Foxe would have laughed, if he hadn't seen the look on the man's face.

'We can't find Lizzie, Mr Garrod. She ought to be getting into her costume — what little there is of it — but she's disappeared. I'm going to try to find a replacement, but we may have to delay the start of the evening's entertainment by a few minutes, while one of the other actresses gets out of her own costume and into Lizzie's.'

'You mean Lizzie Aggs?' Garrod said. 'I just sent someone to find her. Mr Foxe here wants to speak to her urgently.'

'Whoever you sent isn't going to find her, if we can't.' Knight replied. 'I'm telling you, she isn't anywhere in this building. According to one of her friends, she went out maybe two hours ago and hasn't been seen since.'

Foxe intervened. 'Does this friend know where she went?'

'If she does, she isn't telling. All she'll say is that Lizzie got some kind of message and went rushing off. Hasn't come back. This is all I need with barely an hour to go before the performance starts.'

'I'm going to organise a search,' Foxe said. 'You've got enough to do without me in your way. If I get home quickly, I can start immediately. I fear if we don't find this young woman soon, it'll be too late when we do.' With that, he turned away, leaving the other two staring after him.

Foxe's thoughts had turned at once to the White Swan, so he made a detour there, hoping he could pick up the track of where Lizzie Aggs had gone. It proved to be a forlorn wish. The playhouse building was locked and in darkness. It had most likely been that way since the Lincoln company left. He went into the inn but found no trace of her there either. All he could do now was go home and worry. As he told Nicholas over dinner, the young actress couldn't have known what she was stirring up with her lies.

'She's not the daughter of this Margaret Lindsay then?' Nicholas said.

'No, it's a silly and dangerous lie. Margaret Lindsay and her maid, Maude Stebbings, both had babies at the time of the fire. Seeing the room filled with smoke, Maude grabbed up a child and ran for the door but was overcome before she got there. Fortunately, Edwards, who was a young actor and stage hand there at the time, found her and dragged her out into the corridor, then went back and picked up the child. Through his action, both survived. Unfortunately for her, Maude had picked up the wrong child. Hers was a boy. He died in that room along with her mistress, Margaret Lindsay. It must have been agony to realise what she'd done. However, so far as I know, she brought up the child she rescued as her own. I've made enquiries about her. Maude Stebbings is still at the White Swan, employed as wardrobe mistress. The young woman I assume is her daughter works there alongside her.'

'But that young woman is really Margaret Lindsay's daughter, is she? How confusing.' Nicholas said. 'Does she know this Stebbings woman is not her real mother?'

'I have no idea. Whether she does or not, she's quite safe. It's Lizzie Aggs who's in danger.'

'Why? Just because she's pretending to be someone she isn't?'

'It's who she's pretending to be,' Foxe said. 'Don't ask me any more at present. I need to sit and think this through, though I expect I'm already too late. The death of Lizzie Aggs would make a third murder. Each time the murderer kills it gets easier as well. It has to be stopped now. I'm almost certain I know who the murderer is. What's still not clear to me is the reason behind these killings. Still, if Lizzie Aggs is dead, the murderer has made a tremendous mistake. A mistake which, if I handle it correctly, will take the killer to the gallows.'

Nicholas decided to risk one last question. 'Can you tell me what that mistake is?'

'Giving me proof that everything which has happened stems from that night twenty years ago; the night when Margaret Lindsay and Maude Stebbings' son died; the night when an accidental fire set off a chain of emotions and events which have caused at least two, possibly three, murders twenty years later.'

❧

IT WAS ONE OF THE MAIDS FROM THE WHITE SWAN, SENT INTO THE playhouse next morning to make sure no rain had got in during the thunderstorm of the night before, who found Lizzie Aggs' body lying in the middle of the stage.

'Of course,' Foxe said when he heard. 'The playhouse was closed. There was no need to use the storeroom this time.'

The inquest was set for early the next day and, as Foxe knew would be the case, the medical examiner gave evidence the young actress had died from a single blow to the top of the skull, in the same way as Chambers and Postgate had.

Foxe and Alderman Halloran both attended the inquest. Afterwards, they walked together to Halloran's house, for the most part in silence, since both had much to think about. Halloran was wondering how best to avoid this third murder providing more ammunition for the mayor's enemies to use against him. Foxe was trying to decide whether he should bring matters to a head or wait a day or two longer to tie up the remaining loose ends. Surely there was no one left to be killed? Even Lizzie Aggs would still be alive and well, if only she hadn't chosen the wrong lie to try to advance her career.

By the time they reached the alderman's house, Foxe had made up his mind. He had to take the risk. If anyone else died or was hurt, he'd always blame himself.

The moment he and the alderman entered the alderman's library, Foxe spoke up. 'It's time to make an arrest, Alderman. Do you think the mayor will be willing to take action on my word alone? I should warn you that I don't have all the evidence I would like but I think it'll be enough for a jury though.'

'He's been ready to trust you in that way before,' Halloran replied. 'I don't see why he shouldn't now. Who is it you want arrested?'

'Maude Stebbings, the wardrobe mistress at the White Swan.'

'A woman? Are you sure, Foxe? Didn't the medical examiner say Chambers and Postgate must have been killed by a tall man of exceptional strength?'

'He did, but it's the Stebbings woman I believe we want. I know I'm taking a risk, but I'm convinced she did it — I mean I'm sure she killed all three — although I'm still not quite clear what her weapon was. My fear is she'll either kill again — she's done it three times, and I'm sure it gets easier each time — or she'll slip away, and we'll never bring her to justice. In that case, it will be now or never.'

'Very well. You've never let us down before, Foxe.' The alderman went to his writing desk, took paper, pen, and ink and swiftly wrote a note to the mayor. Then he summoned a footman and told him to deliver it in all haste.

'I'm totally confused by all this,' he said, sitting down again. 'You still seem to be ignoring the business with Edwards. You promised to tell me about that, but you haven't done so. To be quite plain, what's been happening at the White Swan feels to me like a melodrama written by someone in Bedlam.'

'You're exactly right,' Foxe replied, 'only hell, not Bedlam. We'll have some time to wait before we hear if the woman's been taken. The theatre's closed at the moment, so they may have to find out from the landlord where she lives and go there. Did you say in your note the Swordbearer shouldn't go alone?'

'When you asked me before to tell the mayor to be ready to order an arrest, you mentioned the Swordbearer should take two sergeants-at-arms. It made sense at the time, because I assumed they'd be facing a kind of giant. Why it should take three men to arrest a woman is beyond me. However, that's what you asked for and that's what I asked the mayor to provide.'

'Thank you. It's this problem of how she carried out the murders. If she has some fearsome weapon, she may try to use it to prevent herself from being taken. Would you like me to fill in the time while we're waiting by explaining about Edwards, as I promised?'

The alderman indicated that this would please him a good deal.

'I'd more or less guessed the answer,' Foxe said, 'then I had a chance to talk to a very old man, once doorkeeper at the White Swan and several other theatres in Norwich. He confirmed my idea and filled in the details. I'm afraid it's a long story.

'There used to be a landlord at the Red Lion who'd invented a trick to bring people in to the playhouse there. Knowing how much people enjoy the chance to witness a spectacular or scandalous event, he used to invent them, persuading the actors and actresses to take part as well.'

'Make up some suitable incident, you mean? Something sensational?'

'Exactly. He'd set a rumour going first. For example, he might say two of the actors were quarrelling and itching to get into a fight. Once the tale was doing the rounds, he'd tell the actors to stage a confrontation sometime during the performance. The first night, there'd be a stand-off and a few insults. That would be seen as proof of the rumour, a few more people would come next evening in the hope of seeing an actual fight. On the second night, he'd maybe tell one of the actors to swing a punch, but make sure to miss. The two of them would put up their fists, while other cast members would rush on to separate them. You could be sure that by the third night, the playhouse would be packed out. No real fight ever took place, but the thought that it might was enough to ensure the company would play to full houses for the rest of the run. Once he invented a story of a ghost — perhaps it's better to say a poltergeist — who caused bits of scenery to fall over. Another time it was a supernatural creature that liked to fondle the actresses' backsides. In the first case, it was easy to instruct a stagehand, out of sight, to knock over a piece of scenery — always one that would do no real harm, of course. In the second, one or more of the actresses would be primed to let out a squeal and claim she'd felt icy-cold fingers stroking her bum.'

'What a rogue! I wonder he got away with it.'

'Yet he did. Many times. Became famous for it amongst theatrical people. What's more, Postgate was working for him at the time.'

'So that's it. Postgate was the one who started the rumour about the ghost.'

'He did. Audience numbers at the White Swan Playhouse have been falling for some time. The competition from the Grand Concert Hall and the Norwich Company of Comedians is too strong. I've also been told Postgate was warned he'd be dismissed if attendances continued to fall. According to my informant, Postgate was a failure as a theatre manager. He upset the people who worked there and couldn't set up programmes to draw in sufficient people. I imagine he remembered what he'd seen at the Red Lion and decided to try it for himself.'

'What you're telling me is the business about the ghost wasn't directed against Chambers at all?'

'Not at first. Remember, Postgate didn't know that Chambers would be there. He was brought in at the last minute to fill a place left by another actor who was injured. I asked my cousin Nicholas to check through the playbills and newspaper advertisements announcing recent programmes at the playhouse to see if we could discover where Postgate got this specific idea. In all the fuss over the third murder, he forgot to give me the answer yesterday. Today at breakfast, he told me he'd found the company who had played at the White Swan immediately before Mr Hunter's troop had included a dramatic monologue in their programme called "The Vengeful Ghost". You see? He could well have got the idea there.'

'Why did he pick on the ghost of that dead actress? Wouldn't it have been better to have a poltergeist, like at the Red Lion? Knock a few pieces of scenery over.'

'Probably. The initial rumour might only have been that the playhouse was haunted. I admit I don't know why he turned on Chambers in particular, unless it was the chance to take revenge for past slights. I've learned Postgate and Edwards and Chambers were close companions twenty years ago or so, getting up to all kinds of disreputable and illegal activities. They were so wild that local people called them "Mohocks", after a group of young blades who terrorised London about ten or fifteen years previously. Chambers was the leader of the group. Maybe Postgate was jealous. Maybe Chambers bullied him or made fun of him. This is all guesswork, you understand. What I'm more certain about is that Postgate switched the ghost story to the death of the actress the minute he knew Chambers was coming.'

'But why? I still don't understand.'

'Postgate was an evil-minded brute. He might simply have wanted to torment Chambers for the fun of it. He might, as I said, have wished to get his own back for some past injury. I suspect he also knew the man was trying to work his way back into favour with managers by giving up drinking. If he could make him upset and angry by pinning the blame for Margaret Lindsay's death on him, he could start him drinking again. Postgate knew the fire at the playhouse had been an accident, so there was no danger of Chambers ending up in court.'

'Did it work?'

'Only partially. The trouble was, Chambers stuck it out. What was worse, he threatened to retaliate by bringing Postgate's past misdeeds to light.'

'Surely it must have been Postgate who killed him then.'

'I've never known Postgate to do his own dirty work,' Foxe said. 'Nor do I believe Postgate intended to go as far as bringing about Chambers' death. I think he asked the wardrobe mistress to arrange something to give credence to the story about the ghost. The trouble is, she went too far.'

'Why?'

'She had once been in love with Chambers, deeply in love, but he walked out on her, went to London to seek his fortune and never looked back. That in itself might have been enough. It's just possible she didn't intend to kill him either. When she did, Postgate was badly frightened. He tried to persuade me to start an investigation, although he knew I hated him. If I had agreed, he would have found some way to make sure I discovered Maude Stebbings was the actual killer. When I stuck to my refusal, he didn't know what to do.'

'And Edwards?'

'In the case of Edwards, Postgate had to do everything himself. The ghost story was still at the front of everyone's minds and Postgate feared Edwards would realise what he had been up to. Remember, the tricks of that fellow at the Red Lion were well known to theatrical people. All Edwards had to do then was tell everyone the truth: the fire at the White Swan had been an accident and Chambers had been on stage at the time—'

'— and Postgate would be exposed as the treacherous brute he was. Serve him right!'

'Postgate set up the business with the dagger as quickly as he could, hoping Edwards would be hurt sufficiently badly to withdraw from the company and go back home. That's why I told you the business with Edwards had nothing much to do with the other killings. This time Postgate got it right. The business with the dagger hurt the man badly but caused no danger to his life. He had to withdraw from the company. At the same time, the ghost story was given another boost.'

'But —'

They were interrupted by the sound of someone knocking at the outer door. A moment later, a footman came to ask the alderman if he was willing to see Mr Gilmore, the mayor's Swordbearer.

Gilmore came into the library, bowed politely to both Halloran and Foxe and launched into his news. 'We took that woman, Your Honour. Found 'er at 'er lodgings. What a vixen that were too! She made a rare fight of it. Broke Pope's arm, she did. Whipped out what looked like an ol' stocking and swung it at 'im. When that hit him, we all 'eard the bone break. Here it is, gentlemen. When we got 'er safe and secure, we found she'd sewed a sort of pouch into her petticoat. She must 'ave kept this thing in there. It were right by the opening she put 'er hand through to reach 'er pocket.'

What he placed on the table was an old stocking. The upper part had been folded over and sewn to the toe, so what was left was shorter, but of double the thickness. About a third of the space in it was filled with sand, with the top sewn shut to keep it there. You could see at once how fearsome a weapon it would make. As she swung it, it would be like a pendulum, crashing down with a greatly increased force.

'There you are, Halloran,' Foxe said. 'This bag of sand is why the medical examiner thought the killings had been done by a giant. I'll bet she swung it round from behind her and over her head, so the end filled with sand would hit the top of her victim's head with maximum force: a force great enough to smash anyone's skull, yet soft enough to avoid breaking the skin. It's all the proof needed to show we've arrested the right person. Display that to a jury and her conviction will be inevitable.' He turned to the Swordbearer. 'Where is the woman now, Mr Gilmore?'

'In the lock-up, Mr Foxe. Icy calm she is an' all. Once she could see 'twas all over, she dropped that sock thing on the floor and let us put the manacles on 'er hands. There was a young woman there with her and she told 'er, cool as you likes, to bring 'er fresh clothes an' some decent food in the morning. Nothing else. After that, she let us lead 'er away. When we gets to the lock-up, she lays down on the mattress and tells us to go away and let her get some sleep. You wouldn't scarce believe it!'

'With your permission, Halloran,' Foxe said, 'and that of the mayor, of course, I'll go and speak with our murderer in the morning. She must know she's no chance of avoiding the hangman. With any luck, if she's that calm, I may be able to get her to tell me some of the things I still don't understand. I can try anyway.'

'Yes, Foxe, you do that. If the mayor objects — and I'm pretty sure he won't — I'll deal with him. Thank you, Gilmore. You can go home now. I assume you've taken Sergeant Pope to see a bonesetter?'

'T'others was doing that while I came 'ere, Your Honour.'

'Off you go then. You too, Foxe. I don't think I can take any more, even if you can. Come and tell me the rest when it's all over.'

❦ 2 8 ❧

Foxe couldn't remember seeing Maude Stebbings before. It wasn't surprising. As wardrobe mistress, she would be behind the scenes, amongst the actors and actresses, or shut away in the room where they kept the costumes. He'd never gone backstage much at the White Swan; never been a regular patron, even before Postgate's presence kept him away from there completely.

Perhaps it was because the cell of the lock-up was so small, but she looked bigger than he'd imagined; bulkier somehow, stockier; a strong, well-built woman, neither handsome nor ugly, with a face which should have inspired trust, had not her eyes been so cold. He guessed she must be in her early forties, though she looked ten years older.

What surprised Foxe most was her calmness. She looked at him as a lady, seated in her own drawing room, might look at a tradesman come to show her items from which she would choose her purchases. He could detect no sign of fear or apprehension. No anxiety, no tension, no concern for the future. She looked him up and down, as he did her, then gave her verdict.

'So,' she said, her voice was surprisingly deep for a woman. 'The great Mr Foxe 'as come to see me 'imself. I suppose I should be honoured.'

The Gaoler bustled in with a stool for Foxe to sit on, taking care to wipe it first with a grubby cloth.

'There, sir,' the man said. 'Sit you there, close to the door. I'll stay within earshot in case you needs me. She's bin no trouble so far; slept most of the night.'

'What else was there to do?' Maude said. 'Knit? Do some sewing? As you see, Mr Foxe, this room lacks amenities to amuse yourself with.'

'Aye, that's a cool one an' no mistake, that is,' the Gaoler said. 'Take as long as you wants, sir. She's got nothing else to do, 'as she?'

'I expect 'e'll stay as long as I'm willing to put up with answering 'is questions,' Maude said. 'An' it's my decision, not 'is.' She turned back to Foxe. 'What d'you want to know? They'll 'ang me, that's obvious. No chance of an acquittal. I shan't deny what I've done anyway. So long as the 'angman turns me off quick and neat, I don't care about the rest.'

As he'd walked to the Bridewell, Foxe had been wondering about the best way to get this woman to talk to him. He saw now he needn't have bothered. Still, he had to start somewhere. Almost on a whim, he decided to begin telling her story for her, in the expectation she would step in to correct his mistakes and fill in any blanks.

'Postgate came to you with his plan to scare Chambers away. Did he know how much you hated Lemuel Chambers?'

'How could 'e? Not that 'e would've cared. I was nothing to our fine Mr Postgate; just a servant to be used. Too old and unattractive to fuck, too tall and strong to knock about, too necessary to the play-house to drive away.'

'He'd already started the story about the ghost, hadn't he? Before Chambers came, I mean. When he heard Chambers was coming, he couldn't resist the opportunity to make the man pay for the times he'd lorded it over him in the past.'

'That was Postgate all right. Vicious little bastard! If Lemuel 'adn't been broken down by his misfortunes and by the drink, Postgate would've fawned all over 'im. Still, I was shocked by the way Lemuel looked: pasty-faced, bloated, all the signs of the regular drunkard.'

'Did Chambers recognise you?'

'Not 'im! When I met 'im in the passageway, 'e looked right through me. I couldn't imagine why I'd ever loved 'im. He hadn't just got over me, 'e'd wiped me out of 'is memory altogether. I couldn't forgive that, could I?'

'I imagine Postgate only asked you to hurt Chambers. Why you? Couldn't he have used anyone else?'

'Oh no. I was perfect for the job. Postgate knew I could walk about the playhouse all day an' no one would notice me. If they did, they wouldn't remember.'

'Just the wardrobe mistress, eh? Always about the place on nobody's business but your own? Did you mean to kill him from the start?'

'It's 'ard for me to be certain,' Maude said. 'It took me a while to get 'im on 'is own. At last, I saw 'im creep into that storeroom. I followed 'im in and 'e was down on his knees, pulling a bottle out from under a pile of painted cloths in the corner. It was when I saw 'im I knew what I wanted to do. God! How I 'ated 'im! You know I followed 'im down to London?'

Foxe shook his head. He hadn't known it.

'After the fire, Lemuel took off for London as fast as 'e could. No thought for me or 'is child —'

'But his child was dead, wasn't he?' Foxe interrupted.

'You 'ave been busy, 'aven't you? More of a ferret than a fox, if you asks me. Yes, I picked up the wrong baby. Not that it mattered to Lemuel Chambers. I could have had ten of 'is children and 'e would still have walked out on me.'

Foxe tried to get her back on track. 'You said you went after him to London.'

'That's right. It took me a while to track 'im down there an' all. When I did, 'e gives me two black eyes and tells me never to come near 'im again. He was going to be a famous actor, 'e was, and 'e didn't want some slut from the streets of Norwich 'anging round him. When I heard, years later, what 'ad become of him, me only thought was it served 'im bloody well right.'

'So, what did you do?'

'What any other penniless young woman, saddled with a baby, 'ad to do in London. I went on the streets. When the baby died, there seemed no reason to stop. I 'ad nothing else to live for. Lemuel's cruelty and the deaths of my little boy and Maggie's baby girl turned my heart to stone. I vowed I'd never love another 'uman being, so long as I lived.'

'Margaret Lindsay's baby died?' Foxe said.

'Ha! You didn't know that, did you? Where did you think she was?'

'The men who arrested you told me there was a young woman—'

'An' you thought she was Maggie's daughter. You should have asked 'em how old the girl is. What they saw was Peggy, my maid of all work. She's 'ardly sixteen. Far too young to be Maggie's child.'

'What will happen to her now?'

'Why should I care? Go back to the gutter where I found 'er, I expect.'

Foxe wanted more than anything else to get away from this woman. He'd never come across anybody so heartless, so self-obsessed, so lacking in any kind of compassion. She disgusted him at least as much as she fascinated him. She complained Chambers had used her and thrown her aside but couldn't see her own behaviour was just as bad. You've got to see this through, he told himself. You owe it to the people this woman killed — murdered with as much feeling of remorse as a farmer's wife wringing a chicken's neck.

'Let's go back to Lemuel Chambers,' Foxe said. 'You found him on his knees, feeling for the secret cache of grog he'd hidden in the storeroom.'

'I suppose you've seen the weapon I made from an old stocking?' Maude said. 'The men who arrested me took it. Neat little thing, isn't it? Plenty of sand in the bags the playhouse uses as counterweights to lift scenery flats up and down. Easy enough for me to slit open two or three, take an 'andful or two of sand from each an' sew the bags up again. A sandbag's a trick I learned in London. I kept my little friend in a pouch I made on the outside of my petticoat, so it would be always to hand. I'd had enough of men lifting my skirts. Enough of 'em wheezing and grunting like pigs as they thrust inside me. Anyone trying that trick would get more'n they bargained for. Maybe I didn't know me own strength. Maybe I'd put more sand in the stocking than was needed. Maybe I wanted to do it. Take your pick, clever Mr Foxe. Whatever I planned, I killed 'im. Don't expect me to be sorry either. I've lived in 'ell on earth these last twenty years. Can't think where I'm going will be any worse. He did that to me.'

Foxe had a sudden thought. 'If Margaret Lindsay's daughter died when you were in London, why didn't you tell everyone the truth when the young actress, Lizzie Aggs, began to claim she was Lindsay's child? You knew it couldn't be so.'

'That little bitch? She couldn't get any of it right, could she? All that nonsense about the second baby being saved. Wherever she got her story from, it was twaddle. The second baby — my baby — died. I wished with all my 'eart I'd died as well, when it happened.'

She leant forward, her eyes blazing. It was the first time she'd shown any animation.

'Maggie Lindsay was my best friend,' she said. 'The only real friend I ever 'ad. I loved 'er, truly I did. I wasn't in the Green Room when the fire started. Maggie told me she was tired and was going to sleep for an 'our. There was a kind of day-bed right underneath the window. Several of the actresses used it. Performances didn't normally finish until eleven o'clock or so. After that the wild ones, including Maggie, might go out with some beau drinking or having sex. It could easily be two or three in the morning before they got to bed. It wasn't surprising they'd snatch a nap later in the day if they could.

'Maggie must 'ave been asleep when the smoke started to come into the room. By the time I got there, the room was full of smoke. Nasty, acrid stuff too; made me eyes water so as I could hardly see. It was real 'ard to breathe as well. That's why I mixed up the babies. I dashed across the room, snatched up the first one I came to and shouted to Maggie to follow me out with the other. I didn't so much as get to the door before I collapsed.'

'I'm not sure I see why it meant you had to kill Lizzie Aggs,' Foxe said softly.

'Then you're more stupid than I took you for,' Maude said. 'Maggie was a real actress, a good one. If she'd lived, she'd 'ave become famous. I'm sure o' that. I asked around about Lizzie. People told me she'd no talent for acting at all. All she was good for was grinning and flaunting what she 'ad. "All teeth and titties," someone told me. Do you think I was going to let a doxy like 'er pretend to be Maggie's daughter, just so as she could get acting parts? She'd 'ave been laughed off the stage and Maggie's memory would have been spoiled.'

'So, you lured her to the playhouse and killed her as you had the others,' Foxe said.

Maude laughed. 'Little fool! I sent 'er a note saying as I could tell her more about 'er mother. She couldn't come to me fast enough. She was standing on the stage, calling out to find out where I was, when I crept up behind 'er. One blow and she fell down all of an 'eap. It was too kind a death, if you ask me.'

Foxe couldn't bear to hear any more. He could understand this woman's hatred of the man who betrayed her. He thought he knew why she had killed Postgate — and he found it difficult to be sorry for him anyway. Someone would have killed him, sooner or later. But this cold-blooded murder of a foolish, innocent young woman stuck in his throat. He was determined to see Maude Stebbings hang for it. He was almost at the end now, he told himself. Might as well see it through, however sordid it had become.

'Why did you kill Postgate?' he asked.

'I thought you could 'ave worked that out for yourself,' the woman said. 'You're supposed to be so smart. After I'd done for Lemuel, 'e was frightened of me. But 'e couldn't turn me in without admitting to what 'e'd been doing. He'd have been charged with being a . . . What d'you call it?'

'An accessory,' Foxe said.

'That's it. I knew 'e'd find some other way to set the magistrate on my trail though.'

'He came to me,' Foxe said. 'Begged me to investigate Chambers' death, but I refused.'

'Of course. If you'd agreed, 'e would have pointed at me. Rat! What a bastard 'e was, an' all! And you want to know why I killed 'im? I should get a reward!'

'Hardly,' Foxe said.

'Look. I knew, if I wanted to stay safe, I 'ad to kill 'im too. Besides, there was what 'e done to Christopher Edwards. Edwards saved my life an' Maggie's child. Wasn't 'is fault she died afterwards in London. That two-faced bastard Postgate made sure he got badly hurt, just to save 'is own job. I owed 'im for that. There was another, better reason too, o'course. D'you know what it was?'

'Edwards knew the fire which killed Margaret Lindsay was an accident. He also knew Chambers was on stage at the time it broke out. Postgate was afraid his grubby little plot against Chambers would be revealed, together with his reasons for doing it. If Edwards had spoken out, he would have been dismissed on the spot. He wanted Edwards away from the playhouse as quickly as possible.'

'You got it! Now, 'ow can you worry about who killed him?' Maude said. 'A man like 'im deserved to die.'

'You're wrong,' Foxe said. 'The only people who deserve death are those who've murdered others.'

'Like me, I suppose. You'll get your wish on that score soon enough. I suppose I'd better go on and tell you the rest. You won't go until you've got all you want.' She took a deep breath. 'It was like it was with Lemuel. I couldn't get Postgate on 'is own at first. 'e was too wary. At last my chance came. I knew 'e used the pile of old cloths in the storeroom as a place to take whores he brought in off the streets. I kept watch and, sure enough, I saw 'im sneak in there with some painted tart young enough to be 'is daughter. I gave them a moment to get started, then followed them in.

'She was down on the pile of cloths with him beside 'er and 'er skirts round her waist. He was sucking on one of her nipples, with his hand up between her legs. She squealed when she saw me, pushed him off an' ran for it.'

'What did Postgate do?'

'What d'you expect? When 'e saw who it was, 'e crouched down on his knees in front of me, begging me not to 'urt 'im. 'e even offered me money. When I 'it him, 'e went down like those bullocks does when the butcher hits 'em with 'is poleaxe. Bang an' they're dead! I kicked 'is body once or twice, stamped on 'im too, though I knew as 'e couldn't feel it. He ought to have suffered a lingering death, not the nice, kind one I gave 'im.'

'No regrets? Not for any of them?'

'None whatsoever. Now, bugger off! I've said all I'm prepared to say and I'm tired. Peggy should be 'ere soon with some fresh clothes and some decent food. I want you gone by then. Gaoler! Mr Foxe is leaving.'

Foxe didn't argue. He'd had more than enough. As he told Alderman Halloran later, if he'd been talking with Satan himself, he couldn't have found anyone with less compassion or sense of guilt. He found it hard to believe, as he left the Bridewell, the life of the city was still going on as normal.

Foxe didn't hurry home. He needed to get back some sense of reality first; to see people laughing and talking and behaving like reasonable human beings. He'd never be able to go into the White Swan again without thinking about everything which had happened there. Despite Postgate being dead, that would be enough to keep him away. It was as well he didn't believe in ghosts. If he did, he'd be imagining the wretched spirits of the three people the wardrobe mistress had killed lingering on in the building. Maybe hers as well.

What a foul affair! He'd had enough for one day. Let the alderman and the others wait twenty-four hours to satisfy their curiosity. What he needed now was a glass of brandy — maybe two or three — and a large slice of Mrs Whitbread's fruitcake.

❧ 29 ❧

Mrs Crombie, Nicholas, and Charlie Dillon came to Foxe's library next morning, eager to be brought up-to-date on all Foxe had been doing. He began by explaining the solution to the murder of Edward Mordifort, just as he had done with Alderman Halloran earlier. It was fairly straightforward from his point of view, but the others had not been much involved in that investigation, so were alternately intrigued and horrified by the tale.

Then, with the Mordifort murder explained, it was time to turn to the murders at the White Swan. Normally, Foxe enjoyed a session like this. It was a chance to show off his skill and bask in the renewed regard it brought him. This time he felt different. He'd done what he'd set out to do: established the facts and procured the arrest of the murderer. It was talking with Maude Stebbings which had left him shaken. Without his intervention, she might well have escaped punishment. That could not have been tolerated. She was as callous a murderer as he had ever encountered. Yet she was also a woman who had been used and mistreated by a series of men, of whom Lemuel Chambers was the worst offender. Fate had dealt her one crushing blow after another. None of which excused her crimes, though Foxe felt they went a long way to explaining them. He was left torn between sympathy for the harsh life she had been forced to endure and a loathing for the pitiless, cold-hearted creature she had become. Maybe cruelty bred cruelty. He didn't know.

Still, after the third murder, that of poor Lizzie Aggs, things were different. No one could feel any qualms about seeing the wardrobe mistress face the executioner for her killing. There was no justification for it whatsoever. He'd also feared more deaths might follow, although he'd been wrong there. There would have been no more — at least, no more resulting from the death of Margaret Lindsay and the child in the room with her that night. Whether Maude Stebbings would have dealt with any future wrongs done to her by using the same means, there was no possibility of knowing. Anyone might kill, given sufficient provocation - though he felt sure each killing made the next one easier to contemplate. Maude Stebbings had probably never been a soft-hearted woman. Twenty years of brooding over the many wrongs done to her had turned her into a monster.

Foxe had spent a good part of the previous evening sorting everything out so he could explain it in a logical sequence. Now he took a deep breath and began at the beginning.

'You need to understand everything that has happened over the past few weeks has its origin in a fire at the White Swan Playhouse; a fire which took place twenty years ago; a fire in which one of the actresses there died, along with a baby which had been asleep in her room.'

No actor ever held an audience more enthralled. No one interrupted; no questions were asked; no comments added. Until he had finished, Mr Foxe's voice was the only one in the room. Even when he reached the end and sat back in his chair, none of the others seemed eager to break the silence.

Mrs Crombie was the first to speak.

'Will they hang her?' she asked. 'Isn't it usual, if a woman is sentenced to death, for the judge to request the king to exercise his prerogative of mercy?'

Foxe nodded. 'Yes, that's what typically happens. I don't think it will in this case, however. Mostly because she's killed three times, but also because the law will consider each one was premeditated, including the first. Unless someone steps forward — someone of suitable medical standing — and persuades the judge she's mad and unfit to stand trial, there can be no mitigating circumstances. She was not defending herself, not in fear of her life, not preventing an attack on any other person.'

'But she was treated abominably!' Mrs Crombie protested. 'Why should any woman put up with that and not fight back?' Then she caught herself back, afraid she had overstepped the bounds of proper conduct for one of her sex. 'Please forgive my outburst, Mr Foxe. Justice must be done, of course. I do not in any way condone such monstrous crimes. It's just . . .'

'I agree with you,' Foxe said, 'but you're forgetting the last murder. The so-called crime for which Lizzie Aggs paid with her life existed only in Maude Stebbings' mind. She could have put a stop to Lizzie's silly impersonation simply by speaking out. As I discovered, there are other people in this city who know the full facts. They, I'm sure, would have come forward to support her. Nothing else was needed, least of all murder.'

'Mr Chambers deserved punishment too,' Mrs Crombie muttered rebelliously.

'Maybe,' Foxe said. 'I don't doubt Postgate too got away with things in the past which would merit a severe sentence. The law won't see things in that way. I don't disregard or minimise the real suffering of Maude Stebbings, the murderess, has endured over the years, but I cannot forgive the murder of Lizzie. Nor, however much sympathy we feel for past wrongs, should we condone what Maude Stebbings did. Let's move on. We can't do anything to change how matters will turn out, whatever we feel about them.'

'I attended the inquest on Lizzie yesterday,' Nicholas said. It was the first time he had spoken. 'The medical examiner confirmed she had died in the same way as the other two. The jury brought in a verdict of wilful murder, though not against Maude Stebbings, since none of what you've just told us was given in evidence. From the comments I heard afterwards, I don't imagine many people in this city will mourn Maude Stebbings' death. To put it crudely, they were out for the murderer's blood.'

'One of the street children brought me a message from Missus Tabby earlier this morning,' Charlie said. 'Well, the message was really for you, master. The Cunning Woman says I'm to tell you you've done the right thing, even if you do feel bad about it. A city can suffer a malignant sickness, just like a person can, and it has to be rooted out. That's all there is to it. Until the balance is restored, it won't be healthy again. Don't ask me what the last bit means, master, but that's what I was told to say.'

'Thank you,' Foxe said to him. 'I think I know what she means.'

Later the same day, Foxe returned once again to Alderman Halloran's house in Colegate. There, sitting in Halloran's library, he and the alderman made a final review of the case against Maude Stebbings.

'She told me she'd plead guilty,' Foxe said. 'If she sticks to her resolve — and I believe she will — there'll be no need for an extensive presentation of evidence.'

'She's due to be brought before the mayor's court sometime today,' Halloran said. 'The mayor will preside with two or three other aldermen on the bench. It'll be largely a formality though. Maude Stebbings will be remanded to the next assizes. This is a serious group of crimes. Everyone will want to be sure there are no legal problems, even if the prisoner does plead guilty. She might change her mind and make a fight of it — her friends, if she has any, might round up a doctor or two to claim she's unfit to plead or something. If they do, it's my guess she'll still hang. Damn good thing too! She sounds like a truly poisonous bitch!'

'Whatever happens, the business is over as far as I'm concerned,' Foxe said. 'I must say I find it a great relief. Talking to the wardrobe mistress, and hearing what amounted to her confession, was one of the toughest and most distasteful things I've done in a long time. With your permission, I'd like to talk about something else now, please — something altogether more pleasant.

'My cousin Nicholas and I had a talk about his future yesterday evening. He's decided he'd like to qualify in the law and specialise in criminal rather than civil cases. I'm quite certain his father will agree. I know he wanted his son to enter the church, but he must see Nicholas has no vocation there.'

'The law is a highly honourable profession,' the alderman said. 'I'd be delighted if a son of mine — if I had one — expressed a wish to take it up. I haven't seen much of young Mr Nicholas myself, but my wife was greatly taken with him — as were my two nieces. None of them are easily impressed by mere show, so that argues a lot for the fellow's strength of character. Good for him, I say! If there's anything I can do to help, you only have to ask.'

'I believe Mr Plumtree has also offered his support and the use of his connections. Between us all, we should be able to find a suitable person willing to accept Cousin Nicholas as a pupil, so he may complete his articles.'

'I have no doubt of it. I'll speak to Plumtree and see if he can come up with any names. Now, Foxe, there's another matter I need to put before you. You may recall me mentioning the Mercantile Club: the group of leading merchants and traders in this city who come together every month to discuss matters of mutual interest. They've expressed an interest in meeting you. I'm to invite you to join us when we meet next. What do you say? It's quite an honour, I assure you.'

❧ 30 ☙

oxe did not quite return to the same way of spending his time as he had before the murders took place. Mistress Tabby, as he must now think of her, was right. He'd begun to take himself much too seriously. He needed to remember he was still a year short of his thirtieth birthday, seriously wealthy, and in excellent health. As she had told him, she hadn't given him those delicious lessons in how to give and receive pleasure so that he could forget them and live like a puritan.

Another thought came to him. After Gracie Catt had left Norwich with her sister, the bordello of which she had been the madam was handed into the charge of a woman Foxe rather disliked. She too had now left Norwich, according to the information that had reached him. Her replacement was a much more pleasant lady by all accounts. There had also been an almost complete replacement of the girls who provided the services and entertainment. Perhaps he should go and see for himself what the place had become. He'd completed two complex and distasteful investigations and surely deserved a reward. Cousin Nicholas was spending a good deal of his time now with Mr Plumtree, so there were bound to be times when he was safely out of the way. The young man had come a long way in the past few weeks, but he might not yet be sufficiently relaxed about the ways of the world to cope with his host spending time and money on enjoying the undoubted skills of high-class ladies of pleasure. Besides, in a few weeks he would be gone, back home at first, then to join his aunt in whatever cottage she had selected for the two of them.

Foxe, sitting at the desk in his library, grinned happily to himself. Pleasures of the kind he liked best lay ahead of him. In the meantime, he would write to his friend Captain Brock to tell him something of what had been happening in the city in his absence.

My Dear Brock,

I trust my last letter reached you safely. I am at last done with the murders of Edward Mordifort and those at the White Swan Playhouse. Although the outcomes were satisfactory, I cannot count either among my more memorable achievements. In the case of Mordifort, the murderers gave themselves away. All that was lacking was the firm evidence to bring about their conviction. The events at the White Swan were much more complex. Even so, I should have been able to sort them out more quickly than I did. I was much too slow to realise the account of events given to me by Postgate was a fiction designed to suit his own ends. When you return home, I'll tell you all about them, if you wish, since the story is far too long to put in a letter.

The White Swan murderess, Maude Stebbings, was tried at the last assizes and was given the ultimate penalty. It could hardly be otherwise. She showed neither fear nor remorse when the judge said she should hang. It was much the same on the day of her execution. A great crowd had assembled, eager to catch sight of this woman who had killed three people in the space of as many weeks. The pamphlet sellers, the vendors of food and drink, the pickpockets and petty thieves, the whores, all those who view any large gathering as an opportunity for profit, were busy amongst the crowd. The noise was tremendous. You would think it was a holiday, not an execution.

Normally, when the tumbril containing the condemned person appears, it's greeted with a cacophony of jeers, yells, and catcalls. Not this time. It sounds incredible, even as I write it, but as each part of the crowd caught sight of the woman to be executed, sitting upright and unafraid in the cart, her eyes fixed firmly on the gallows set up by the Castle Ditch, the noise they made stuttered, lessened, and finally ceased. By the time she stood in the back of the cart and the executioner placed the noose around her neck, the only noise to be heard throughout that whole, vast assembly was the sound of weeping. She made no speech, sought no prayers from the parson present, said nothing to the executioner by her side, looked at nothing save the clouds and a flock of birds wheeling over the marketplace.

The executioner urged the horse forward and the woman was launched into eternity, still silent, still unafraid. A moment later, there came a great sigh from the crowd; a noise much like a gust of wind makes as it stirs the branches of a forest. It was over.

A common highway robber was the next to be brought up to the gallows, but the crowd had lost interest by then. They began to drift away, first in twos and threes, then in their hundreds. By the time the robber had been turned off from the cart, little more than a handful remained. All in all, it was one of the most remarkable events I have ever witnessed.

Peter Mordifort and his sister were sent for trial to the Old Bailey, probably because of the status of the family, though it might have been for fear a Norwich jury would be biased. Whatever the reason, they too were convicted. Peter Mordifort, true to what he told me when he was arrested, pleaded guilty. His sister tried to proclaim her innocence, but with him determined to give evidence against her she had little chance of persuading the jury to acquit. I understand they did not even choose to retire but delivered their verdict in moments. The sentences were inevitable and neither judge nor jury made any recommendation for mercy. I'm glad I wasn't at Tyburn when the sentence was carried out. I gather the crowd was especially hostile on that occasion. It could hardly be otherwise, I suppose.

Now, at last, my life has returned to its normal pattern. Cousin Nicholas is still here, though much occupied with making his arrangements to begin legal training. Thanks to the good offices of Alderman Halloran and Mr Plumtree, he has secured his pupillage in fine chambers in Thetford. I believe the partners there are much in demand, both at the assizes held there and at those held in Bury St Edmunds. They also serve Quarter Sessions and Petty Sessions over a wide area. His father has agreed to pay the costs of his pupillage, as I knew he would.

It may amuse you to hear of the success of a small deception I have under-taken to assist my Cousin Harriet to live independently. The story I concocted went like this. Looking for something amongst my father's old papers, I came across the draft of a letter he intended to send to his attorney, changing part of his Will. He wrote that he wished to set aside sufficient funds to provide his niece Harriet Foxe with an annuity of one hundred pounds per annum. Unfortunately, he died before the letter could be sent and the Will amended.

My letter to Cousin Harriet was a small masterpiece, though I say it myself. In it, I explained how I felt honour bound to see my father's wishes carried out as he would have wished, and had therefore instructed my attorney to set aside sufficient money in trust to allow the annuity to be paid. I added that I hoped she would forgive me for the delay in carrying this out. It was only ignorance of my father's wishes that brought this delay, not any reluctance on my part.

She and her brother have swallowed this pack of lies without hesitation. On her part, she wrote assuring me she holds me free of any blame. Indeed, she is convinced there was no obligation on my part to make so generous a provision for her, which she attributes entirely to my kindness of heart. Her brother, on the other hand, wrote me a stern lecture on the importance of family duty, urging me to make sure I am not so careless of my obligations in the future.

The result is Cousin Harriet is now seeking a suitable small house, in or near Thetford, where she may set up home. Nicholas will lodge with her, which will be convenient for them both. He tells me he is due to receive a small legacy from his maternal grandfather when he comes of age in a month or so, so he'll be able to help pay his way until his studies are complete and he can set himself up in practice. I think you will agree this is a most satisfactory outcome.

Here I must cease writing, for I have already expressed myself at far too great a length and you will be bored with my ramblings. I must also prepare myself to meet with the members of the Norwich Mercantile Club, no less. They have summoned me to their meeting this evening, for what purpose I do not know. At least I am promised a good dinner and an abundance of fine wine.

I trust that you and the lady in your charge are both well and enjoying the sights of Rome and the surrounding countryside. Please take care to give Lady Julia my kindest regards.

I am, sir, ever your most obedient servant and devoted friend,
Ashmole Foxe

AUTHOR'S NOTE

Theatres

In the eighteenth century, to be called a theatre the building had to be licensed by Act of Parliament — a status which cost a good deal of time and money to obtain and which was only granted to two theatres in London at the outset. Outside the capital, theatrical performances took place with permission from local magistrates, usually in a building attached to a local public house, which might be roughly converted to include a stage and seating and given a name like 'playhouse'.

In major cities like Norwich, such playhouses gradually gained better seating, theatrical boxes and maybe a gallery. Even so, most remained simple, rectangular structures built of wood, a far cry from what we would class as a theatre today. Most also lacked permanent companies of players. Instead, troops of actors travelled from location to location on a set 'circuit', performing for a few days at each one. Since being classed as a travelling actor could get you declared a 'rogue and vagabond' and thrown into prison, these groups also assumed other names, often including the term 'comedians' or simply 'So-and-so's Men', using the name of some helpful patron.

The White Swan Inn in Norwich, close to the market place, did exist, though it is long gone now. Its yard was the site of what was, for a time, the principal theatre in the city, the White Swan Playhouse, home of the 'Norwich Company of Comedians'. It wasn't the only pub/theatre complex though; there were about five in all, including the one attached to the Red Lion, which is also mentioned in this book.

The city's first purpose-built theatre wasn't erected until 1757. Initially, it was called the New Theatre, but, since it wasn't licensed, the name was rapidly changed to The Grand Concert Hall, which is how it appears in this book. Only in 1768 was the requisite licensing act passed and the theatre renamed the Theatre Royal — the name its successor building retains to this day.

Left-handedness

At the time when this book is set, left-handedness was seen as a fault to be corrected, especially amongst the upper classes. Children who were naturally left-handed were always trained to use their right hands instead. As a result, few beyond the immediate family would even know someone was born left-handed. That is why everyone assumes the murderer of Mr Mordifort used his right hand — and why Dorothy Henson's strong left arm was not thought of earlier.

ABOUT THE AUTHOR

William Savage is an author of British historical mysteries. All his books are set between 1760 and around 1800, a period of great turmoil in Britain, with constant wars, the revolutions in America and France and finally the titanic, 22-year struggle with Napoleon.

William graduated from Cambridge and spent his working life in various management and executive roles in Britain and the USA. He is now retired and lives in north Norfolk, England.

www.williamsavageauthor.com
www.penandpension.com

ALSO BY WILLIAM SAVAGE

ALSO BY WILLIAM SAVAGE

THE DR ADAM BASCOM MYSTERIES

An Unlamented Death

When the body he trips over in a country churchyard proves to be a senior clergyman, Dr Adam Bascom expects a serious inquiry to follow. Instead, it looks as if the death is to be left unsolved.

The Code for Killing

Dr Adam Bascom, called to help a man who's been brutally assaulted, is drawn into solving a series of murders in a world of deceit, violence and treachery.

A Shortcut to Murder

18th-century Norfolk physician Dr Adam Bascom longs to get back to his medical work. Fate, however, is determined to keep him off-balance as he is asked by his magistrate brother Giles to investigate the death of Sir Jackman Wennard, rake, racehorse breeder and baronet.

A Tincture of Secrets and Lies

A Quack doctor leads Dr Adam Bascom into a mystery which includes a series of local murders and a plot to destabilise the country, and ends with Adam directing a thrilling climax on land and sea.

51501048R00128

Made in the USA
Columbia, SC
19 February 2019